W9-BAF-356

HarperMonogram is pleased to present a unique selection of "keepers." Throughout this year we will bring back enduring romances that readers have told us they will always remember. Here is another chance to discover these gems—sizzling, tender, charming, passionate, captivating romances that you will want to have on your bookshelves and by your bedside forever. Written by some of romance's bestselling and most popular authors, these are heartfelt stories of hearts broken and sins forgiven, lost love found, and new love discovered. HarperMonogram knows that romance readers want only the best. So here is your chance to discover why the best deserves to be kept in your hearts and your homes always.

"The most delicious, thrilling, and rambunctious time-travel adventure to come in a long time."
—*Romantic Times*

Books by Suzanne Elizabeth

When Destiny Calls
Fan the Flame
Kiley's Storm
Destined to Love
Destiny Awaits
Till the End of Time
Destiny's Embrace
Destiny in Disguise

Published by HarperPaperbacks

Destined to Love

⊰ SUZANNE ELIZABETH ⊱

HarperPaperbacks
A Division of HarperCollinsPublishers

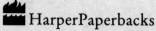

HarperPaperbacks

A Division of HarperCollins*Publishers*
10 East 53rd Street, New York, N.Y. 10022-5299

If you purchased this book without a cover, you should be aware
that this book is stolen property. It was reported as "unsold and
destroyed" to the publisher and neither the author nor the
publisher has received any payment for this "stripped book."

This is a work of fiction. The characters, incidents, and
dialogues are products of the author's imagination and are not to
be construed as real. Any resemblance to actual events or
persons, living or dead, is entirely coincidental.

Copyright © 1994 by Suzanne E. Witter
All rights reserved. No part of this book may be used or
reproduced in any manner whatsoever without written
permission of the publisher, except in the case of brief
quotations embodied in critical articles and reviews.
For information address HarperCollins*Publishers,*
10 East 53rd Street, New York, N.Y. 10022-5299.

ISBN 0-06-108549-9

HarperCollins®, 📖®, HarperPaperbacks™, and
HarperMonogram® are trademarks of
HarperCollins*Publishers,* Inc.

Cover illustration by Jean Monti

First printing: September 1994
Special edition printing: May 1997

Printed in the United States of America

Visit HarperPaperbacks on the World Wide Web at
http://www.harpercollins.com/paperbacks

❖ 10 9 8 7 6 5 4 3 2 1

For Lila Marie, my friend and sister.
Because I somehow had to make up for
that lost trip to Disneyland.

Within every lonely heart lies the timeless gift of love and the whisper of undiscovered destiny. . . .

1

San Jose, California 1994

Her hair was a disaster.

Josie had tried to tame it in the dressing room, but the rain and wind had wreaked irreversible damage during the dash from her car to the building. The largest can of hairspray in the world couldn't plaster down the spiked clumps of black hair she now had sprouting from her scalp.

She'd forgotten to bring her power lipstick, the deep wine-rose color that said "That's right, I've got lips and I'm not afraid to use them." So much for first impressions. Now she was bound to come across as meek and homespun—two things she definitely was not.

Perspiration was beginning to bead on her upper lip, and as Josie sat on a velvet-covered stool, alone in a bare, twenty-by-twenty room, with hot lights beating down on her from every direction, she was struck by the oddest impulse: to stand up and do a Gene Kelly impersonation on the hardwood floor.

Okay, so she was having a hard time taking this whole thing seriously. What kind of man searched for the woman of his dreams in the library of a video dating service, anyway? And with the way she looked at the moment, she had to be some poor soul's nightmare, not perfect date material, as her friends were so fond of telling her.

Her friends. This whole thing was *their* fault. If Yvette, Linda, and Vickie hadn't gotten themselves happily married in the past three years, they wouldn't be all over her to do the same. Always a bridesmaid, never a bride—she had heard the damn saying so many times, she felt as though it were tattooed across her forehead.

"Just relax, Dr. Reed, and tell me your heart's desire."

Josie started at the sound of a woman's voice. She hadn't been aware that anyone else was in the room. A small face peeked out through the distant shadows at her and smiled, and Josie silently congratulated herself for not making use of the hardwood floor. It would have been embarrassing to have someone witness that.

"Dr. Reed? Your heart's desire?"

"How about Mel Gibson, Tom Cruise . . . and just a touch of Clint Eastwood?"

Wishful thinking. After living among the male species for twenty-eight years, Josie Reed knew that such a man did not exist.

She squinted into the bright lights, which were looming over the videocamera she was suppose to spill her guts to, and licked her dry lips. If she didn't get at least one decent date from this ridiculous lark, she was never going to hear the end of it from those happily married friends of hers.

The woman continued to smile out from behind the tall tripod and camera. "Nervous?"

Josie adjusted her position on the stool and tugged on the lapels of her emerald-green jacket. "A little, I suppose."

"Your first time?"

Josie laughed. "Yeah, I'm a virgin video dater."

"You're not so unusual, Dr. Reed. Many young women are growing tired of the rat race and looking to find more discriminating ways to meet men."

"You mean instead of parading themselves through sleazy dance joints and singles bars, they're choosing the more subtle approach of flaunting themselves on videotape?"

The small woman's smile seemed to freeze as she stepped down from the crate she'd been standing on. "I get the impression you don't have much hope for this dating service."

Josie hadn't meant to insult the lady, or her business, but the only thing she was hoping for was that this whole ordeal be quick and painless. She was running her life just fine, thank you, and certainly didn't need a man mucking it up.

"To be honest, Valino's Video Dating Service was suggested by my friends," she answered. "This is actually the last place I thought I'd ever find myself."

"They say people tend to find what they're looking for in the last place they'd ever think to search."

"A date for Friday night is all I'm after."

"A date?" The woman stepped closer. "Tell me, have you ever met a man who could really make your heart pound?"

No. And if she ever did, she'd run him out of her life as fast as she could.

"You know, love is a remarkable thing, Dr. Reed. It can turn the coldest day to warm, the saddest heart to joy, the darkest soul to light—"

"It makes the world go round," Josie finished for her. She wasn't interested in love. It was invariably attached to "commitment," and that word alone made her nervous. She was here for a date. One date. And then, she hoped, Yvette, Vickie, and Linda would consider their work done and leave her to her perfect life of solitude and independence.

The woman persisted. "Don't you harbor *any* hope for eventually finding your soul mate?"

Josie blinked and peered harder at her, trying to see better through the bright lights and cloying shadows. "That's an interesting term, considering fifty percent of all marriages end in divorce. And I consider myself pretty lucky so far for not getting trapped into playing mommy to some insecure male who can't even keep track of his own underwear."

The woman blanched. "Is that really how you view the sanctity of holy wedlock?"

"Sanctity? Try using that term on the ninety percent of married men who spend all their free time boffing someone besides their sacred spouse. Did you know that married men live longer than single men? And that single women live longer than married women? Does that tell you anything? It tells me that men are sucking the life out of their wives."

The woman moved forward into the light, and Josie could see the sharp angles of her face. "We're just full of important facts, aren't we, Doctor?"

"I'm nothing if not a realist, lady. Marriage isn't for me."

"Certainly you must be lonely, or you wouldn't

have let your friends talk you into coming here."

Josie glanced away. "Loneliness is something I can handle. And I'm doing this for my friends, not me."

"For them? But what could they possibly gain by sending you out on a date?"

She shrugged. "Some small measure of satisfaction, I suppose. Like giving a dollar to a wino. Now, can we get this over with? It's been a long day and I'd like to go home and take a hot bath."

"Wait, Dr. Reed." The woman inched a little closer. "What if I told you that I knew exactly where you could find the perfect man for you?"

"*Perfect man*? Isn't that what they call an oxymoron?"

The woman was undaunted by her sarcasm. "What if I told you he lived in New Mexico in the nineteenth century?"

"Isn't it just like a man to be in the wrong place at the wrong time."

"What if I told you I could send you back there to be with him?"

Josie stared at the woman in a whole new light. She'd never come face to face with an honest to goodness schizophrenic before. "I'd ask if you could bottle the trick and share the profits with me."

"Dr. Reed, tell me, would you go back in time to be with the one man who could make you happy for the rest of your life? To be with your soul mate?"

Josie gave a short laugh. "Let me get this straight, lady. You're asking me if I'd like to go back to the nineteenth century, a time of primitive living and female suppression, give up everything I've worked my whole life to achieve, and all for a man?"

"He is everything your heart desires, your perfect mate—"

"I'd rather eat ten pounds of pancakes and run in the hot sun! What is this? I come in here looking for a date and—"

"All right, Miss Reed."

Josie's attention snapped to the door, where the broad Italian man who'd signed her in in the lobby strode into the room. "Sorry to keep ya waitin' so long, sweetheart."

"Well, this nutty camerawoman—" Josie glanced to where the tiny woman had just been, then peered into the shadows. The woman was gone, which was an odd thing considering there was only one door in the small room and this man had just used it.

"Camerawoman?" he questioned with a raise of his bushy brows.

"A tiny woman with short brown hair and a string of pearls. . . ."

He gave her a skeptical look, then said, "We don't have any women workin' here, honey."

"The name is Dr. Josie Reed—not sweetheart, not honey—and I think you'd better check the employee roster, Mister . . . ?"

"Valino. As in Valino's Video Datin' Service. And I can assure you only me and my three bruthas work here." He glanced at the form in his hands, which Josie had filled out when she arrived. "So you're a docta, eh? Why didn't ya put that on your profile?"

"I did."

He held up the piece of paper, looking smug. "No, you didn't. You left the little box that says 'profession' blank."

Josie snatched the form from his hands. Mr. Valino occupied himself by cleaning his teeth with his tongue while she glanced over her handwriting and, sure enough, found that she had left the box blank. But how could that be? If she hadn't written her profession on the form, then how had that woman, whoever she was, known she was a doctor?

"Puttin' your profession on there might up the ante." Mr. Valino's mouth twisted into a grin. "Not a man I know that don't like playin' docta."

Josie's jaw tightened. She handed the form back to him. Great, she thought, I'm putting my love life in the hands of Andrew Dice Clay. "There was a woman in here talking with me. If she wasn't an employee of yours, then who was she?"

The man saw Josie's scowl and held up his hands. "Hey, I'll look into it. Now, you about ready, sweetheart?"

Josie gritted her teeth while he strutted over to the camera and positioned himself with a hop and a few rolls of his hips. She wasn't going to back out. Whether good or bad, she was determined to get a date out of this whole bizarre experience. If anything, she'd have some unique memories for when she was old and gray.

And alone.

Josie jammed the car into fourth and sped up the entrance ramp and onto the freeway toward home. It had been another long night at the hospital, and she hadn't even bothered to take off her green cotton scrubs before leaving at the end of her double shift. She'd just grabbed her clothes from her locker and fled. Two fatal car accidents, three shootings, and a messy leap from a two-story building; she supposed that was enough to make anybody want to run for the hills.

But at least tonight she could go straight home and to bed, instead of having to worry about another dating fiasco like the one she'd experienced the night before. Perfect man? Try perfect joke! That was the only way to describe her first and *final* experience with the wonderful world of video dating.

Harvey Maxwell, computer technician, had chosen her two days after she'd made her video profile, and despite the fact that he seemed far off the mark from her tastes, her "friends" had decided that she should at least meet the man once and check him out.

So, like a brainless fool, she'd called him back. He'd sounded sane enough on the phone, and Josie had agreed to dinner and a movie.

Only they never made it to the movie.

He'd picked her up wearing the funkiest shirt she'd ever seen: purple silk, with pictures of banana splits plastered all over it. Josie was sure she'd gain five pounds just staring at the thing all night. And, good God, his pants. Harvey Maxwell was definitely a man who lived under the assumption that he weighed a bit less than was actually fact, and Josie would have given twenty bucks to anybody who could explain just how the hell he'd packed himself into those jeans.

She'd sat for two hours at Emille's, fiddling with her nouvelle cuisine—"food for the anal retentive," Vickie called it—listening to the man talk about a computer program he was working on for plumbers, how they'd be able to unstop a pipe on screen before ever attempting the dreaded "real-life situation."

Great, Harv, Josie had thought to herself while feigning polite interest, the world can definitely sleep better now.

The guy was a creep, from his slicked-back hair to his glossy loafers, and any man who wore gold chains and a pinky ring was definitely not her type. During the course of their two priceless hours together, he made crude remarks to their waitress, commented on the posterior of every woman who had the misfortune to wander past their table, and entertained Josie with dirty jokes while his mouth was full of veal chops.

Josie doubted she had said three words all evening, and she was equally doubtful that Harv had even noticed. Toward the end of their meal, after the waitress had taken their dessert order, thrown Josie a sympathetic look, and escaped into the back kitchen, Harv finally stopped talking about himself long enough to ask Josie a question about herself.

"So," he said with an oily smile, "you're a doctor. I think that's really great."

A baboon couldn't have missed the condescending tone in his voice. "And you're certainly beyond any medical help," she grumbled under her breath.

"No, no, I really mean that. I think it's great that you've found a little something to keep yourself busy."

She snorted. "Yeah, medicine is just a little hobby I picked up after eight years of higher learning."

"Well, I for one think a college education is over-rated," he said seriously, and then laughed. "I didn't even finish high school, and look at me!"

"Do I have to?" Josie said to herself.

Their chocolate mousse arrived, and Josie hoped for a reprieve, but good old Harv didn't miss a beat. He went on and on about how he hadn't spent a single second in a classroom after the ninth grade and had managed just fine. Josie felt that point was debatable.

Then, with a spoonful of chocolate dessert floating around in his mouth, Harv asked, "So . . . how much do you pull in a paycheck?"

Josie closed her eyes. Then she set down her spoon,

calmly picked up her purse, and stood. "It doesn't matter, *Harv*. The king of Arabia couldn't pull in enough to support that gut you're cultivating."

With that she'd turned and left, envisioning all three of her friends hanging side by side from the tree in her front yard.

Josie slammed her hands against the steering wheel now, unable to remember the last time she'd felt so frustrated. She was a normal, healthy woman. Men were supposed to be an important part of her life, but even the ones she found interesting she ended up chasing out of her life eventually. The last one she'd dated had merely mentioned the idea of marriage "sometime in the very distant future," and she had gotten cold feet and stopped returning his calls.

Tears burned her eyes, and she squeezed the wheel in a death grip to hold them back. "Damn!" she said. "What is wrong with me?"

"Nothing."

The voice startled Josie so much that she swerved her car into the next lane, making the tires screech.

"Dr. Reed! Watch out!"

She straightened the car, then quickly turned her head to see the camerawoman sitting next to her on the passenger seat. The woman was still wearing the same gray skirt and jacket and the same strand of pearls from the week before.

"What the hell are *you* doing here!"

"You called me."

"Lady, I don't even know you!"

"You said, 'What is wrong with me?' And I was compelled to answer."

"Well, I didn't think I had an audience!"

Josie pulled off at the next exit and sped down the

freeway ramp. She took the first left, into an empty 7-Eleven parking lot, pulled up short beneath a lamp-post, and cut the engine.

She frowned down at her street clothes, which had somehow appeared in a wadded-up pile in her lap—evidently the woman had tossed them there to make room for herself in the passenger seat—and then stared out the windshield. "Would you like to tell me exactly what you think you're doing in my car?"

"I can help you. I can give you what you need, Dr. Reed, what your soul is crying out for."

Josie gave her a sharp look. "What I need is a good night's sleep."

The woman leaned closer. "Within each person's lifetime there exists one other who is the perfect match for him or her. However, an unfortunate mistake has been made. You were born in the wrong century. Your true mate exists in another place, another time."

Josie glared at her. "Are we back to this again?"

"Trust me. Let me guide you to your soul mate, to the place where you truly belong. Let me help you to find your true destiny—"

"Look, fairy godmother, I appreciate your concern, but I'm afraid a new dress and a pair of glass slippers isn't going to fix what's broken here. Cinderella doesn't want to go to the ball! She can actually get along just fine without Prince Charming!"

"You're wrong, Dr. Reed. Neither one of you can get along without the other. If you stay apart much longer, the consequences will be tragic. All you must do is agree to meet him."

"To meet him?" Josie laughed. "You mean another blind date?"

"I guarantee you, this man is nothing like Harvey Maxwell."

Josie leaned back against the headrest and sighed, too overwhelmed to ask how the woman knew about Harv the wonder date. She watched the gas station sign across the street flicker on and off and thought about how she'd come to be sitting in her car, in an empty parking lot, listening to some crazy woman talk about sending her back to the past. First her friends, and now this. It seemed the whole world was out to see her married or committed to an institution—whichever came first.

"Agree, Dr. Reed. Simply agree—"

"If I agree, will you stop hiding out in my car?"

"Absolutely."

"Then all right, fine." She adjusted the small pile of clothes in her lap, pulled her medical bag closer, and closed her eyes. "Zap me," she said, thinking that if she played along, the woman might go the hell away. "Zap me back to the land of the dino—"

Josie's hands flew out to her sides to take hold of the wooden door frame she suddenly found herself standing in. She heard a dull thud and glanced down at the plank floor to find her medical bag and her wadded-up jeans and T-shirt lying at her feet.

Her head began to spin, and fear, deep and strong, coiled inside her as she struggled for an explanation to whatever had just happened to her. The sound of muffled voices caught her attention, and she looked up to stare in stunned silence at two men standing by a bed across the room. They were awash in the dull yellow glow of a lantern and were so intent on the form lying on the bed that they were oblivious of the fact that they had company.

"He's out again," the heavyset man said.

The tall, balding man nodded. "With that infection, he likely won't make it to morning."

"Then there ain't nothin' for it, Doc?"

The tall man sighed and began rolling up the full white sleeves of his shirt. "Get the saw, Deputy Green. I'm taking the leg."

2

The saw?

Josie watched as the short man, dressed in a torn red shirt, baggy pants, and suspenders—obviously a necessity rather than a fashion statement—reached toward a small table and turned up a gas lamp. The musty smell of stale air, mingled with the fumes of burnt kerosene, filled Josie's nose, but her eyes focused intently on what the short man picked up and held out to the one called Doc.

The lamplight hit something metallic, but instead of glinting brightly, the metal was dull and rusty, and Josie began to doubt her own sanity. What in God's name had happened to her? And what kind of man would turn a rusty saw on another human being?

"What about morphine, Doc?" the short man asked.

"Shipment hasn't come in from Santa Fe," the other one replied. He tested the blade and then wiped it on the front of his shirt. "I'm running low. He'll have to do without."

Josie would have shouted a protest, but her throat had gone dry and tight, making any sound impossible.

"Be just wastin' precious medicine usin' it on the likes a him, anyhow," the one named Deputy Green said.

She dug her fingernails into her palms, trying to wake herself up from the nightmare.

"Tie his hands to the bedpost, Deputy. I'll get his feet. You might want to stuff some cloth down his throat so he doesn't frighten the folks outside."

Josie wasn't waking up. And in the back of her mind a fear niggled that maybe, just maybe, that strange little woman had done exactly as she'd said.

The logical side of Josie refused to entertain the idea that she'd been sent back to the past, however, and she bit the inside of her cheek until she tasted blood. The sharp pain not only proved she was awake, it also pumped some much needed adrenaline into her muscles and got her heart going again.

"Just below the hip, Deputy Green," Doc was saying.

Josie glanced down at her medical bag and knew what she had to do. Without a second thought, she kicked aside her jeans and T-shirt, snatched the bag from the floor, and marched up to the two men.

"Is this some kind of sick joke for my benefit? Or have I stumbled onto the find of the century—the real-life Dr. Jekyll and Mr. Hyde?"

They turned to her and exchanged bewildered looks. The man Josie assumed was some poor excuse for a doctor had a curling black mustache and tiny brown eyes, while the other man, Deputy Green, had a smashed round nose and was missing a front tooth.

The deputy was the first to speak. "Young fella, you best get on outta here. The doc don't need to be bothered at the moment—"

"Bothered? Oh, I wouldn't dream of interrupting the doctor's little carving session. However, that man there on the bed might appreciate it if I intervene on his behalf—just until he wakes up and can tell you two to go to hell all by himself."

She made a move toward the bed, but the two men stood together to block her way. Their effort was futile: she paused only long enough to give them a glare before shoving past them. What she found on the narrow bed, sprawled in damp sheets, was enough to make her breath catch. His hair was long and dark blond. He had high, fine cheekbones and a perfect roman nose. He was broad-chested and long-legged and probably the best-looking man she'd ever seen in her life.

He was also flushed with fever. Josie tried to ignore the sexy dark stubble covering his sculpted jaw in order to study him from a more professional point of view.

The entire front of his shirt was plastered to his chest with dried blood. His denim pant leg was slit clear to his crotch, exposing a wound in his right thigh that was seeping a yellow-green drainage.

She bent to his face and felt his heat, caught his sun-and-sweat smell, and detected only a subtle, fragile tremble of warm breath on her cheek.

"Gunshot?" she asked as she dropped to her knees and settled back on her heels to open her bag for her sphygmomanometer.

When she received no answer to her question, she wrapped the pressure cuff around his bulging upper arm. "*Gunshot*?" she demanded again.

"Yes," the doctor finally answered after clearing his throat.

Josie pumped the inflation bulb and watched the mercury rise and fall. The man's blood pressure was alarmingly low. She leaned over him and tore open his grimy shirt, sending buttons flying. The doctor behind her made a sound of protest, but her stony glare over her shoulder stifled any inclination he might have had to interfere.

She put her stethoscope in her ears and listened to the steady but shallow thrumming of her patient's heartbeat. His chest and airway sounded clear. Then she bent to run her fingers over the planes of his chest and abdomen. Despite his condition, the man was rock hard, and she actually had to take a deep breath to steady her hands. For several long moments she searched for bullet holes, until she was satisfied that the dried blood on his shirt wasn't his own.

"When did this happen?" she asked. Again, silence reigned as she searched in her bag for an ammonia inhalant. "Either answer my questions or get out! When did this happen?"

"A—a few days ago," Deputy Green answered. He and the doctor both seemed entranced by the contents of her bag.

"Where's the other one?"

"Uh . . . other one?"

"This isn't all *his* blood, Deputy Green. Where is the other gunshot victim?"

"Oh. That's from his horse. S-say, is . . . is you a doctor of some kind, li'l fella?"

Josie rolled her eyes but chose to ignore that rather absurd question. She broke the ampoule of ammonia beneath the injured man's nose. He groaned and twisted his head away, and she was satisfied that he was unconscious only from the fever and not from any serious injuries invisible to her trained eyes.

She proceeded to make a bodily assessment, feeling the steely length of his arms for broken bones and then moving to his thick, corded neck. She was relieved to find no other injuries besides the one in his thigh. His fever was raging, however. He was clearly septic.

She moved her examination down to his long legs and removed the rest of his severed pant leg with the sharp scissors in her bag. Making use of a large ceramic bowl and pitcher of water resting on the floor beside her, she thoroughly cleansed his wound with strips of sterile gauze. The leg was badly infected, but it certainly didn't need to be removed.

Josie prepared a syringe with penicillin and injected it into the man's strong thigh. He let out another faint groan, and she quickly followed the penicillin with an injection of morphine, which she didn't happen to feel anyone was beneath deserving.

Next she probed his wound. His perfect features clenched, and his full lips parted.

"I need some alcohol," Josie said.

Almost immediately a bottle of Irish whiskey appeared in front of her face. "Need a glass, li'l fella?"

Josie gave the plump man a sidelong glance. "I meant alcohol for sterilization, Deputy Green."

The man looked completely baffled. "This here is all I got."

The injured man began to roll his head from side to side, as if he were looking for some escape from the pain. Josie snatched the bottle from Deputy Green's hands. "What's his name?"

"His name?"

"You know, the word you call out to get his attention?" she snapped. She'd never had much patience for incompetent people.

"Uh . . . Mitchell."

She turned back to her patient. "I'm here to help you, Mitchell. And I hope you'll keep that in mind during the next few seconds."

She uncorked the bottle, braced herself, and poured the fiery liquid into the open, seeping wound in the man's thigh.

With a growl, and in one swift, powerful move, he lurched upright and took hold of Josie's arm. She dropped the bottle to the floor as she was yanked up close to the coldest, meanest expression she had ever seen. His dark, deep-set eyes were full of rage and pain, and she felt an impulse to fight for her life surge through her.

Suddenly his eyes narrowed and he stared at her, long and hard. The silent moment filled her with a strange current of excitement and a palpable sort of fear, both of which she found hard to tamp down.

Like a cautious wolf, he sniffed her, and she wondered, cynically, if he planned to lick her next. Then his eyes widened and his lips curled up to reveal even white teeth. "Get this woman away from me!" he roared with more strength than she would have expected him to have.

His harsh, raspy voice echoed against the four timber walls, and the two men behind Josie backed off to the other side of the room. Despite her urge to do the same, Josie stood her ground. Power emanated from the man's every pore. He was slick with a fevered sweat, dark circles rimmed the bloodshot brown of his wild eyes, and still he had a presence that could strike fear into those around him. But Josie refused to be daunted.

She reached her hand out to his bronze shoulder in an attempt to reassure him, but he only shoved her away, nearly knocking her from the bed. There was a loud snicker, and she stole a glance behind her at the two men hovering near the door.

"You best watch yerself," Deputy Green said. "He'll eatcha in one bite."

Josie righted herself and looked back at her patient. "Not once he understands that I'm here to help him. Do you understand that, Mitchell? That I'm here to help you?"

The man's wild eyes gradually began to clear, and he sank back down on the bed. "Where's . . . the doctor?" he rasped.

"*I* am your doctor."

Their eyes met, and his answering expression told her that he didn't buy her claim for one minute. After spending the better part of her adult life waging war on men who thought her capable of little more than a soufflé and a few babies, Josie had a store of pride that got the better of her at times like these. "*I* am the doctor who is going to save your life, Mitchell. But, if you prefer, the doctor behind me has his rusty saw ready. And he does seem to be in quite a hurry to chop off your leg."

Mitchell's hard gaze darted past her toward the far door, and she watched his expression change as he struggled not only with the dilemma of having her as his doctor, but with the growing effects of the morphine. Finally he looked up at the ceiling. "Man's a butcher," he said in a hoarse whisper.

"Then we do agree on something."

His gaze returned to her, but his lids were beginning to grow droopy and heavy.

"Get some rest, Mitchell." She set her hand on his forehead to check his temperature, even though he tried to turn away from her touch. "I promise, when you wake up both you and your leg will still be here."

Her back and neck were taut from fatigue as Josie stepped out of her patient's room and into the lobby of the most primitive hospital she'd ever seen. Instead of the normal smells of alcohol and floor wax, she could detect only stale air and dust. And talk about an uncomfortable wait; three tired-looking patients were sitting on a long, crooked log resting against the far wall, with not a magazine in sight.

The three patients, dressed in odd, ratty-looking clothing, looked up at her and stared as she walked past them. "Amish," Josie muttered to herself as she reached the door. Somehow she'd wound up in the middle of an Amish town. Intent on finding some fresh air and peace of mind, she stepped outside.

The late afternoon sun beat down on her as she walked across a board porch and descended it to the dirt road. She stretched her arms above her head to relieve the spasm in her lower back, and a warm breeze fluttered through her short hair. She closed her eyes and took a deep breath.

A pungent scent filled her nose. She cringed and opened her eyes. A sudden cry of panic lodged in her throat, and amid deep shouts and curses, she jumped back up onto the board sidewalk just as an old-fashioned wagon pulled by two gigantic black horses practically ran her down.

Josie caught her breath as the conveyance rolled past, and the bearded driver leaned down from his seat to shout crude things at her. Having grown up in the big city, Josie simply couldn't resist; she jabbed her middle finger in the air and told him to go straight to hell. She'd never realized the Amish had such a colorful vocabulary.

Just then the long rifle strapped to the side of the man's wagon caught her eye. She wasn't exactly up on her religions, but she felt sure that the Amish were a passive society and most certainly didn't carry weapons.

"What the hell is going on here?" she whispered to herself.

For the past two hours she'd put aside any questions about where she was, intent on cleaning and stitching up the unconscious patient. She'd worked in what she'd been told was the best medical facility for a hundred miles. But now, as she began to take in the rather odd sights surrounding her—the wagons, the horses, the clapboard buildings—the memory of that strange little woman and her strange little questions returned to her and forced the breath out of her lungs.

Evidently she was losing her mind.

She stepped back out into the dirt road, and the same breeze touched her face. This time she recognized the pungent smell of manure. She shielded her eyes and stared at the weathered buildings lining both sides of the road, which stretched out toward the distant mountains for about five city blocks.

A big sign reading "The Montana House" hung over the double doors of the building directly across the street from where she stood. Next to that, on the corner, was a stucco building with "Juan Patron's House and Saloon" painted in black letters over the door. A glass of beer, it boasted in its one wide window, was only a nickel. A nickel for a beer? she wondered. Quite a bargain. And then another sign caught her eye: "Lincoln Post Office."

Lincoln? Lincoln, Nebraska?

Frantic whispering sounded behind her, and she turned to see four women standing on the boardwalk. They were all decked out in bright, old-fashioned dresses and armed with frilly decorative parasols. And they were staring directly at her, whispering and giggling behind their hands like giddy high school cheerleaders.

"Great," Josie mumbled to herself. "The welcoming committee."

The sudden sound of a gunshot blasted in her ears, and her attention jerked up the street just in time to see a man drop to the ground. Forgetting about the four women, she broke into a run toward the fallen victim. Blood was everywhere. She dropped to her knees beside the injured man and checked for a pulse, not surprised when she didn't find one. He'd been shot in the chest and had probably been dead before he hit the ground.

She rose and stared at the people on either side of the street who'd paused to take a look. "This man is dead," she called to them. But none of them reacted. "Well, somebody call the damn police!" she shouted.

"I am the damn police."

She turned to see a round-faced man in a gray jacket. He was smirking at her through a heavy dark beard, and the gun in his hand was still smoking from the bullet he'd fired into the man at her feet. In stunned silence, Josie stared at the silver star pinned to his chest. "You're the . . . the—"

"The marshal."

She nodded slowly, cast a glance at the oddly dressed people still staring at her from every direction, and began to stumble backward down the street, back toward the security of the hospital. As she reached the boardwalk, the world began to tilt crazily beneath her feet, and she paused to bend her head down to her knees.

"Pardon me, ma'am?"

Josie kept her back bent but craned her neck around to look up at the man standing beside her. He was huge and dressed in leather chaps and gloves, a sweat-stained gray shirt, a red bandanna, and a wide-brimmed hat. His face was tanned and creased, his eyes no more than wrinkled slits beneath white bushy brows, and he smelled worse than the pile of manure resting a few feet away.

Her attention fell to the gun he wore in the thick, cracked-leather belt spanning his hips, and slowly, with practiced control, she straightened.

"You is a *ma'am*, ain'tcha?"

Josie wasn't sure if she could trust her voice yet, but she made an attempt to answer. "The last time I checked."

"Ask her who cropped her, Jeb!"

There were two other men standing behind the first, both filthy, with greasy hair and rotted teeth. The man directly in front of her shifted his weight to his other leg. "You get yourself scalped, little lady?"

Josie raised her hand to her short hair.

"Or do all you newfangled, eastern lady doctors wanna look like men?"

"How 'bout them Chinamen clothes!" one of the others put in, laughing.

Josie looked down at her green scrubs. According to what she'd witnessed so far, she was apparently a bit off the mark from the latest style.

"Heck, Jeb. Maybe she is a he, one of them Ching-Chong Chinamen, hornin' in on the livin's of decent white men!"

The one named Jeb gave a lecherous grin. "Well, boys, I guess there's only one way ta find out fer sure."

He reached out and grabbed hold of Josie's arm. She was still too stunned by all she'd seen to react as the man pulled her up against his big dirty chest and began pawing at her breasts. The two other men moved closer, whooping and hollering their approval, while the people milling in the street barely paused to take notice.

Josie couldn't believe the things that were going on in whatever this place was. Now she supposed it was her turn to get killed while nobody lifted a finger to help? Well, not while she had a breath left in her body! She'd had about all she could stand from this weird little town, and she certainly wasn't about to become a victim of some western movie reject, who probably had the equivalent of a bullet for a brain!

Even though her enemy was bigger than she, Josie knew there was always one sure way to bring a man to heel. With this in mind, she took a handful of what lay nestled between Jeb's bulky thighs.

Jeb's eyes bulged, and Josie squeezed just a little harder, eyeing his companions, who wisely decided to stand back. "I'm going to ask you a few questions,

Jeb," she said through clenched teeth. "And you're going to answer me, plain and clear—understand?"

"Y-yes, ma'am," he responded quickly.

"Where am I?"

"L-Lincoln City."

"Lincoln City, Nebraska?"

"No, ma'am. N-New Mexico Territory."

"Territory?" She tightened her grip on Jeb. "When!"

"When?"

"What is the date!"

"June the twenty-ninth!" he said with a note of confusion.

"What *year*, you idiot!"

"Year?" When she twisted a bit more, he shouted, "Eighteen eighty-one!"

With a shocked gasp, Josie released him and stumbled back against a street post. A small crowd had gathered behind her on the boardwalk, and she turned to one particularly kind looking older woman. "Is this real?" she asked her. "Is this really real?"

The woman gave her a disconcerted look while the words of the camerawoman rang through Josie's mind:

Would you agree to go back in time to be with the one man who could make you happy for the rest of your life? To be with your soul mate?

She brought her hands to her face. Her cheeks were as cold as ice.

Agree, Dr. Reed. Simply agree.

"I was only kidding!" Josie burst out. The woman standing close gasped and pressed back into the crowd. "I wanted a date for Friday night! Just one lousy date! Not Daniel Boone! Not Custer's last stand! Not 1881, for God's sake!"

She spun around and ran into the middle of the

street. "How in the world did you do all this!"

"Do what?" Jeb asked.

Josie ignored him. "Put me back!" she shouted.

"Pu'cha back where?"

"Shut up, cowboy! Little woman, you come here this minute and zap me back!"

"I'm thinkin' that spendin' time with that outlaw injun has fevered up her brain," she heard one of Jeb's friends whisper. "'Pears to me *she* needs a doctor."

"Yeah, we best get outta here." Josie turned to see Jeb and his companions backing away. "Whatever she's got might be catchin'."

It was then that Josie realized what a fool she was making of herself, standing in the middle of a dirt road, shouting up at the empty sky like a madwoman. Ignoring the people who were still staring at her, she stalked back toward the clapboard hospital, hoping to find an empty room where she could scream down the heavens in private.

"Li'l fella?"

She whirled around to see the rotund Deputy Green moving out from the center of the onlookers. "I—I mean, ma'am," he added. He took off his hat and began twisting it between his dirty hands. "Doc sent me over ta find out how the prisoner's farin'."

Josie narrowed her eyes and leaned toward him. He took a faltering step back. "Don't you mean *patient*, Deputy Green?"

"Uh . . . no, ma'am. I do mean prisoner. That breed runs with the kid. Me and a posse hunted him for days afore catchin' him."

Her patient was an outlaw? "Great," she said. "Life doesn't get any better than this, Deputy Green. No, it surely doesn't."

"Doc Primrose'll gladly take over, ma'am. If you'd just see yourself clear to leavin' his hospital. He's over talkin' to the marshal as we speak—"

"You mean he's off complaining that I didn't let him hack off your prisoner's leg."

"Pardon, ma'am, but Mitchell's just a breed. Ain't no sense in you—"

"A *breed*, Deputy Green?"

"An injun. Half white." He moved so close that she could smell his rancid breath. "The mixing of the blood does somethin' ta their brains. Vicious killers, each and every one of 'em."

"In other words, I shouldn't be wasting my precious time and energy trying to save his life?"

The man nodded firmly. "Especially since he'll be hung fer sure, anyhow."

"Hung? What's that, Deputy Green, another wonderful bit of news? Well, is there anything else I should know, like maybe the sun will turn to blood tomorrow and Beelzebub will come charging into town riding a great white monkey!"

"Ain't no call to get nasty—"

"Tell me, Deputy Green. Has the *prisoner* had a fair trial yet, or are you planning to forgo all that mess and just get on with killing him?"

"I believe the word you're meanin' to use is *execute*, ma'am. Execute—"

"I suppose that would depend on which end of the rope you're on, now, wouldn't it? If you will excuse me, despite the fact that I've been beamed into a bad episode of *Gunsmoke*, I do have a patient to look after!"

Deputy Green's brows dropped down as she brushed past him and headed for the door. "A white woman ought not to take such an interest in a savage," he grumbled.

She paused on the threshold and glared back at him. "Then I guess you haven't heard, Deputy. *I* am a China-man!"

3

Josie rested on her pallet on the floor with her legs bent up in front of her. Nothing moved within the darkened hospital room except the flicker of the lowered lamp flame as it cast dancing shadows on the walls and on the man still sleeping in the bed.

Her arm resting on her knee, she chewed her thumbnail, contemplated the floor in front of her, and listened to the crickets chirp in the growing darkness outside. She considered her options—of which there were very few.

She was sitting right smack dab in the year 1881. There was no doubt about it. And she didn't have a clue, or even a clue to a clue, how to get herself home.

A low moan brought her to her feet, and she crossed the small room to stand beside the bed of her patient. He was resting as comfortably as possible: on clean sheets, with regular injections of morphine, and with a cool mug of water at the ready.

The penicillin she'd been giving him was already beginning to have an effect on his fever, and she was more than satisfied with the condition of his leg.

Unfortunately, in order to make him so comfortable, she'd had to strip him herself. The hospital nurse had refused, and Dr. Primrose, as she'd come to know the tall, mustached "butcher," was above such things.

Josie was beginning to believe that if she hadn't come along, this man Mitchell, outlaw or not, would have died from neglect, if not improper care. He was an outcast, a so-called breed, and apparently warranted no better treatment than a stray dog.

So she'd wrestled with his heavy body by herself and had managed to remove his filthy shirt only after many long minutes of struggle. After that she'd dealt with the remains of his pants with the help of her trusty scissors.

His hard, virile body had been revealed, inch by bronzed inch, making her hands shaky again. Criminal or not, Mitchell was a man any woman would find attractive. But she wasn't just any woman. She was his doctor, and she had to remind herself of that fact constantly.

Now he was lying under the sheet, nude, and Josie was doing her damnedest not to envision him that way.

When she heard another faint groan she bent over him. "Can you hear me?" she whispered, feeling his brow. He was surprisingly cool to the touch. "Can you hear me, Mitchell?"

"Get away from me."

His raspy growl sent her back a step. "Well, it's nice to know you're getting some of your strength back."

She reached for his wrist, intending to take his pulse, but he wrenched his arm free, bellowing, "I can die without your goddamn help!"

Finally he turned his head toward her, and their gazes clashed in the wavering light, one pair dark and feral, the other bright and determined. She held his stare until he was forced to blink in order to refocus his eyes. He was still groggy from the morphine, which seemed to have made him incapable of doing much but shout at her.

"But can you *live* without my help?"

He rolled his head back to the center of his pillow and closed his eyes. He was clearly too tired to argue with her; Josie couldn't help wondering how much resistance she would have come up against if he'd had full control over his faculties.

She stared at his profile for a moment, and then reached over to turn up the lamp. "I need to check your bandages."

"You touch me . . . and I will snap your neck," he said without so much as cracking open an eye.

The room brightened in a yellow glow. "Somehow I doubt you have the strength to snap your fingers."

"Don't bet on it, lady."

She crossed her arms and stared down at him. "How am I supposed to help you if I can't touch you?"

"Who said I need your help?"

"That leg of yours appears to be screaming my name. Are you going to let me check its bandages, or shall we let it rot off?"

He hesitated.

"Of course, you've always got one other perfectly good leg. Why keep a spare?"

Without warning, he yanked aside the sheet, revealing every inch of his sleek, sinewy body. Josie caught her breath, and despite her greatest efforts to prevent it, she felt her cheeks go hot. She quickly averted her eyes, but not before catching a glimpse of a hard, ribbed stomach, tight corded thighs, and more man than any woman could possibly need.

She returned her attention to his face, but his dark good looks coupled with the dangerous narrowing of his eyes only made her breath come faster. And then she got mad.

"Is this supposed to impress me?" she snapped. "Or maybe send me screaming from the room?" She leaned over him, very aware of the threatening glitter in his eyes. "I think it's time you and I got a few things straight, Mitchell. You may be able to frighten people with a blink, but it takes more than a snarl and a growl to scare me off. You are my patient. And if I have to pump you so full of sedatives that you float, just in order to do my job, then don't you think for one goddamn second I won't do it!"

He held her stare for a long tense moment. "You apparently kept yourself busy while I was asleep."

The thought then occurred to Josie that maybe he hadn't exposed himself on purpose. Maybe he hadn't even been aware that he was completely bare beneath that sheet. "Some—somebody certainly had to get you out of those filthy clothes," she said, suddenly feeling self-conscious. "And despite what you might be thinking, I am only trying to do my job to the best of my ability."

"Then get to it."

She retrieved her scissors from the lamp table and then, giving his face a final cautious glance, tugged at the coarse sheet to cover what the little devil on her shoulder kept daring her to look at.

She removed the thick layer of gauze that spanned his big leg from knee to upper thigh, always aware of the string-tight tension in the room. Mitchell kept his attention on the ceiling the entire time, even when her shaky hand slipped and nudged against the concealing sheet.

He was healing nicely, she noted as she examined her neat stitches and the clearer drainage coming from his once inflamed wound. She, however, was doing much worse, with her pounding heart and her dry throat.

She wrapped his leg again while he lay silent and unmoving, then pulled the sheet up to cover the rest of him, including the imposing span of his muscular shoulders. "You're a fast healer."

He didn't respond, just stared straight up as though intent on ignoring her very existence.

"If it makes any difference, I'm sorry they intend to hang you."

His attention snapped to her face, and he stared at her with raw horror in his eyes. "What did you say?"

"You mean you don't know? These primitive bastards plan to hang you."

She thought she saw a spark of panic cross his face, but then his jaw hardened and he looked away again.

She closed her medical bag and set it on the floor by the bed. "You know, when a person does something wrong, they usually end up paying for it." She couldn't help but wonder what he had done to deserve to hang. "No one is beyond justice," she added.

"It appears no one is safe from it, either."

His answer surprised her, and she was about to ask him what he'd meant by it when the door swung open and the cold-eyed marshal strode into the room. He wore the same gray jacket and wide-brimmed hat, and his shiny silver star was pinned to the front of his shirt for the whole world to see.

He and Mitchell exchanged glares, and then the lawman turned to Josie, his sharp gaze flicking over her surgical scrubs. "You must be the doctor from the east who Primrose has been crowing to everyone about. District Attorney Rynerson would like a word with you first thing in the morning."

Josie's heart tripped. A district attorney? So far she'd allowed the people she'd come into contact with to assume she was from the east, but what if she was questioned more in depth about her origins? What if this DA wanted to know the name of the medical school she'd attended or the hospital where she'd spent her residency?

"Why?" she asked.

"Because he's in charge of this investigation, Doctor, and you will do exactly as he says." He turned to the doorway and called, "Deputy?"

A thin, wide-eyed boy of no more than sixteen rushed into the room. "Yeah, Marshal Riggs?"

"Shackle the prisoner."

"What!" Josie couldn't possibly have heard right.

The deputy moved toward Mitchell with a heavy set of rusty iron manacles in his hands, but Josie darted in front of him. "Wait just a minute! This man nearly *died* less than twelve hours ago! Don't you think shackling him is a little excessive?" The deputy pushed past Josie without apology. "My patient is barely strong enough to keep his eyes open, Marshal, let alone pull off a daring escape!" she cried.

Despite her protests, Mitchell's wrists were shackled to the iron headboard. He did nothing to resist but simply looked up at the ceiling and acted as if it were the most normal thing in the world to be chained to his bed.

Once his task was completed, the deputy left the room, and Josie, outraged, turned to the marshal, who was still standing in the doorway. "He doesn't even have the strength to stand, for God's sake."

"Will he live?" Riggs asked her.

"What the hell do you care?"

"Will he live?" the marshal demanded again.

"No thanks to you."

"Good. Wouldn't be any fun hanging a dead man. Remember, Doctor, tomorrow morning in the district attorney's office."

"You can bet I'll have quite a bit to say to this Rynerson!" she shouted after him as he strode into the lobby. "You might want to tell him to pop a few aspirin before I get there!"

She slammed the door and turned to lean back against it. Mitchell was still staring at the ceiling. They'd chained him like an animal.

She moved forward to check his manacles and noted the rusty cuff, the old-fashioned keyhole, and the heavy chain that wound through the cast-iron bars of the bed's headboard. "Are they too tight?" she asked.

He didn't answer. Instead he closed his eyes and began breathing deeply through his nose. For one brief moment she thought he might have fallen asleep.

"Turn down the lamp," he finally said.

"Just let me—"

"Turn down the goddamn lamp," he growled.

"Fine."

She turned the lamp off completely and stepped over

to her pallet of rough, woolen blankets by the far wall. She'd saved Mitchell's leg—and probably his life—but he was making it very clear that he didn't appreciate the gesture.

In the darkness she took off the lime-green shirt and pants of her scrubs and pulled on her jeans and favorite T-shirt, which she'd fortunately brought back to the past with her. Then she lay down on her makeshift bed.

She was intent on getting some sleep, considering what little she'd had in the past couple of days between her date with Harv, overtime at the hospital, and now this. But too many things were racing around in Josie's head. All of her problems, combined with the occasional *clink clink* of Mitchell's chains, were making peace a hard thing to come by.

She finally did manage to fall asleep, however, but only after determining that tomorrow she would find out just exactly what she was doing in the year 1881.

The next morning Josie asked the first person she saw on the street for directions to District Attorney Rynerson's office. After the small, elderly woman had finally managed to tear her eyes away from Josie's jeans and T-shirt, she sent Josie past a row of shops peopled with gawking men and women. One mother actually went so far as to hide her little boy behind her skirt as Josie walked past.

Though Rynerson's office building was small, it would have been clearly discernible from Mars. It was painted a brilliant white, gleaming amid the older, weathered buildings like a new tooth in the mouth of a hillbilly. Out front hung a gigantic sign that read "Rynerson, Attorney at Law."

She stepped up to the threshold, gave a quick knock, and pushed open the door. The room that greeted her was barely large enough to accommodate the immense oak desk situated by the window, let alone the floor-to-ceiling bookcase that practically blocked the doorway.

Seated behind that desk was the district attorney, a formidable-looking man in a heavy black suit complete with a white stand-up collar. He had a dark mustache, a pale, almost waxen complexion, and crystal green eyes. As she strode into the room he looked up, dropped his pencil, and proceeded to stare at her clothing much the same way the people on the street had. Despite the fact that he'd sent for her, he didn't seem the slightest bit pleased to have her standing before him.

Not waiting for an invitation, Josie sat down on the wooden chair across from him.

"Dr. Reed, I presume," he said with a blatant note of distaste.

"District Attorney Rynerson, I presume," she replied in much the same tone.

Josie had come prepared to do battle. Her patient had barely slept at all the night before, and her own rest had been interrupted frequently by the sporadic rattling of his chains. She'd been greeted at first light by that damn Marshal Riggs, who'd stated *cheerfully* that Mitchell was to be placed in jail immediately after Dr. Primrose had finished a thorough examination of him. Just the thought of that butcher laying hands on a patient of hers had been enough to send Josie flying out the door and straight to the DA's office.

"Our marshal tells me that ya've done an excellent job healin' the prisoner," he said with an accent that seemed to be a combination of Irish lilt and cowboy drawl.

She remained silent, allowing him to size her up for another long moment.

Finally he sat forward on his chair. "You from Vanderbilt?"

Hoping he was speaking of the historically famous Vanderbilt University, she responded, "Yes."

"You don't sound like a Southerner."

"I'm originally from New York." As good an eastern city as any.

He seemed to not quite believe her. "And what is it that has brought ya so far west, Doctor?"

She hedged. "What brings anybody out west?"

He nodded at length, his thin mouth vanishing behind his mustache. "Greener pastures provide well durin' the spring, but in my experience it's only the woman with a good man beside her who goes on ta see all four seasons."

It took a great deal of effort for Josie to keep her mouth clamped shut after that ridiculous statement, but starting an argument about the autonomy of women certainly wasn't going to help matters at the moment. She only hoped Gloria Steinem wasn't sitting up in heaven, waiting to be born, shaking her head in disappointment at hearing all of this.

"Will ya be with us long?" Rynerson continued.

"Actually, I'm not sure how long I'll be here."

"You're certainly welcome to stay as long as ya like. However, Dr. Primrose has suggested to me that ya might be better served to find other places to occupy yourself besides his hospital."

Josie had never appreciated being given orders, subtly or otherwise. "I have a patient in his hospital—"

"That is bein' taken care of as we speak."

She eased forward on her chair, leaned her arms on

the polished desk, and looked the district attorney in the eye. "My patient isn't well enough to be taken from his hospital bed, Mr. Rynerson."

"I think Dr. Primrose should be the judge—"

"As a matter of fact, Mitchell was practically dead when I arrived yesterday. Your noble doctor was about to hack off his leg with a rusty saw, and without benefit of morphine."

Rynerson narrowed his eyes and sat back on his chair. "Your concern for your patient is admirable. However, Mitchell is a prisoner of this county and will be treated as such. He belongs in jail until his trial."

Josie smiled coldly. "Surely even you realize that a man with such a severe infection couldn't possibly survive in a chilly, damp cell for very long."

The DA's mouth tightened, but he said nothing.

"And I doubt you want him dead just yet, or your faithful marshal would have killed him instead of going to all the trouble of bringing him in and handing him over to Dr. Primrose for patching up."

"I've been told that Mitchell was quite alert last night—"

"You take him from that hospital bed, Rynerson, and lock him up in a cell, and he'll be dead before you even get your scaffold built."

Rynerson blinked, the only sign that what she'd said had bothered him. He studied the top of his desk, moved a wooden cigar box a little to the left until it lined up with a stack of leather-bound books. Finally he looked back at her. "You take your job very seriously, I can tell."

Josie held his intent gaze and nodded.

"That in mind, Doctor, I have decided to take your professional opinion to heart, and will inform Marshal

Riggs that the prisoner may stay within the walls of his hospital room until it is decided that he is well enough to be remanded to the jail. There will be a guard posted. Any trouble, and I will see both you and your patient locked up myself."

Josie stood and held out her hand. "I understand."

The district attorney stood as well. He merely stared at her offered hand. "You're a very odd woman."

"I'll take that as a compliment."

His gaze traveled over her jeans and lingered on her T-shirt. "I'm sure you will."

Josie hurried outside and walked down the street the way she'd come, ignoring the people who paused to stare at her. Primrose had undoubtedly had his grubby hands all over her patient by now, and if he so much as—

"Mornin', ma'am."

"Good morning, Deputy Green."

The large man smiled hesitantly and fell into stride beside her. "Been ta see Rynerson, have ya?"

"Yes, I have. And I'm sure you'll be annoyed to hear that I've convinced the DA to let my patient remain in the hospital until he's well."

Josie hopped over a large mud puddle and continued her hurried pace down the street, the deputy bustling along beside her. "Ye're a feisty li'l dickens, ain'tcha?"

"What's the matter, Deputy? Afraid my dickens might be bigger than yours?"

"Doc"—he darted forward, trying to keep up with her—"Doc asked me to entertain ya outside until he's finished with the prisoner."

"Oh?" She climbed the porch of the hospital and reached for the door. "Do you belly-dance?"

"Well, no—"

"Damn, *that* would have been entertaining."

She strode through the hospital's outer hall, with its hardwood floor and horizontal log bench, and continued to Mitchell's room.

"Uh . . . " Deputy Green's hand came down on the knob before Josie could get her fingers around it. "Doc was real specific about you—"

"I don't care what *Doc* was, Deputy. Rynerson has given me full charge over Mitchell—and if you don't get your hand off this knob, you're going to get a mouthful of my fist!"

He jumped back quickly, and she pushed the door open.

Dr. Primrose was standing by the bed. He looked at Josie and then at Deputy Green as the cumbersome man barged into the room behind her.

"Sorry, Doc. I tried ta keep her out, but she—"

Josie's forward motion ended abruptly when she saw what was happening before her. "What in the *hell* do you think you're doing, Primrose!"

4

"I did my best ta keep her out, Doc."

Josie shoved past the doctor and ran to the bed. Primrose stumbled out of her way while tugging down the edges of his brown silk vest. "Now see here!" he said in a huff.

Mitchell was still stretched out on the bed, his hands shackled above his head. His face appeared impassive, but Josie could see the telltale ticking of the muscle in the side of his jaw. Clamped to the inside of his right arm was the most horrendous metal contraption she'd ever seen. And it was dripping his blood into a pail on the floor.

"What the hell is that!" she demanded.

"It is called a leech, madam. And if you had received a decent medical degree, you would know that it is the only way to purge poisons from the blood."

With careful fingers Josie released the sharp-toothed

instrument from the bleeding flesh of Mitchell's inner arm. She set the device on the table and reached for her medical bag. She took out gauze pads to stanch the bleeding, all the while grinding her teeth together so hard that her jaw began to ache.

"How do you justify healing a man by draining him of what little blood he has left?" she asked tightly. "Where did *you* get your medical degree, Primrose, Physicians R Us?!"

Dr. Primrose's dark eyes narrowed. "It is the only way to seep the infection from his body, but *you*, apparently, are not aware of that!"

"In that case I'm pleased to be ignorant!" she shouted back. "Say, I've got a novel idea, Primrose, let's treat the wounds he has instead of inflicting more!"

"The savage will die if he's not bled!"

"Does he look like he's dying!"

"That he still lives is merely a fluke!"

She clenched her teeth together again, her temper barely under control. "Well, the district attorney doesn't agree. He's remanded the patient into my care until *I* decide he's healed."

The ends of Primrose's waxed black mustache twitched. "That is impossible."

Josie checked Mitchell's newest wound and was relieved to see that the bleeding had stopped. She set the bloody gauze aside. "No, that's a fact. Now I want you out of this room." Despite the fact that Primrose towered over her five-foot-two-inch frame by about six inches, Josie advanced on him and shoved him toward the door. "And if I catch you in this room again . . . I'll be leeching the Primrose family jewels!"

"We shall see about this!" Primrose cried as he left the room, with Deputy Green fast on his heels.

Josie slammed the door behind the two men and took a few deep breaths. Then she looked back at Mitchell. He was still lying quietly on the bed, but his intent black gaze slid from the ceiling to her face as she approached.

"Let's see what other damage the good doctor managed to do," she said, lifting the sheet back a few inches to check his leg. She was relieved to find the bandage on it undisturbed.

"He didn't get that far," Mitchell said.

She looked back at him, at his manacled wrists, and wondered if his shoulders were cramping from their continued forced position. "The good doctor was apparently in too much of a hurry to dig that vise from hell into your arm."

She let the sheet drop back over his leg and leaned across him to check his manacles. The red, raw skin she found made her curse out loud. "These need to be cleaned." She stood back from the bed. "But I won't be able to do an adequate job as long as you're wearing those things. . . . I suppose I could stuff some cotton along the inside to protect—"

"Do you have a hairpin?"

She gave him a bewildered look. "A hairpin?"

"Picking a lock's an easy thing, Doctor," he said with a faint twist of his lips.

It was the closest she'd ever seen him come to a smile, and her heart nearly stopped. Forget that he was an outlaw, it was crime enough that he was so damn good-looking!

"Whadayasay?" he persisted.

She tore her attention from him and looked over at the closed door. "I don't think I should—"

"You don't strike me as the kind of woman who

worries a whole lot about what she should and shouldn't do."

"And you don't strike me as the kind of man who'll sit tight and wait to be hanged."

As quickly as it had come, the warmth in his gaze fled, leaving only his usual indifferent stare.

"Look, Mitchell, I can't just set you free. We'd *both* end up in jail."

When he didn't respond, she began to question her decision. His wrists did need to be looked after, and she wasn't his jailer, she was his doctor. The man was so weak he could barely lift his head. Where could he possibly go? "All right," she finally said. "But if anyone comes through that door, I want your arms up to that headboard so fast they break the speed of sound."

"A hairpin."

She ignored the urgency in his voice, telling herself he was only anxious to have his hands free, like any normal human being. After a quick look in her medical bag she produced a scalpel that she hoped would do the trick.

Placing a knee on the bed beside him, she bent her head and began working on the first rusty lock while he kept his eyes on the door.

The lock finally clicked, and the manacle popped open. There was a slight clanking sound as Mitchell gathered his arms to his chest and rubbed the sore muscles of one forearm. She held her breath, but the guard who was supposed to be posted outside the room didn't enter.

Then Mitchell held out his free hand to her. "Give me the knife."

Josie hesitated, beginning to think about what, exactly, she was doing. She was setting a criminal free—a murderer, for all she knew. Dare she give him something that could easily be used as a weapon against her?

She searched his face, looking for an answer in the depths of his unreadable gaze. Finally she decided to trust her instincts and set the scalpel in his open palm.

With calculating dark eyes he looked down at the razor-sharp instrument and then back up at her. A sudden fear struck her in the pit of her stomach as his expression turned stone cold. "You're lucky I don't kill old men and fools," he said.

Since she wasn't an old man, that apparently left her in the fool category. "Those are awfully ambitious words for a man who can barely lift his head."

He didn't spare her another glance, but she was stunned when he sat up in bed to work the other lock. She backed up a step, wondering what he would do once he was completely free. But then he wavered, his big body swaying slightly to one side, and she dashed toward him, catching him just before he fell sideways on the bed.

Her arms went around him, and he landed hard against her chest, his head knocking solidly against her chin. He was incredibly heavy, but somehow she managed to push him onto his back. His breath was quick and choppy.

"Exertion isn't good for you, Mitchell. In the end it will only hamper your progress."

He ignored her advice and struggled to rise again, but he ended up crumbling onto his back after only a few moments of effort.

Josie stood and watched as he brought his heavy breathing under control. Truthfully, she was a little perplexed that he was still so weak after being on penicillin for over twenty-four hours. Then, begrudgingly, he held out the knife and his remaining manacled wrist to her.

She gave him a cool look. "You need a fool's help?"

With a low growl, he threw the scalpel across the room. "I won't beg you, Doctor, if that's what you're after!"

Josie caught her breath at his violent outburst and instantly looked toward the door. She half expected the guard and the entire town to come barging in, but, surprisingly, the knob didn't even jiggle.

Calmly she retrieved her scalpel and then, just as calmly, sat down on the edge of the bed to work the other lock loose. Soon he was completely free, but after seeing how weak he was, she didn't give his liberation a second thought.

As he lay stiffly beside her, she used a cloth from the ceramic bowl of fresh water to gently clean the injured skin around his thick wrists. "You're going to be leaving here with more wounds than when you arrived," she said.

"And with one hell of a long neck."

Her ministrations stopped, and she stared at the creased palm of the large hand she held. His long fingers flexed, grazing the inside of her wrist, and sparks shot up her arm. "Have you even considered that the trial might go in your favor?"

He snorted. "With a jury of my *peers*?"

Recalling that he had been called a "breed," she looked at his face and the dark, noble features that marked him an outcast. She began washing his other wrist. "So ask for a change of venue, to be tried in another town."

"It won't be any different anywhere else."

She finished her cleaning and wrapped each of his

wrists with a thin layer of gauze, then followed with his routine shots of penicillin and morphine. Finally she went to sit on her pallet, to try to straighten out her own thoughts.

She couldn't decide what was more cruel: leaving this man to his wounds so that they dragged him, half-dead, to the gallows, or healing him only to allow him to feel every fiber of that rope around his neck, every instant of it tightening and cutting off his air, every crack and snap—

She wouldn't think about it. She was doing her job, and that was what mattered.

The morphine acted quickly, and she soon heard Mitchell's deep, even breathing. She looked up to where he lay motionless on the bed, and the image of his dark, angry eyes returned to haunt her. How could the life of such a potent man be snuffed out with only the simple pull of a wooden lever?

Josie checked to be sure her green scrub shirt was baggy in the front and pulled down past her bottom in the back, and then she cautiously stepped inside Juan Patron's House and Saloon. She had to maneuver around several drunken men in order to get to the bar, but somehow she managed without tripping in the dim light.

The place was small and dark and smelled of unwashed bodies, too much alcohol, and smoldering cigarettes. She'd come to find food for herself and Mitchell, but the dismal interior was making her wonder if they'd both be better off without it.

The straggly-haired man behind the bar caught her eye. His lower face was covered with stubble, and a thick cigar was hanging from his mouth. "What d'ya need here, boy?"

"Hell, Juan," a voice called out. "That ain't no boy. That there's our new doc. Ain't that right, Doc?"

"Yeah," another voice said. "The new doc here is healin' up that breed what runs with the kid so's we can hang him while he's still kickin'."

Male laughter rumbled from the table in the far corner, and Josie turned to find Jeb and his two cohorts grinning drunkenly over their mugs of beer.

"Ain'choo a mite young to be a doc?" Juan asked. He spit a glob of tobacco into a filthy brass spittoon at Josie's feet.

More laughter came, and Juan narrowed his eyes on the men. "You boys findin' somethin' funny?"

"I hear you serve food here?" Josie said. She moved to lean her arm on the bar but caught herself just in time; the scarred oak was filthy.

"Yeah, yeah, we serve food here. You got the *dinero* to pay for it, son?"

This was greeted with more laughter, but Josie had the distinct impression that if she whirled around to confront the men, and this dirty, burly man realized that she was a woman, all hell would break loose. "Dr. Primrose told me to put it on his account," she responded.

Actually, she and Dr. Primrose had yet to have another conversation since their confrontation that morning, and she was taking quite a chance in even assuming he had an account in this saloon. However, when it came to *dinero*, she was a little short.

The bartender narrowed his eyes. "He did, did he? Maria! A plate of enchiladas!"

"Two," Josie said.

"Huh?"

"Two plates, please."

"Make that two!" He turned back to her. "And you tell the good doctor that he owes me a dollar for that whore he had last night. Say . . . he didn't share her with *you*, did he? 'Cause tha'd be double."

The laughter started up again behind her, and Josie took a deep breath. "No. He didn't share her with me." She smiled. "But I know for a fact that those three gentlemen back there each had a turn. I suggest you speak with them."

The laughter stopped as Juan came out from behind the bar with a vicious look in his eyes. "Three dollars, boys!"

"Three what!"

"What fer, Juan?"

"We didn't do nothin'!"

"That's the same thing ya said when I caughtcha sneaking bottles of whiskey from the back shed last week! Now, I know you boys shared with Primrose last night—"

"Shoot, Juan, I ain't never had to pay for it my whole life," Jeb said.

"Which is gonna be cut mighty short if you don't hand over the cash!"

A plump Mexican woman came from the back room carrying two plates full of tortillas covered with a rich red Mexican sauce. Josie thanked her, took them, and quickly headed for the door.

"You ain't gonna believe that crazy eastern lady over us, are ya, Juan?" Jeb whined.

"What crazy eastern lady?"

"The one standing over yonder with her hands full of Maria's prize enchiladas!"

At that point every male in the place stared at Josie.

She hurried over the prone men in the doorway and out the swinging doors, praying that nobody would get it into his head to chase her.

She dashed across the street and made it into the hospital safe and sound. However, when she reached her patient's door, Deputy Browne, the large guard assigned to sit outside, stood up and refused her entrance.

"Primrose isn't in there again, is he?" she asked.

"The sheriff is having a word with the prisoner, Doctor, and would appreciate it if you could wait outside."

Sheriff? Dread rose up in Josie as she remembered Mitchell's unshackled wrists.

"Deputy, these plates are awfully heavy. Could you hold them for me while I wait?"

The man smiled. "Why, certainly, ma'am. Smells like Maria's prize ench—"

As soon as the man had his hands full, Josie rushed forward and flung open the door. Inside, a lean, dark-haired man was sitting on the edge of her patient's bed. The two of them were having what appeared to be a very serious conversation.

The sheriff rose when she entered. "Didn't I tell you no visitors, Deputy?" he said.

The guard gave his boss a helpless look while standing there holding two hot plates of food.

"I am this man's doctor, Sheriff, and you have no right to question him without my express permission." Josie hurried forward and was relieved to see that Mitchell at least had his hands up over his head.

The sheriff gave her a crooked smile that twitched the ends of his neat mustache. "Of course you're his doctor. I should have guessed."

"And you'll have to guess at the answers to any

other questions you'd planned to ask him because I am asking you, kindly, to leave."

"Am I to understand that you don't normally ask kindly?"

He smiled past her at Mitchell, but when Josie turned to look at her patient she found Mitchell's expression as impassive as usual.

"I think you'll find that manners matter very little to me, Sheriff, when one of my patients' health is at risk."

"I suppose that's how it should be. I could only hope that my own doctor would be so dedicated."

"I appreciate your understanding. Now, if you'll please lea—"

"You are aware that he's a danger to you and the rest of the town, aren't you, ma'am? Don't you think it would be safer to tend to him in jail?"

"Sheriff, this man is not going to jail or anywhere else until I decide he's well enough to get out of that bed. And, quite frankly, that may not be for a very long time."

The sheriff took a deep breath and addressed Mitchell. "She's a stubborn little thing."

"And she'd like to feed her patient," Josie responded.

The sheriff bowed slightly. "Then I'll leave this man in your very capable hands."

He left the room. The guard handed her the plates of food and followed, closing the door behind him.

Josie turned to Mitchell and set his plate on the edge of the bed. "That was very, very close."

Mitchell didn't respond. He rolled to his side, picked up a fork, and started eating.

"Listen, if this is going to be a regular occurrence, lawmen dropping in unexpectedly, maybe we should reconsider—"

"Everything's fine."

Fine for him! He wasn't the one risking his neck by freeing a prisoner! "And what if he'd checked your manacles just a little closer? Trust me, Mitchell, a jail cell wouldn't agree with me. I get nervous when I get a parking ticket."

He paused in his eating to give her a curious look but said nothing.

"I know, I'm running off at the mouth. But I'm a little anxious about all this, okay?" she snapped. "I think I'm holding up rather well considering I've been dumped out in the middle of nowhere with nothing but hanging-happy marshals, ruthless criminals, and, oh, let's not forget Dr. Frankenstein to keep me company!"

"Relax. Sheriff Garrett was just checkin' up on me."

"And what about the next time he checks up on you? What if they find you unchained and come after *me* with a pair of— Wait a minute . . . did you just say Sheriff *Garrett*? As in Sheriff *Pat* Garrett?"

"Are you two old friends?" he asked dryly.

Josie didn't answer, her mind was too busy putting together the pieces of the puzzle. If that was Pat Garrett, and this was 1881, Lincoln City, New Mexico, then . . .

"Holy history lesson, Batman," she said. She looked at Mitchell, her eyes wide. "They said you run with the 'kid.' That wouldn't by any chance be *Billy* the Kid?"

He looked up from his plate and studied her. "Another friend of yours?"

Josie backed up a step. "What the hell was that woman thinking?" she said out loud. "No, no, I know what she was thinking. She was thinking she'd drop me in the middle of a war and get me killed! I wouldn't go along with her silly little back-to-the-past blind date, so now she's hoping I'll get shot up in some gory gunfight between Billy the Kid and Pat Garrett."

"Lady—"

"You run with Billy the Kid, and *I* set you free!" she shouted at him.

"You seem a little upset."

She glared at him. "Well, I'm not going to stand for this—not for any of it! This is *my* life! I am in control of it! And nobody is going to send me skipping through time unless I agree to skip!"

With that, she turned on her heel and stomped out of the room.

5

Josie sat in the darkness in an empty field behind the town, beneath a sky full of stars. The air was chilly, and she was growing cold, but she refused to give up until that fairy woman responded to her pleas and sent her back to good old 1994 where she belonged.

"Look, I just want to go home," Josie said into the cool night air. "You don't have any right to keep me here against my will!"

She'd been there for almost five hours, begging, whining, yelling, cursing. The sun had long since set, and the town had long since gone to bed. But even if it took her all night, she was going to reach that damn woman!

"I'm assuming there's some method to this madness." She listened but heard nothing other than the crickets and the occasional yip of a coyote. "At least have the decency to pop in and tell me what I'm doing here!"

"I intend to, as soon as you calm down, Dr. Reed."

Josie spun around to see the woman standing a few feet behind her. "Well, it's about time!"

"I refuse to talk with you if you refuse to be rational—"

"Rational!" Josie lurched to her feet. "I ought to—"

The woman vanished in the blink of an eye, and Josie panicked. "Wait! I'm sorry. I'm sorry. Okay, I'll be rational."

"That's more like it." The woman reappeared. "Now. What is the problem, Doctor? I certainly hope you're not one of those cases that will have me dashing to and fro holding your hand through all this."

Josie tried to phrase her next question *rationally.* "Assuming, of course, that I haven't died and gone to hell, exactly what is *all this*?"

"I thought we'd discussed that already—"

"Refresh my memory."

The woman sighed. "It is your true destiny, Dr. Reed. This is the place where you truly belong."

"Funny, I don't feel like I'm sitting at home with my feet up. . . . Maybe I should take another look around. Oh, yes. This whole town must be my TV— because I sure as hell feel like the new *Dr. Quinn!*"

"Here is where you'll find your soul mate. Your perfect man."

"I said a *touch* of Clint Eastwood, lady. But then I guess I should be glad I didn't say a touch of Daffy Duck."

"I'm sorry, but your particular brand of humor escapes me."

"As has your mind."

"Your sarcasm is not appreciated."

"Neither is your interference!"

"I have only done what is best for you. Please remember that you agreed—"

"You tricked me into that agreement and you know it! Now put me back!"

Josie took a threatening step forward, and the woman moved a step back. "You cannot go back—"

"Don't you *dare* tell me that! If you do, I'll go out of what's left of my once very stable mind!"

"Dr. Reed, please remain calm," the woman said sharply. "I don't deal well with hysteria."

"I used to be a calm person. Until the day I became Lincoln City's lady sawbones! Put . . . me . . . back!"

The woman gave her an annoyed look. "It's always the same, you know. 'Take me back. Take me back.' Just once I would like to be appreciated for my efforts."

"So I'm not the only unhappy Cinderella on your wish list?"

The woman sighed. "I'll need at least a week."

"A *week!*"

"No, there's that problem in Kansas. You'll have to give me two weeks."

"Two—why not just do it now!"

"Dr. Reed, many different elements are affected by dimension changes. I cannot just snap my fingers. These things take time."

"And what am I supposed to do for two entire weeks?"

The woman arched a brow. "There's that patient of yours. He could certainly use your help."

"Mitchell? If there's one thing I've discovered since I got here, it's that it is hard to put your heart into making a man well when they're only going to hang him in the end."

"That's funny, I was under the impression that you never put your *heart* into anything."

"Let's leave my love life out of this, shall we, fairy godmother? You say two weeks? What if something happens to me between then and now? This isn't exactly Club Med, you know. This is a pretty dangerous place."

"I suggest you keep your head down."

"Great. And how do I know you'll keep your promise? How do I know you'll be back here in two weeks?"

The woman drew in an insulted breath. "Dr. Reed, despite your opinion, I am a very respectable woman. I do not lie, nor do I break promises."

"Maybe not, but I get the distinct impression that you bend things very neatly to suit your purposes."

"I will be back in two weeks. Do try to work on that prickly disposition of yours."

In a blink, she was gone.

Josie stormed all the way back to the hospital. Two weeks? Two weeks of outdoor plumbing. Two weeks of Dr. Primrose and Deputy Green. Two weeks of living in fear that Sheriff Pat Garrett would discover that she'd picked the locks on his prisoner's manacles.

She had to get Mitchell back into those chains. Maybe they could agree to take them off a few times a day so he could stretch and she could treat his sore wrists.

Inside the hospital she was brought up short at the sight of the empty chair outside Mitchell's room. Was it customary for Deputy Browne to go off duty from his watch at night?

Just then a heavy thump came from inside Mitchell's room, and the hair on the back of Josie's neck prickled. Maybe her patient had fallen out of bed?

Slowly she opened the door and poked her head inside the room. The bed was empty.

"Mitchell?"

She heard the metallic click of the hammer being cocked before she even saw the gun staring her in the face. A strong hand closed around her upper arm, yanked her inside the room, and slammed the door closed behind her.

Josie stumbled forward and was hauled up against a hard body. She didn't have to look to know who it was holding her. The sun-and-sweat smell of him filled her nose, and the bronzed wall of his bare chest burned where it pressed against her.

She swallowed thickly and tipped her head back to stare up at the grim line of her patient's mouth. "Mitch—"

He shoved her against the closed door, knocking the wind out of her, and clamped his hand tightly over her mouth. "Welcome to the party, Doctor," he whispered into her face. "I've been expecting you."

6

Josie's patient was apparently not as weak as she'd been led to believe. That fact became clearer with each passing second as Mitchell's hard, muscular body pressed her against the door and his fingers dug like clamps into her cheeks. She had to struggle to breathe.

"Don't make a sound," he whispered into her face.

With the cold bore of a gun resting against the side of her neck, Josie certainly didn't have to be told twice. She nodded, and he relaxed his grip on her mouth.

"How many guards are outside?" he demanded.

She glanced at where Deputy Browne lay sprawled on the floor, minus his shirt and pants. "None," she answered hoarsely.

The marshal obviously hadn't bothered with more than one guard outside Mitchell's door, because he had assumed his prisoner was shackled. Josie wondered desperately what would happen to her once it was discovered that she had been the one to unchain him.

"Not one sound," Mitchell warned again, pressing the gun a little harder to her neck.

Josie nodded, and he stepped away from her. He slipped the gun into the waistband of the gray woolen pants he'd stolen off Deputy Browne and gave her a final cautioning look as he pulled on the deputy's white shirt. Then he leaned against the iron footboard on the bed to pull on his boots. He was flushed beneath the dark stubble on his face, and Josie knew that without his nightly dose of morphine he had to be in a great deal of pain.

"This is insane," she finally whispered, risking his wrath.

He glanced up and gave her a sharp look. "Be quiet."

"They'll catch you," she continued. "Just like they did the last time. You're too weak to get very far."

He reached for his second boot and began pulling it onto the foot of his injured leg. "Apparently not as weak as you thought."

Josie clenched her jaw. "I took those manacles off because I trusted you to stay put!" she whispered furiously.

"I guess you learned a valuable lesson."

"They're going to throw *me* in jail when they find out I set you free!"

He was having a hard time pulling on his second boot. His features were drawn, his lips thinned and pale. "I suggest you keep that in mind," he said in a strained voice. He grunted when the boot finally jerked into place. Amazingly, he could stand without staggering, but he was still flushed, and beads of perspiration were gathering on his brow.

Without thinking, Josie reached out to feel his forehead to gauge his temperature. He caught her wrist, his fingers like hot iron. "Don't," he said.

"You look like hell," she replied as he slowly forced her arm down. "Without regular doses of penicillin you're going to die, Mitchell. The infection isn't completely gone from your body."

"Then I guess there's only one thing for me to do."

Still holding her arm, he reached down and picked up her medical bag. Then he pulled her toward the door. Cautiously he peeked out into the lobby, but Josie knew without looking that the hospital was empty. Mitchell was the only patient, which made her the only doctor in the house.

When he handed her her medical bag and pushed her through the door in front of him, she started to drag her feet. "What are you doing?" she demanded. "Where are—"

His arm squeezed around her ribs and effectively cut off her air. "You keep quiet and you just might survive this. Now move."

He shoved her out the front door and off the porch, and before Josie knew it they were moving stealthily down the empty street. Her stomach began to twist as she realized that she was his hostage.

They walked two blocks to the darkened livery, and he pushed her inside and up against a stall. She was pinned to three splintery rungs by his hips as he took a bridle from the wall. While he worked the leather straps and bit over a horse's head, Josie prayed silently that because she'd been so quiet and cooperative, he'd let her go unharmed when he was finished.

Finally the horse was bridled, but instead of releasing her, Mitchell leaned harder against her and whispered, "Let's see if we can do this nice and easy." He opened the stall and led the horse out toward the livery's double sliding doors. "Get on."

"Can't you just let—"

"Get on!"

Josie turned to face him with wide eyes. "I . . . I don't know how to ride a horse."

"Then you're about to learn."

"I won't let you take me with you," she said bravely. Even in the darkness she could see his ruthless eyes glowing.

"I don't recall asking your permission."

Josie opened her mouth to shout for help, regardless of the gun he still had, and Mitchell clamped his hand over her mouth again. Then he whispered something that turned her blood cold. "What excuse will you give them, Doctor, when they ask you why you set me free?"

A tangible feeling of dread raced through Josie. After the stink she'd put up about protecting him, she knew nobody in town would believe her if she said she hadn't meant for him to escape. They'd probably hang her in his place just to even the score.

She went weak with despair, and he removed his hand from her mouth. "This can't be happening," she whispered.

"Do you get on? Or do I throw you on?"

Apparently she hesitated a moment too long with her answer. Mitchell's arm snaked around her back and yanked her off the ground. Their faces came level, and she gazed into his relentless stare.

"You're going to have to learn to pay attention, lady. Or you won't be alive long enough to do me any good."

That said, he practically threw her onto the bare

back of the horse, leaving it up to her to hold on. But Josie hadn't been bluffing when she'd said she didn't ride, and it took all her balance—and every ounce of mane she could grab—to stay on board.

Mitchell swung up behind her, with only a faint grunt of pain, and clucked at the horse. The animal lurched forward out of the livery barn, and Josie almost fell off. But her captor clamped an arm around her middle and hauled her back against his hard chest, bracing her between his thighs.

They reached the field Josie had stood in only an hour before. She stared in desperation at the spot where the fairy woman had been, wondering how she was ever going to get away from this villain to keep the scheduled meeting two weeks from now.

Soon after, they crossed a narrow, shallow river. And then, with a kick of his heels, Mitchell sent them charging into the forest and disappearing into the night.

Mitchell hadn't said a word to Josie since leaving the livery, and they'd traveled in silence all night long. At eight in the morning, according to Josie's watch, she noticed that the journey was proving to be too much for him. They'd been riding for over seven hours, and he was beginning to lean more on her than she was on him. Still, he showed no signs of slowing down, even for a short rest.

At first she'd thought he would take her into the surrounding mountains and "lay low" until he'd healed completely. But now she was sure, by his grueling determination, that he had a definite destination in mind.

She kept glancing down at his right thigh, burning

with the temptation to give his wound a good slap, then jump to the ground and charge off into the concealing forest. But she doubted she could ever survive in the wilderness on her own, and she doubted even more that she'd ever find her way back to Lincoln without a dependable guide.

She looked up at the tall lean pines driving straight up into the blue sky above her head. The forest was so thick that hardly a ray of morning sun shone through the heavy branches, making it damp and chilly below the foliage canopy. Their horse continued to plod along, amid ferns growing soft and full beside rocks covered with clinging blue-green moss.

Josie checked her wristwatch again just before one in the afternoon, and that was when Mitchell swayed dangerously behind her, almost knocking her off the horse. The large black animal beneath them stopped, his ears pricked back in confusion, and Mitchell's arm tightened around Josie's ribs. The action gave her little security, however, considering that if Mitchell toppled, she'd end up falling with him.

"You need to rest," she said. "It isn't going to do either of us any good if you keel over and die now. We have to stop."

No sound came from behind her. Just when the silence had grown so heavy that Josie thought she might have convinced him, he kicked the horse beneath them into motion again.

"You're going to kill us both if we continue on like this," she said.

"It's not much farther, Doctor."

The sound of his voice alarmed her. It was nothing more than a thin rasp. "It's not much farther to your grave, either!"

She didn't care anymore that he was a bloodthirsty criminal with a gun stuffed down the back of his pants. She was tired, hungry, and frustrated with her lack of control over this whole damn situation. She was at the whim of a man whom she didn't know, didn't trust, and didn't care to be spending any quality time with. When she got her hands on that fairy god-mother, she was going to strangle the life from her!

By the time they broke through into a clearing a few hours later, Mitchell was practically prone over the top of her and Josie knew she wasn't going to be able to walk right for days. She looked up, saw a small log cabin in the center of a lush green meadow, and sighed with relief. "Please tell me this is it."

They rode up to the cabin and stopped. Mitchell straightened slowly, and Josie supposed she had her answer when he swung down behind her and into the foot-high grass.

She glanced around at the thick shelter of tall piñon trees that circled the clearing on all sides, and at the sparkling stream that trickled a few yards away, before returning her attention to the log cabin. "Have you led me right to your hideout, Mr. Desperado? Shouldn't you have blindfolded me or something?"

Mitchell ignored her sarcasm and steadied himself against the horse's side. The thought occurred to Josie that she should dig her heels into the animal's flanks and get herself the hell out of there. But where would she go?

Mitchell began walking unsteadily toward the cabin, making his point clear: it didn't matter a whole lot to him at the moment whether she got down or not.

With a sigh, Josie decided that the only thing for

her to do was to dismount as well. She slipped the handle of her medical bag over her wrist, eased one cramped leg over the back of the animal, and then slowly slipped to the ground.

She stood perfectly still for a moment to make sure everything on her body was in proper working order. Then she took her first step toward the cabin and dropped to the ground like a sack of potatoes.

She swore and looked up to see Mitchell struggling up two long plank steps. He rested against a splintered porch post for a moment and then dragged himself inside the cabin.

Stiffly Josie managed to climb to her feet and straighten her aching back. She walked, slowly and decidedly bowlegged, toward the cabin, climbed the same two steps—with about half as much grace as Mitchell had—and practically fell inside.

Streams of golden sunlight poured in through the single front window, making patterns in the dust swirling in the air. The whole cabin couldn't have been larger than Josie's living room at home. There was a thin-legged table beneath the window with two matching chairs; a threadbare couch in front of a cold, stone fireplace; a wobbly dresser against the wall in the back; and a large homemade bed in the far corner.

"Home sweet home," she muttered.

Mitchell was sprawled on his back in the center of the bed, his breathing loud and deep. He'd barely made it inside before falling fast asleep.

Josie hobbled to his side to check his temperature and found him warm to the touch. She opened her medical bag and made a quick slit in his stolen pants to check his bandages and wound. She was pleased to see that none of her stitches had torn.

She gave him his shot of penicillin and then added a shot of morphine to keep him out until she'd had a chance to get some rest. Then she covered him with a blanket from the foot of the bed and took one for herself.

Dust flew up all around her as she sat on the faded brown couch. Was it her imagination or was her life getting more and more complicated with each passing second?

She looked across the room to where her patient lay, quiet and heavily drugged. He'd be out at least until the next morning, which gave her time to catch up on her own rest. Careful not to stir up any more dust, she stretched out on the couch and closed her eyes. She had to figure a way out of this mess. In the next thirteen days she would somehow have to find a way back to Lincoln in order to catch her return ride to 1994.

7

Josie's sleep that night was interrupted by a bad dream that brought her leaping to her feet. She rubbed her eyes and blinked at the dim gloom of dawn spreading through the room from the front window, then glanced back at the filthy couch she'd slept on. She stretched and tried to remember where she was.

The past three days returned to her in one blinding flash, and she let out a low groan. Carefully she rotated her shoulders and relaxed the knot that had a grip on her back, while staring around the quiet cabin. One quick look behind her told her that Mitchell was still out cold.

Now was her chance to escape him. She took a few steps toward the door, her sore inner thighs screaming at the idea of mounting that horse again, and then paused with her hand hovering over the wooden latch.

It would be twelve days until the guide returned for

her. If Josie even managed to make it back to Lincoln in one piece, how could she possibly go undetected by the authorities in such a small town for such a long period of time? An image of her ducking down dark alleyways plastered with Wanted posters of her face flashed through her mind, and she jerked her hand back from the door.

She looked back at Mitchell. He must have forced her to come along because she'd made the stupid mistake of telling him that he'd die without her precious shots of penicillin. With that in mind, Josie felt she could assume that he wasn't about to hurt her—for the moment, anyway.

She decided the best thing she could do was stay put. And maybe she could convince her patient to get her back to Lincoln by the fourteenth in return for her gracious assistance.

Her stomach growled. She hadn't eaten since dinner the night before last, and there was no kitchen in the cabin. She'd have to wake the bastard up just to find out how to eat.

She decided food could wait at least until she'd answered the call of nature and cleaned up in the stream outside. If Mitchell wasn't awake by the time she came back, she'd make just enough noise to change that fact.

She opened the door and went out onto the porch. The first thing that greeted her was the horse, standing there, free as a bird, munching on the tall spring grass. His satiny black body was glistening in the early morning sunshine, and his bridle was dragging at the ground, mocking her inability to make use of him. She clenched her jaw and walked past him to the trees a few yards away, with morning birdcalls echoing all around her.

The stream was wider than she'd expected, nearly six feet across. She crouched down to stare at her reflection in the glittering ripples. Her hair was a mess, and her face was so smudged with sweat and dirt that she barely recognized herself.

She bent down, dipped her hands into the water, and splashed her face. It was ice cold but refreshing as it dribbled down her chin and neck and dampened the front of her T-shirt. She washed her arms and rinsed her hair and then sat back on her heels.

What she found staring at her from the opposite bank made a scream catch in her throat. Not only was it huge, it was the ugliest thing she'd ever seen. It watched her with watery pale blue eyes, then bared its sharp yellowed fangs and let out a low growl.

Josie fell backward, and the brown-and-yellow-splotched animal began moving toward her. She screeched, scrambling to her feet as it lunged. But when it reached the edge of the water it backed up quickly.

An image of *Cujo* racing through her mind, Josie did some hasty backing up of her own. Her wet hair was dripping down her face and into her eyes, but she ignored the distraction as she scampered backward toward the sanctuary of the cabin as fast as her legs could carry her.

The animal used a fallen tree to cross the stream. Then it began stalking her with increased energy, its head lowered.

The edge of a step slammed into Josie's heel, and she spun around. She jumped over the porch in one bound, dashed inside the cabin, and slammed the door closed just as the wild beast charged.

Shaking with fear, she backed to the center of the cabin, trying to catch her breath while keeping her attention glued on the flimsy door latch. She hoped it would hold.

A sound came from behind her, and she turned around to face Mitchell. He was sitting up on the bed, his arms crossed over his muscular bare chest.

She narrowed her eyes, hating the way he looked so calm in the face of her fear. It was, after all, his fault that she was here in the first place . . . his and that damn fairy's. And if it came down to it, by God, she'd feed *him* to that ravenous beast!

Without the effects of morphine or pain clouding his mind and his vision, Kurtis Mitchell took himself a good long look at his strange lady doctor. FRANKLY, MY DEAR, I DON'T GIVE A DAMN. That's what it said across the front of her odd, half-sleeved shirt, right above the large satirical drawing of a woman's smiling face. And he couldn't think of any other sentence that summed up Dr. Josie Reed any better than that.

She hadn't given a damn what Dr. Primrose might do when she'd taken on the task of healing a half-breed criminal. She hadn't given a damn what the risk might be to herself when she'd gone to Juan Patron's to find her patient some food after the nurse at the hospital had refused to feed him. And she certainly didn't give a damn what people thought of her, as evidenced by her outlandish haircut and the fact that she strolled around wearing a faded pair of boy's denims.

She was a beauty, he could add that to her list of pluses, even with her dark hair cropped above her ears, which only made her deep blue eyes seem clearer and more alive.

At the moment her wet hair was dripping water into

her ears and down her neck, and those round blue eyes of hers, set in skin so white and flawless it almost glowed, were wide and sparkling with anger.

She straightened her spine so tight it looked as if somebody had just rammed a pole up her ass. Then she said, "Don't just sit there looking aloof. We're about to be eaten by some mutant bear! You're the one who dragged me here—now do something!"

Kurtis frowned. That was right, he had dragged her there. But he'd been out cold for what looked to be the better part of a day. So why the hell hadn't she escaped when she'd had the chance? Could it be that she hadn't given a damn about her own safety or reputation and had stayed to see him restored to health?

As she continued to fume, he stared at her flaring nostrils and her compressed lips and wondered why she, a white woman, kept going out of her way to help him, a half-breed and suspected criminal.

Then he remembered the bug he'd put in her ear about what explanations she'd give for unlocking his manacles, and any favorable feelings he'd been nurturing about his lady doctor fell by the wayside. Her staying here had nothing to do with him and everything to do with her fear of what the authorities might do if they ever caught her.

His gaze traveled up her denim-clad legs, over her narrow hips, and lingered on her full breasts beneath her damp shirt. To think that when he'd first set eyes on her, when she'd poured that fiery whiskey onto his wound, he'd mistaken her for a boy. One look into those thick-lashed eyes, however, one whiff of the flowery scent clinging to her skin, and he'd quickly realized his startling mistake.

It had been a few seconds since the beast outside had

made any noise, and she took in a long breath, which only pushed her breasts higher against the thin material of her shirt. She held out her hand and took a step toward the bed. "At least give me your gun, Mitchell. I probably won't hit the monster, but I guarantee it'll think twice about sticking its ugly face in here."

Kurtis looked over at the door, where patches of yellow-and-brown fur could be seen through the cracks in the unsealed wood. Suddenly there was a faint snarl, then a whine, and then a giant paw began digging frantically at the threshold.

"Jesus!" she blurted. She scrambled up onto the bed, hopped over Kurtis's legs, and pressed herself so hard against the wall, she was bound to have splinters clear to her spine.

"All bets are off!" she shouted at him. "It's every woman for herself!"

Her eyes widened as the flimsy latch bounced and lifted with a thud. He could tell she was holding her breath as the door creaked open.

"At least shoot at it or something! What kind of a cold-blooded killer are you?"

The door opened completely, and the huge dog loomed in the doorway, its head lowered, its hackles raised. The doctor let out a little squeak as the animal slowly shuffled across the floor toward them.

Kurtis gave the dog an impatient stare. "Stop messin' around, Bart."

The dog straightened instantly and trotted over to him. Kurtis responded by scratching the dog's chin. He wished the whole world were as easy to manage.

The bed shifted, and he looked up to find his doctor glaring down at him. "Are you telling me that that gargoyle belongs to you?"

To the best of his knowledge, he hadn't *told* her a thing. "Stay out of his way and you'll be fine," he replied.

"Which brings me to the question of the day, Mitchell. I don't suppose you'd like to explain to me just what the hell I'm doing here?"

He met her icy glare and found it interesting that he could see apprehension lurking in the back of her eyes despite her show of courage.

"Look"—she jumped off the bed, careful to land a good distance away from the dog—"I think I've been more than reasonable, waiting around here for you to wake up and give me a few explanations. I could've easily jumped on that horse and left you and that injured leg of yours a long time ago."

"Then go."

Her stern expression slipped. She looked surprised for a moment, but then a spark of pure stubborn intent flashed in her blue eyes and she started for the door.

For one brief moment Kurtis thought she might actually leave, and he would have to get up, despite the ache in his leg, and haul her back by a handful of her short silky hair. But then she suddenly spun around to face him.

"If I make it back to Lincoln, I plan to tell them exactly where you are!"

He didn't answer.

"And then you'll be charged with kidnapping!"

"They can only hang me once."

Her inky black brows arched. "And I'm taking the horse. So when they come after you, you won't be able to get away."

He looked up at the ceiling and then closed his eyes. She couldn't ride worth a damn, and she was terrified at what might happen to her if she returned to Lincoln. She wasn't going anywhere, and they both knew it.

"Damn it, just tell me what the hell you want from me!" she cried.

He listened to the sound of her stomping back across the floor toward him. Bart growled, and Kurtis said his name softly but firmly. She stopped at the edge of the bed, and after a few moments of heavy silence Kurtis decided that if he was going to get any peace at all during her stay, he was going to have to say something.

"You're here to keep me alive, lady. Do your job, and everything will work out fine."

"All right, Mitchell. We'll play it your way for a while. You have seven days left of injections. One week. And then you, your dog, *and* God himself won't be able to stop me from leaving!"

He cracked open his eyes and watched the enticing sway of her firm, round backside as she strode toward the door.

"Oh, and I suggest you keep that dog out of *my* way, or I'll skin him and use him as a blanket!" With that, she went out and slammed the door behind her.

Kurtis gave Bart a sideways glance. The dog was watching him with pale blue eyes, no doubt wondering why this loud female had been brought into their fold.

"She wasn't serious."

All the same, the dog dropped his face down onto his paws and let out a soft whine.

8

Josie picked her way across the stream's rocky bank, grumbling to herself. She'd been more than serious with her threat; she was leaving in seven days, and nothing and no one was going to stop her. She'd saved Mitchell's life, for God's sake, and he was showing her about as much gratitude as Dracula with a stake through his heart!

That prehistoric dog of his was bound to eat her the first chance it got. Josie stole a quick glance over her shoulder to make sure it wasn't sneaking up on her. She'd never been overly fond of dogs, and this particular canine sort of summed up all her complaints.

She paused to check her watch. It was past time for Mitchell's shots. One thing she knew for sure: she was dependent on him just as much as he was dependent on her—no matter how much she detested the idea. She didn't know the first thing about surviving in the wilderness, couldn't even start a campfire without burning down the whole forest. So regardless of how ungrateful he was, she knew she had to keep Mitchell healthy and alive.

When she reached the cabin she paused on the porch to take a bracing breath. She was going to need every ounce of her limited supply of patience not to slip the guy a little rat poison in his next injection.

The door swung open before she touched the latch, and there he was, all six feet and so many inches of him. He'd taken off the deputy's shirt, leaving himself bare from the waist up. His gray woolen pants were slit up one side, revealing a dark-skinned calf, a sinewy knee, and the white bandage she'd wrapped around his thick thigh.

The top of Josie's head came only to the breadth of his strong, rounded shoulders. Her eyes widened at the sight of the bronzed expanse of his muscular chest as he took a long, slow breath. "Where are you going?" she demanded a little too weakly.

He gave her a dismissing look and tried to hobble past her. Josie sidestepped, gripped the porch post, and blocked his path. "I said, Where are you going?"

His responding glare told her, loud and clear, that she was treading on dangerous ground. He braced his big hand just above hers on the post and leaned down over her. "Get out of my way."

She refused to let his imposing size or the distinct flaring of his nostrils intimidate her. "Answer my question."

"To take a piss."

"Thank you."

He gave her a mocking look. "Next time I'll wet the bed waiting for your permission."

"Next time I can at least help you out of the house if you take the time to ask."

He took a deliberate step forward, but Josie still refused to budge. "Move," he said.

Just to spite him, she lifted her hands and wiggled her fingers. "Is this movement enough?"

His stubbled jaw tightened. "Don't push me, lady."

"Don't tempt me, Mitchell. And before you threaten to do grave injury to my life, I think you should keep in mind that if you kill me, you won't live long enough to dig my grave. You must have some will to live, or I wouldn't be here," she added pointedly.

"Let's just say that that will varies from moment to moment."

She widened her eyes. "You mean I might get lucky some morning and wake to find you chewing on the end of your gun?"

"*You* might be chewing on the end of that gun if you don't get the hell out of my way," he growled.

She laughed off his threat, and his chest expanded again, the warm, smooth flesh coming close to pressing against her chin. "If you want to recover from that gunshot wound, you'll follow my orders to the letter. You'll stay in bed unless it's absolutely necessary to get up, and you'll take your shots like a good boy. Understand?"

Their eyes locked, and he studied her with that dark, savage gaze of his.

"Do you understand?" she repeated.

"Lady, I understand that your shoes are about to get very wet."

She wouldn't have put it past him to pee all over the leather uppers of her white Nikes, so she quickly stepped aside.

He brushed past her and struggled with the two porch steps, landing hard on the last and pulling in a sharp breath. Josie didn't make a move to help him. She wasn't feeling particularly charitable at the moment and knew she'd only get a snarl for her trouble anyway.

She watched the play of muscles across his bare back as he limped toward the trees a few yards away, and then the doctor in her called out, "Try to keep your weight off the leg as much as possible!"

He peeked out from behind the trunk of a pine. "Maybe you should come and watch to make sure I do it right!"

She turned her back on him then, grumbling about his lack of appreciation, and walked into the cabin. The dog was lying by the tall dresser, looking like a big yellow-and-brown rug with fangs, appearing uninterested in the world. But Josie wasn't fooled by his complacent stance.

When she reached for her medical bag, which sat on the table by the grimy front window, the dog's pointy ears perked. She froze as he looked up at her and didn't relax until his watery blue eyes had slid closed once again.

Suddenly anxious for Mitchell's return, Josie moved to the window and attempted to clear a spot on the pane with the bottom of her T-shirt. The only thing she accomplished was a dark smudge on the front of the shirt.

Mitchell finally came back into the cabin a few minutes later, his long hair damp from washing in the stream. He leaned against the doorjamb, feigning interest in the spot she'd tried to clear on the window, but Josie could tell he was pausing to catch his breath. His lips were thin and pale, indicating that he was in pain again. She supposed it was up to her to make the first move, because she doubted he'd ask for morphine if his nose was falling off.

She opened her medical bag and began preparing two syringes. "Everything come out okay?" she asked cheerfully.

Her supplies were running low. She was going to have to start reusing needles.

"I don't need any more morphine."

"Right. And if you grind your teeth together any harder, you'll need dentures. Struggle your way to the bed over here, and I promise I'll be gentle."

When he made no move to follow her instructions, she turned toward him impatiently. "Look. I'm tired and I'm hungry, and I'm in no mood to keep playing power games with you! Do you want the shots or not?"

He stared at her. She was about to toss the syringes into her medical bag and forget the whole thing when he took one painful step toward her. She saw the flinch in his eyes and couldn't tear her attention away as he clamped his jaw and limped forward. She held her breath until he finally landed with a heavy thud onto the bed.

Well, damn. She'd actually felt a spurt of admiration for him for one brief second.

She crouched down, brushed aside his sliced pant leg, and jabbed the needle into the long muscle in his thigh. "I know the morphine makes you tired, but it eases the pain and helps you to rest."

She gave the puncture in his leg a rub. "This is the last shot of morphine I'm going to give you. It can be very addicting. You stay in bed today and by tomorrow you shouldn't need it."

Next she injected him with the penicillin. "The

penicillin shots we'll continue through the next week to fight off the infection. You won't be running the hundred-yard dash right off the bat, but I think you're going to heal pretty well. You'll have to start slowly, by building strength in the leg so you don't injure the atrophied muscles. I'd say that in two, maybe three weeks, you should be almost back to normal—"

"No."

She looked up at his face. "No?"

"One week."

"In one week you can expect to be limping around without much pain."

He gave her a hard stare.

She straightened and tossed the syringes back into her bag. "Look, you can demand to be up to one hundred percent in one week all you want, Mitchell. When it comes right down to it, it's up to you and your leg, not me."

There was a long pause in which she could practically feel the tension in the room building. "One week," he said again.

He was looking up at her with that drilling glare of his, and Josie began to reconsider her decision to stay. She had the sinking feeling that if Mitchell wasn't completely healed in one week, she'd be tree fertilizer.

She could knife him in his sleep . . . just one fast slash with the scalpel.

Josie was down on her knees, scrubbing the cabin's front window. Mitchell had fallen into a drugged sleep an hour or so after their last confrontation, and she'd been more than relieved not to have his black stare on her for the time being. He was a little less than happy that she couldn't give him any guarantees about being up to par in a week. In fact, at one point he'd even insinuated that he'd feed her to his dog if she didn't do exactly as he commanded.

She stood from her crouched position and arched her back to relieve an ache. The windowpane still wasn't spotless, but at least now she could see the trees outside. She stared out at the sky for a moment, at the crimson of the sunset, and wondered for the first time since her arrival in the year 1881 if she was missed in her own time. But then again, 1994 didn't exist yet. None of her friends, not even their parents, had been born.

God, she missed her friends. Not only their companionship but their familiarity, the comfort of being around people who knew you and understood you.

She tossed the filthy rag into the bucket of murky water, where it landed with a splat. Bart lifted his head and stared at her suspiciously. That was the only way the dog ever looked at her, though, even when she'd been feeding him handfuls of beef jerky all day—which she hoped had kept him from envisioning her as his next meal.

The thought of a meal made her stomach growl once again. She was starved for something besides hard crusty rolls and bruised apples. A search through the root cellar out back had uncovered all kinds of canned foods, but Josie hadn't been able to figure out a way to get the cans open.

She'd spent most of the day by the creek, gnawing on mushy apples, wishing she had a good book to read along with a nice turkey sandwich. Finally the boredom had led to industriousness, and she'd decided to clean the cabin while her patient slept.

She heard a noise behind her and turned to find Mitchell wide awake and staring at her. "What's for supper?" he asked, his voice thick with sleep.

"Good evening to you, too," she responded sarcastically. "I take it you're hungry?"

He didn't answer as she walked to the bed and reached out to check the low-grade fever he'd been running all day. "Your fever's gone. Stay in bed and we'll keep it that way."

Before she could move back from him, he took hold of her wrist and hauled her so close she could see tiny flecks of gold in his coffee-colored eyes. She gasped as her bare feet slipped on the dusty wooden floor beneath her, forcing her to brace her free hand against Mitchell's bare chest to keep from falling completely over him.

"No fires," he said, glancing toward the cold fireplace.

Then you'd better keep your hands to yourself, she wanted to say; one touch from him could light an inferno in her to rival a volcano. Instead she pried his steely fingers from her arm and took a step back, trying to remain composed. "Don't sweat it. I'd make a miserable Girl Scout."

His dark brows drew together in a brief, confused look, giving her the impression that he had no idea what she'd meant. She supposed half the time she must sound to him like a person from another planet.

"And as for supper, I'd be happy to whip you up a bowl of cold corn, but my teeth aren't strong enough to open the cans."

He gestured toward the dresser with a jerk of his head. She reached out to open the top drawer, and her eyes widened at the arsenal she found: some guns, knives, even several sticks of dynamite. And of course, right where it should be, a can opener. The weapon to use when all other options had been exhausted.

She turned back to Mitchell, can opener in hand, and found him regarding her suspiciously. "What's the matter, Mitchell?" she asked. "Afraid I might knife you in your sleep?"

"The thought occurred to me."

"Good." She started for the door. "You hold that thought close to your heart, and I'll just skip my way out to the root cellar, like a good little woman . . . *and fetch you some grub,*" she added with a blatant drawl.

"Take Bart with you."

She stopped and looked over at the huge dog sitting at full attention by the bed. "I'd rather go it alone, thanks."

"Take him. The sun's going down, and renegades roam at night."

"I'd rather take my chances with the renegades."

"Bart, go!"

In a flash of yellow-and-brown matted fur, the dog was at her heels. Josie smiled tightly as the animal stared up at her, its pink tongue hanging out of its mouth, strings of saliva dribbling onto the floor. "Do you ever close your mouth?"

It tilted its head and whined, causing a blast of hot spicy air, not unlike the odor of rancid jerky, to come blowing up into her face. She grimaced and looked back at Mitchell.

"Take him if you don't want to lose the rest of that hair," he said.

"Tell me something, Mitchell. If I did happen into a circumstance where I might lose the rest of my hair, what makes you so sure that your faithful beast, here, would help *me* and not the renegades?"

"I guess we'll just have to take that chance."

"And you do so enjoy taking chances with my little life, don't you?"

"It's somethin' to do."

She arched a brow. "One would think a big bad man like you could find better ways to occupy yourself."

His dark gaze slid over her body. "It's possible that I might yet," he replied.

That heated stare had been nothing if not suggestive, and Josie's traitorous body burned at the possibilities. "Don't get your hopes up," she replied.

He continued to stare at her, and then a slow smile crept over his face. "Too late."

9

Josie slept terribly that night, only to wake up to a patient even more determined to thwart her.

"We'll be leaving after breakfast."

She looked up from where she was crouched in front of him, poised to give him his penicillin shot. "What? Why?"

"Because I want to keep my trail cold. Be ready."

She stood and threw the used syringe back into her bag. "Forget it, Mitchell. I'm not going anywhere else with you. I'll give you some needles and all the medicine you need, but this is one trail I plan to keep nice and warm—"

He sprang toward her from the bed and grabbed her arm. "Look, lady, you seem to be confused about exactly who is in charge here. Well, let me enlighten you." He hauled her up against him, bringing their hips into solid contact, and she gasped, pressing her hands against his chest.

The ice in his eyes seemed to melt in that moment, and his intent gaze slipped downward and focused on her mouth. "You'll do as I say." He pulled her up onto her toes, until their faces were mere inches apart.

"Or?" she said breathlessly, staring into his eyes.

"Or I'll tie a rope around your waist and drag you along behind me."

She wrenched her arm free and shoved back from him. "Remind me to put that one on a greeting card!"

Then she stormed out of the cabin in the direction of the creek, where she sat down, Indian style, in the sunshine, and dropped her forehead into her hands. The man refused to see reason! Damn it, she couldn't let him haul her around the countryside, or she'd never find her way back to Lincoln and that damn little woman! Maybe she should give the horse a try, after all, and leave her patient and his leg to fend for themselves.

She grumbled on for a few more minutes, until she felt the penetrating heat of his stare on her back. A glance over her shoulder told her he was standing right behind her. He'd sneaked up without making a sound, which led her to believe that he *was* making a remarkable recovery.

She turned back around and squinted up at the sky. The morning was bright and beautiful, and for the first time in her life Josie felt utterly confused and helpless. She hated herself for that weakness, but she hated the man responsible for those feelings even more. "How long have you been standing there?" she asked him.

"Long enough to hear you mumble something

about stealing my horse and taking your chances in the wilderness."

"Did you catch the part about my eating your dog to stay alive?"

He stepped around her and hung a jagged-edged mirror on a nearby pine tree but said nothing.

"You know, you really are a bastard."

Mitchell didn't bat an eye at that assessment of his character. He pulled off his shirt, bent down to the water with a bar of soap in his hands, and worked up a thin lather.

She found it hard to take her eyes off the rippling planes of his back. "I hope you know that if I could stay on that horse for more than five seconds, I'd be gone from here so fast you'd think I never was here."

He straightened, careful not to lean on his leg. Then he stepped in front of the mirror, smeared the lather over his stubbled jaw, and pulled a straight razor out of his back pocket.

"Careful you don't slit your throat," she said. "I might not be inclined to lend a hand in stitching you up."

He studied his refection. Obviously he had the uncanny ability to ignore her whenever he chose, no matter what she did, no matter what she said, and that fact really galled her.

He touched the razor to his throat.

"Sure I can't help?" she asked too sweetly.

Mitchell didn't hesitate in his task, and she finally gave up trying to bait him. She rested back on her hands and watched him shave the dark stubble off his face and neck.

Her attention was drawn to his powerful shoulders. The muscles in his bronze-colored back flexed and relaxed as he moved, and the motion soon held her spellbound.

Then she looked down to the pants he'd stolen from the deputy in Lincoln. They were tight and a bit short. But they hugged his hips and athletic thighs and showed off the high, tight curve of his backside.

Here was a butt her friends would go wild over. "Go for it, Jos," she could hear them saying. "That baby was made for grippin'."

And the worst part was that Josie could actually imagine herself doing just that. She could practically feel her hands clamped around his steely rear end, her fingers digging into the bare, hard flesh, pulling his hips closer to her, urging him—

The mirror. Their eyes collided in the reflection, as did her heart against her ribs, and she knew beyond a shadow of a doubt that he was well aware of what she'd just been appraising so intently.

To hide her guilt, she decided to go on the offensive. "Don't you have any pants of your own?"

He wiped the blade off on the leg of the pants. "Not any that I'd appreciate you cutting to pieces."

"Aren't those just a bit tight?"

He paused in his motions. "When it comes to appearances, I don't think you have a lot of room to talk, lady."

"Is that another hair remark? Because if it is, I'll have you know that where I come from—"

"Your hair suits you."

Josie blinked and watched as he eased down to his knees in order to rinse his face in the creek. Had it been her imagination or had the man just paid her a compliment? He quickly dunked his whole head under the water, then sat back to push his fingers through his long, wet hair.

"What did you say?" she asked.

He stood, letting the water drip down between his shoulder blades to disappear beneath the waistband of his pants, and looked at her through damp, spiky lashes. "I said your hair suits you."

She waited, instinctively knowing there was more.

"It's ridiculous. Just like you."

She clenched her teeth as he wiped the water from his face, wondering how long it would take them to find his body out here in the middle of nowhere. "Would you care to elaborate?" she asked tightly.

"Do you harbor a secret wish to be a man, Doctor? I mean, your hair, your clothes, your profession—"

"Afraid I might make a better one than you, Mitchell?"

He let out a short laugh.

"Because the only time a man ever says something like that to a woman is when he's feeling threatened."

"Or confused."

"I enjoy being a woman—love it, in fact. Life is complicated enough without two heads running the show."

He gave her a twisted smile and looked in the mirror to wipe the remaining patches of lather off his face. "I suggest you keep your eyes off my ass, Doctor, and firmly planted on the ground in front of you so you don't fall all over that arrogance of yours."

"Your ass looks remarkably like your face, Mitchell. Are you sure you're sitting on the right end?"

He turned back to her with a patronizing look. "Down to childish taunts, now, are we?"

She clamped her lips shut as he limped toward the cabin. No one in her life had ever gotten the better of her, especially in an argument, and her frustration quickly turned into fury.

She ran forward and caught Mitchell by the arm before he could reach the cabin steps. "I've agreed to stay and make you well, but I'll be doing it right here! You want to leave? You go alone!"

In one quick motion he spun her around and slammed her against the splintery porch post. "This discussion again?" he asked, his hard stare drilling through her.

Josie dug her feet into the ground and attempted to push him away, but he was stronger than she'd ever imagined, holding her in place with just his forearm across her upper chest.

"Let me try once again to make things just a little clearer for you," he said. "When it comes to medicine you're the boss. When it comes to where we go and what we do, *I* say what goes." She struggled against him, but he stood his ground. "Do we understand each other, *Doctor?*"

"You won't hurt me, Mitchell!" she shouted up into his face. "I'm the only thing that stands between you and hopping on one foot for the rest of your miserable life!"

He stared down at her for a long moment and then once again, just as before, something in him changed. He pressed his big body closer, his attention slipping down to fasten on her mouth. "You've got the fangs of a viper," he said softly. "Anybody ever tell you that?"

His deep, smooth voice combined with his proximity made Josie's heart leap, much to her disconcertment. However, she managed somehow to retain her outward composure.

"In fact, I find myself wondering whether or not you actually bite," he continued.

"I may not be as strong as you, Mitchell, but I'm amazing with a scalpel—even in the dark. So if you don't want to wake up some morning minus a few fingers, I suggest you take your hands off me."

He smiled faintly at her threat, his gaze still attached to her mouth. "We'll be leaving after lunch, Doctor. And I do mean *we*."

Josie urged the big horse closer to the porch and climbed to the second step. Then she took the reins in one hand, a fistful of black mane in the other, and pulled herself on board.

Fortunately the animal had the sense to stand still while its inexperienced rider settled herself. And then, with a nudge of her heels, Josie urged the horse to walk.

Mitchell was asleep, and she was leaving. She was going to find her way back to Lincoln, explain everything to Sheriff Garrett, and then wait—quietly—for that little fairy woman to come and take her home.

The horse continued at an ambling pace toward the tree line and Josie did a remarkable job of staying seated, even though each step slid her a little to the right. She calmly corrected her position each time she slipped, however, and began calculating how long it would take her to reach Lincoln at such a lumbering speed.

Suddenly Mitchell cut in front of the horse, and the animal stopped, throwing back its head and snorting in confusion. "What do you think you're doing?" he asked, reaching for the animal's nose.

"I think that's pretty obvious. I'm leaving."

She gave the horse a kick with her heels. It shuffled but wouldn't budge past the man holding its head.

"Move," she said to Mitchell.

With a crooked smirk, he raised one hand and wiggled his fingers.

"Get out of my way, you savage bastard!"

His jaw tightened. "Get down off the horse, Doctor, before you hurt yourself."

"I'd rather break my neck than be dragged through hell with you!"

"Another few feet and you might get your wish. Now get down."

Josie glanced back at the cabin. How could it be that she'd ridden less than ten feet?

She released a long sigh and let her shoulders drop. "Okay. I suppose you're right." As she'd expected, he relaxed his guard—and she dug the heels of her sneakers into the horse's underbelly.

The horse burst forward with lightning speed and Josie almost fell to the ground, but she tightened her grip on its mane and held on for dear life as it charged toward the dense trees.

She could hear Mitchell shouting behind her, but the thought of slowing down never crossed her mind. She was actually staying mounted and began to think that maybe she *could* ride all the way back to Lincoln.

Then the horse went crashing into the woods, and the very first tree they passed reached out a long thick branch, hit her square in the chest, and knocked her onto her back.

As she lay there on the ground she tried to pull the wind back into her lungs, feeling stupid and frustrated and listening to the horse race on without her. Footsteps pounded through the foliage toward her, and she closed her eyes, hoping that if she played dead, Mitchell might go away and leave her alone for once.

She heard him drop down beside her in the pine needles, but she refused to open her eyes. "Doctor?" he said.

She flinched slightly when he took her chin in his fingers and turned her head toward him. But she kept her eyes shut even when he began patting her cheek.

"Doctor?"

When she didn't respond Mitchell swore heatedly and slipped his arms beneath her shoulders and knees. In the next second Josie was swept up against his hard chest and carried through the air.

She heard the uneven thud of his boots on the porch and the high pitch of Bart's whine, then felt the softness of the lumpy mattress as she was laid down upon the bed.

"Come on, lady. Wake up."

He touched her face, and she could feel the heat of his fingers as they traced a faint path over her cheek. Then he brushed his thumb over her mouth, and her lips parted of their own accord. To cover the slip, Josie grimaced and moaned a little, slowly cracking open her eyes.

Mitchell straightened and stood over her. That cool expression Josie had grown so used to came over his face once again, and he crossed his arms over his chest. "Didn't I tell you you'd hurt yourself? Now, do I have to tie you up or will you promise not to try something that stupid again?"

"I'm not a child—"

"Then stop acting like one!" He leaned forward to glare into her face. "I've asked you to do one simple thing: your job. And if you'd keep your mouth shut and do it, things would be a hell of a lot easier around here."

"If you're looking for a slave, then you've kidnapped the wrong woman, Mitchell. I don't do submissive."

"Don't go near that horse again. I want your word—"

"You won't get it."

The muscles in his jaw pulsed. "I knew this was a mistake from the very beginning."

"Oh, well, I wish you could have come to that priceless conclusion *before* you kidnapped me and left it to look like I'd helped you escape."

"Are you going to keep clear of that horse or not?"

Josie refused to answer. She had him over a barrel as far as she could see, so she turned her head and stared straight up at the ceiling, mimicking his own stubborn stance.

"Fine. I guess it's time you learned that there's more than one way to skin a cat, lady."

"Is that supposed to frighten me?"

He didn't answer, but the expression on his face made her very, very nervous.

10

"Get in."

Josie crossed her arms and stood her ground. "Forget it."

Mitchell bent over and threw aside the top blanket on the bed. "If you're not in there by the time I count to three, I'm going to pick you up and throw you in."

She arched a brow. "Unless you're prepared to grow another set of testicles, I wouldn't suggest trying that."

The two of them had spent most of the day arguing about her dash for freedom, and he'd refused to let her out of his sight the entire time, even insisting on accompanying her on her trips to answer the call of nature. Fortunately her claims of a piercing headache had kept him from packing her up and taking her off deeper into the mountains.

But now he'd come up with the brilliant idea that the only way to keep her from trying to escape him in the middle of the night was to force her to sleep beside him.

His eyes narrowed. "One . . . "

Josie remained where she was, with the couch as a solid barrier between them.

"Two . . . "

"Three," she said for him.

His jaw clenched. "Bart!"

Josie had forgotten about the dog, he'd been so quiet all day, but at the sound of his master's voice, he leaped up from his place by the door and lunged at her.

She yelped and dashed toward Mitchell, the only one who seemed to be able to tame the beast, and he instantly clamped his arm around her waist. With one giant heave he tossed her in the middle of the lumpy mattress.

Josie struggled into a sitting position. "It's not as if I could go anywhere in the dark!"

He reached over and shoved her onto her back. "You budge off that bed before I do and I'll tie you to it." Then he sat on the edge of the mattress and began pulling off his boots. "I don't trust you, Doctor, it's as simple as that."

Josie glared daggers at his back. "And I'm supposed to care one way or the other?"

The lamp went out, and she felt the dip of the mattress as he lifted his legs onto the bed.

"I'm a very light sleeper, by the way," he said after a moment.

She lay stiffly beside him in the darkness. "We'll see."

"Your family should have married you off before you garnered this wild streak in you."

"Beautiful. Look, I've got friends a-plenty trying to fix me up, pal, I don't need my kidnapper joining the club. Besides, marriage is for fools," she added, watching the way the moon cast a golden glow across the ceiling.

He grunted. "You sound like my brother."

She turned to look at him, although she could see nothing but the faint outline of his profile in the darkness. "You mean there are more of you?"

"Unfortunately."

Pursing her lips, she turned back to the ceiling. "I never had a brother. Or a sister, for that matter. . . . "

"You can have one of mine."

"Do I detect a note of sibling rivalry? What, does your brother wear your clothes and steal your girls?" She allowed herself to smile because she knew he couldn't see.

"Nope. He robs people."

"Your folks must be so proud of the two of you."

"Go to sleep, Doctor. We'll be leaving at first light."

"You know, I've always wondered why cowboys do that. Why can't you guys just sleep late, enjoy a nice breakfast, maybe even a lunch, and start out whenever the need strikes you?"

"That wastes daylight."

"The dark isn't so bad."

"It is if you're a horse who's carrying a sleeping rider over unsure terrain."

"That's not good, huh?"

"No . . . not good."

An owl hooted outside, and she heard Bart's toenails scrape against the floor as he adjusted his position. "Mitchell?"

"Hm?"

"I don't suppose I should ask you what, exactly, you did that's got men wanting to hang you . . . should I?"

"Nothing."

"What?"

"I said nothing."

"Nothing," she whispered to herself.

There was a moment of silence, and then he went on. "Doctor, don't you know that everybody claims they're innocent, no matter how guilty they really are?"

She let out an impatient sigh. "Well, *I* happen to be innocent. And I don't appreciate that you've dragged me into the royal mess that is your life."

"Oh, now, not so fast. *You're* innocent? I could swear it was you who used that little knife on both my manacles."

She jerked her head around to stare at his profile. "That's different—I didn't intend for you to escape."

"Frankly, my dear, I don't think *they're* going to give a damn."

"Will they shoot me? I mean if they catch us, will they shoot first and ask questions later?"

"The posse? Maybe."

She suddenly had the unmistakable urge to cry. "But you won't let them shoot me, right? I mean, I saved your life, for God's sake. You'll return the favor, right?"

There was a long pause, and Josie held her breath waiting for his answer. If he didn't intend to protect her, then she wouldn't stand a chance against a posse of armed men.

Finally Mitchell said, "How can I protect you if

you're here in the cabin and I'm out there somewhere on the trail?"

Josie clamped her mouth shut before she said something really nasty. The bastard had actually managed to win in the end, by dangling her own life in front of her nose.

It wasn't long before she heard the deep, even breathing that told her he was asleep. Just to test the waters, she tried to sit up. His arm shot out and shoved her back down.

"Don't push your luck, Doctor."

She fell back to the bed and swore that if she ever returned home, she was going to take karate so she could defend herself from men like him. And damn it if she wasn't going to learn how to ride a horse.

The next morning Josie opened her eyes—and froze. She was sprawled, chest to chest, over Mitchell. And if that wasn't enough, her face was pressed into the side of his neck, her fingers were tangled in his dark blond hair, and her knee was nudging between his thighs. He smelled so strong, warm, and male.

When she lifted her head, subtly trying to push herself away, his arms tightened around her back.

"You're a bed hog," he said in a sleepy voice.

"Could you let go of me, please?"

"Probably."

She looked into his half-open eyes. "Sometime in the near future?"

His big hand slipped down to her lower back, pressing her even closer. "Give me a minute."

Josie could feel his morning arousal pushing up against her stomach, and desire began to twine itself through her treacherous body. She tingled where he touched her, and her chest tightened to such a point that it was hard for her to breathe. But when he took a grip on her backside she had to force herself to speak. "You want to . . . you want to keep that hand, Mitchell, I suggest you move it."

He gave her a twisted smile but didn't let her up. "For someone who claims *I'm* cold-blooded, you sure have got a lot of threats to throw around." He skimmed one hand up her back, and she went as stiff as a board. "Has anyone ever told you you've got too much starch for your own good?"

Yes—Yvette, Linda, and Vickie had, to name just a few. She didn't take it from them, though, and she wasn't about to take it from him. She placed both hands against his chest and shoved. He refused to let her budge even an inch.

"Don't you ever smile?" he asked, molding her completely against him.

"Is that your idea of the perfect woman, Mitchell? A pretty little ball of fluff that giggles and laughs at all the witty things you say?"

He hooked his fingers beneath her arms and slid her higher up his body, until her face was mere inches from his, until she was so close to his mouth that his warm breath was gliding over her lips like a balmy breeze. "Go ahead, Doctor," he whispered seductively. She blinked and realized she was staring at his mouth. "Take yourself a little taste."

She quickly jerked her head back, and he let out a deep rumble of laughter. "I think you're fighting yourself more than you're fighting me," he said.

"Let me up."

He arched a brow.

"Let me up, *please*."

As soon as his tight hold slackened, she arched up and scrambled to her feet. Her heart was pounding and her palms were sweaty—damn the man for having this effect on her!

She cleared her throat, determined to change the subject. "Where do you plan to drag me today?"

He didn't answer, just tucked his hands beneath his head and watched her sit down on the couch to pull on her shoes.

"Don't ignore me, Mitchell." She tied her laces. "More than anything, I hate it when you ignore me."

"I don't think it would be possible for anyone to ignore you," he replied.

"Then answer my question." She finished with her shoes and stood. "Where do you plan to take me now?"

"Don't worry about it. Who's Nick?"

"Nick?"

He pointed to the floor at her feet. "Nick." She looked down. "And what am I supposed to guess?" he added.

"Guess— Oh, I get it." She was wearing Guess jeans. Laughing, she straightened and turned back to him. "It's pronounced Ni-kee, and they're just brand names."

"Why would you want to brand your shoes and your denims? They got clothes rustlers where you're from?"

"The brands are the names of the people who made them."

"A fellow in Santa Fe made my boots, but you don't see me running around with Clyde plastered all over the sides. And while we're at it, where in the hell did you get that shirt?"

Josie glanced down at her I-don't-give-a-damn T-shirt and smiled. "Some friends gave it to me. They said it summed up my personality."

He raised his brows and looked away. "Perceptive friends."

"Hey, you're no prize yourself, pal, so don't go casting stones."

He ignored this comment. "Go get us some apples for breakfast."

"Get them yourself. I'm not your wife."

His mouth twisted into a wicked half smile, and his attention slid from her face to her breasts. "Yeah, but someday soon maybe we'll pretend a little."

Josie felt heat rush to her cheeks, but she refused to acknowledge even to herself what the mere idea of making love with him did to her already faltering restraint.

She strode out of the cabin and down to the creek, hoping to cool the desire that continued to pulse through her veins. Bart was already there, lapping up water as if there'd be no tomorrow, and Josie moved a few yards upstream to wash up.

She hadn't been at the creek more than two minutes when she looked into the water and saw Mitchell's reflection behind hers. The playful glint was gone from his eyes, leaving him looking as cold as usual, and she assumed that he hadn't appreciated her leaving the cabin without his permission.

"I'll be in to give you your shot in a minute," she snapped at him.

He reached out and took hold of her arm, pulling her around to face him. At that moment Bart began to growl, low and threatening, like the first time she'd seen the dog at the creek.

"Oh, is this it? Is this the moment when you feed me to your dog because I refused to fetch you some lousy apples!"

"Doctor, I want you to do exactly as I say—"

"Stuff it! I'm fed up to my eyeballs with doing what you say!" Bart was beginning to make such a racket that Josie had to shout to be heard. "And shut that dog up!"

She looked down at the animal and saw, to her amazement, that Bart wasn't even looking at her. He was staring off into the distant trees, his fangs bared and his hackles raised.

Then Josie looked up and squinted at the tree line. Mitchell's hand was still clamped around her arm, and the air had grown chilly and eerily quiet. "What's going on, Mitchell?"

"Posse."

It wasn't so much the word, but the way it was said, low and ominous, that made the hair on the back of Josie's neck prickle. She took a step toward him, and that's when Bart let out one final bark and turned tail and ran.

"So much for your brave guard dog."

"He knows to get when the getting's good." With that, Mitchell took hold of her hand and ran, full out, toward the cabin.

"Cover the front door, boys!" someone called from far behind them.

Mitchell leapt onto the porch, dragging Josie along behind him, and burst inside the cabin. He pushed her to the floor, shoved the table and couch against the door, and began dragging the large dresser across the room to block the front window.

In her fear and confusion Josie couldn't move or

make a sound, until a bullet shattered the front window and a startled screech escaped her throat before she could stop it.

Mitchell looked back at her. "Keep your head down," he whispered.

"It is already," she snapped. "You keep yours down. I won't be up to piecing it back together after all this."

"Can you use a gun?"

"As a paperweight!"

He got down and reached beneath the bed. "What about a shotgun?"

Josie stared at the double-barreled weapon he pulled out from under the bed. "A *monkey* could shoot something with that, Mitchell."

He handed it to her. "Just don't point it at me."

"*Come on out, Mitchell! We know the two of you are in there! You and the doctor come out with your hands high!*"

Mitchell crouched down behind the dresser. "Go to hell, Marshal!"

Josie gave him a glare. "Don't you think aggravating them might be the wrong thing to do at the moment?"

"I think they're already pretty aggravated, lady." As if to punctuate that fact, a bullet flew in the window and embedded itself in the wall above Josie's head. "But I'm open to suggestions," he said with a flash of a smile.

"They're going to kill us, aren't they?" she whispered hoarsely.

His cocky attitude seemed to slip a bit. "You being a woman, they're sure to go a little easier on you."

A little easier? Maybe they'd be sure to shoot her

straight through the heart so she wouldn't suffer? "How many men do you think are out there?" she asked.

"Five or six at least."

Another shot rang out.

She looked at the dresser, more specifically the top drawer. "I think I have an idea. But you have to promise me something, Mitchell. You have to promise me that if I get us out of this mess, you'll get me back to Lincoln by the fourteenth."

He gave her a pointed look. "You got a date?"

"You could say that."

Another shot splintered the top of the dresser. "You think this plan of yours will work?" he asked.

"If I know men—and believe me, Mitchell, I know men—then, yes, this plan will work."

11

"We have a deal, right?"

Kurtis watched as his doctor jammed two sticks of dynamite into each of her front pockets. He still couldn't believe she was doing this. Women didn't take chances with their lives, especially when there was a perfectly capable man around to take the heat. But she was right. If they both wanted to come out of this alive, her plan was the only way.

"This should be easy, right, Mitchell? Like taking candy from a baby?"

Despite her show of courage, he could tell by her wavering voice that her confidence was lagging. "How well do you play poker, Doctor?" he asked her.

Her smile was brief, but damn sexy. "You'd lose what's left of your pants."

He arched his brows. "Remind me to make you prove that point someday."

There was an odd quiet moment as they stood there staring at each other, almost as if the whole world had stopped for one brief second, and then she held her arms out to her sides. "Can you see them all right?"

He checked to be sure the dynamite in her pockets was clearly visible and that the long fuses draped her narrow hips. Another shot came through the window and whizzed by where they stood behind the dresser, and they both flinched. They'd been formulating their plan for the past ten minutes, and in that time the walls of the cabin had been riddled with bullets.

They could both be killed. Josie was just as aware of that as he was, and his admiration for her was growing by leaps and bounds. He'd never met another man or woman like her. She was scared, he could see that by the liquid glow in her brilliant blue eyes, but she wasn't backing down from what she knew had to be done. Instead of wasting time thinking about the danger, she was jumping in with both feet. She took a deep breath and gave him a tremulous smile. "Wish me luck, cowboy."

Kurtis reacted on impulse, and in the instant that it took for her to figure out what he was doing, he closed his mouth over hers. The kiss was wet and deep, and instead of pushing him away, she surprised him by tucking her fingers into his hair and pressing herself closer. He opened his mouth, and her lips parted easily beneath his, making his heart kick like crazy in his chest.

It was when the muscles in his legs started to tingle that he finally eased away from her. By the flush to her face, he could tell that she was just as stunned as he was at the intensity of their embrace. She quickly turned away from him. He took a moment to gather his scattered wits and then smiled at her rigid back. The woman was one surprise after another.

She cleared her throat and picked her doctor's bag up from the floor. "Ready?"

"As ready as I'll ever be."

He hooked his arm around her middle and pulled her back against his stomach. His other hand was sweating, and he wiped it on his pants before picking up the twig they'd wrapped with a tight, thick packing of gauze from her medical supplies.

He took a match from the tinder box in the dresser and lit the end of the makeshift punk until it smoldered. "I'm coming out!" he called to the men outside. "Hold your fire!"

"*Hold your fire! Hold your fire!*" echoed around the meadow.

The doctor pressed back against him, and Kurtis gave her a reassuring squeeze. They'd survive this, he swore. And when it was all finished, he'd be testing those passionate waters of hers again.

He reached for the door and pushed her out onto the porch with him. At least seven rifles were cocked and leveled on them from behind the distant trees. He looked down to find a man lying in the grass not ten feet from the porch, his rifle aimed and ready.

"It's Marshal Riggs, Mitchell!" a man shouted from the pine by the creek. "I've got a warrant for you! Throw down your gun!"

"The only weapon you should be worried about, Marshal, is the one I've got flaming in my hand!" Kurtis called back. "If you haven't noticed, the woman, here, is in a bit of a pickle!"

There was a moment of silence while the marshal

sized up the situation. And then, "What have you got in mind?" Riggs called.

"I have in mind to loose myself of her, that's what! She has more than served her purpose—and she is one hell of a pain in the ass!"

During the following moment of silence, Kurtis adjusted his arm around Josie's middle and gave her hip a subtle caress; he could feel her fear quivering through her body and tensing her muscles against him. "Ready?" he whispered to her.

"Do it," she breathed back.

With careful hands, he slowly let the red-hot tip of the makeshift punk ease down toward one of the sticks of dynamite in her pocket. "You ever see a woman explode, gentlemen?" he called to the distant posse.

Murmurs came from the trees, especially when Josie gripped his arm and began to struggle, weakly, against him. "Nooo!" she screamed. And then she started to sob. "Help me. Please . . . please help me!"

Her heart-wrenching cries surprised even Kurtis at first, and he had to remind himself that she was only pretending to want help.

"Now, you don't wanna go and do that, Mitchell!" the lawman called. "That woman saved your life!"

"That's right! And I'm not about to let you take it from me now!"

"He won't do it!" a familiar voice yelled. "He'd blow hisself up right along with her!"

"Green's right!" shouted another man. "He ain't gonna kill hisself!"

Kurtis lifted his chin in his best proud Indian stance. "I'd rather die in the battlefield than swing at the end of the white man's justice!" he called back.

"Every one of you back off, or so help me, I'll light this fuse and send this sweet little lady to kingdom come—piece by tattered piece!"

Josie enunciated his threat by moaning, going weak in the knees, and hanging from his supporting arm. She reached a hand out to the man lying in the tall grass. "Please help me," she whispered.

The man lifted his head and stared at them, as though he were working up the courage to give the damsel in distress a hand. Kurtis tightened his hold on Josie; she wasn't going anywhere but with him. "Don't even think about it, friend," he said to the man. "Now, pick yourself up and get the hell out of here."

The man climbed to his feet and scrambled away.

"Pull back, men!" the marshal shouted.

"I want a horse!" Kurtis called. "And I want it fast!" An animal was brought forward, saddled and ready to ride. And then it was time for the fun to start.

Kurtis lit the fuses.

Josie let out a convincing startled shriek, and a low rumble went through the crowd of men in the trees. He held her tightly as she struggled against him, trying to work her hands free of his grip so she could pluck the dynamite from her pockets.

"I'll pull the fuses when I'm damn sure we're not being followed!" Kurtis called out.

He threw down the lit punk in his hand, hauled Josie up onto the horse, and took off toward the back woods.

"Hold your fire!" he heard the lawman behind him holler. "You might hit the woman!"

Kurtis rode with Josie straight into the concealing trees and disappeared over a ridge. The woman had outsmarted a posse of six armed men, for Christ's sake, and frankly he wasn't sure whether to be amused or insulted. She'd just proven beyond a doubt that when it came to helping a woman, men were nothing but a bunch of blind, glory-seeking jackasses.

Any second now she was going to slip and tumble to a bashed-up, bloody death.

Josie gripped the pommel between her legs and peered down over the sharp, sandstone cliffs beneath her. The trail cutting into the side of the mountain was so narrow, their horse was practically walking pigeon-toed.

Her plan to escape from the cabin had gone off without a hitch, and they'd been riding upward for almost four hours now and hadn't seen hide nor hair of anyone, let alone a horde of rifle-toting men. The posse, it seemed, had been ditched—for the moment, Mitchell kept reminding her. He had yet to thank her for saving his life again.

She focused her attention on the narrow trail and wondered, not for the first time, just where they were heading, Mount Olympus? Mitchell certainly wasn't offering up any explanations about their destination, and she was beginning to wonder if they were lost— and without a call box in sight!

She looked down into the shadowed, pink-and-purple sandstone pit of hell and gave the horse beneath her a gentle pat on the neck, willing it the sure-footedness to get them safely up the mountain. And then, finally, the path veered to the left and, to Josie's eminent joy, widened into a flat, solid trail.

She broke into a relieved smile, her eyes following the trail as it stretched out toward a sheltered plateau . . . and that's when her relief melted away. Slowly making their way toward them were a pack of braid-wearing, buckskin-clothed, savage-looking Indians. Ten or so grass huts were resting on the plateau in the distance, and she assumed that she and Mitchell had wandered into an Indian village.

"Oh, my God," she said. She kicked at the horse beneath her. "Quick, quick, turn us around!"

Mitchell had a tight grip on the reins, and the animal didn't respond. "Relax," he said, and swung down from the horse.

Josie watched, astounded, as he strode forward and clasped the forearm of one of the tall, fierce-looking men. He and the Indian exchanged a greeting and then looked back at where Josie still sat on the horse.

Over twenty Indian women and children dressed in soft animal skins pressed closer, staring with dark, expressionless eyes at Josie, while movies filled with bloody Indian massacres spun through her head. She gripped the reins, determined to leave Mitchell and ride like the wind at the first sign of hostility.

Mitchell was saying something to the half-circle of men in a language Josie couldn't understand—and she hated him all the more for that when the men turned their attention back to her and laughed.

One of the women grew brave enough to reach out and touch her athletic shoes, and Josie resisted her impulse to jerk back in fear.

"Why are we stopping here?" she finally said in a raspy, insistent whisper.

Mitchell said something else to the men, and they all had another good laugh.

"Get back on this horse and get me out of here!" she hissed.

One of the Indian braves made a gesture toward her

and spoke a few unintelligible words, and the laughter continued. "What did he say?" she demanded to know.

Mitchell turned to her with a twisted smile. "Wind-in-Leaves says for you not to worry. A scalp like yours would bring shame to his family."

Another hair remark? "Well, you can tell your good pal Windy Leaves that I'll take my hair any day to that mop of infested braids he's got dangling over his two huge ears!"

At Josie's angry reply, the entire group of women and children took a collective step back, looking stricken. The men's expressions went stone-cold hard, and Josie paled. If she'd known they'd understand her, she wouldn't have spoken quite so loudly.

"Don't raise your voice to me, Doctor," Mitchell warned in a conversational tone. "You challenge me here, and I'll have no choice but to publicly put you in your place."

"I beg your pardon?" Josie retorted. "And what, pray tell, is my place?"

His dark stare sharpened. "Behind me . . . or beneath me."

Her mouth dropped open. "I'll be beneath you on a cold day in hell!"

"I'm going to warn you one more time, Jos—"

"And the only time I'd stand behind you is to shove a knife between your shoulder blades, you faithless—"

His jaw set, he strode toward her and yanked her off the horse. His retaliation had been swift, and it actually wouldn't have been quite so bad if he'd simply let her fall to the ground in a heap. But, instead, he hefted her over his shoulder and began carrying her into the fold of circular huts.

Josie let out an indignant scream, and he whacked

her on the bottom to keep her quiet. No one was even attempting to help her. In fact, everyone they passed looked rather pleased.

The ground spun past as Mitchell trudged through the encampment, into one of the huts, and then dumped her on a pile of furs. With a low growl, Josie surged to her feet and took a swing at him.

The last thing she'd expected was to connect with anything, but to her surprise, her fist landed squarely against his hard jaw. She yelped in pain and clutched her bruised knuckles. He didn't even blink.

"You could at least have the grace to flinch!" she shouted at him.

"You're lucky you saved that little swat for the privacy of my wickiup—"

"*Your* wickiup?"

"This is my late mother's village."

"Oh, I get it. And I suppose if I'd hit you in front of your Indian friends, you would have had to shoot me with a dozen poison arrows to save precious face!"

"I would have knocked you to the ground."

She raised her chin and looked him square in the eye. "And I would have climbed back to my feet and hit you again."

His nostrils flared, but she continued to stare him down. "Now, would you like to tell me why you've brought me to a place where white people are eaten for lunch? Am I to be the main course? Josie stew?"

"These are my people. We'll be safe here."

She arched a brow. "I thought white men made a game out of raiding Indian camps."

"Not without a full-scale army battalion, they don't." He moved a step closer, and Josie took a reflexive step back. He stepped closer again, and Josie's foot tangled in the furs on the floor, sending her stumbling. Mitchell reached out and caught her by the shoulders before she could fall.

She braced her hands against his broad chest and tried to stamp out the memory of their earlier kiss that suddenly surged forth in her mind. "So I'm safe from a posse. But what about your friends outside?"

He raised his hand and toyed with a tendril of short hair lying against her neck. "Apache warriors respect the property of their brothers."

His caress moved to her neck itself, and she tried to shrug his hand away. He persisted in touching her, though, a small smile twisting one side of his mouth.

"I'm not your property," she pointed out. "I'm your doctor. Remember?"

He took her chin in his hand and pressed his thumb against her bottom lip as if he were testing a ripe cherry. "I wouldn't tell them that. One of them's likely to get it into his head to make you his, and I'm not sure I'm ready to fight for you yet."

Fight for her? "I can take care of myself."

His smile broadened into a full-blown grin, and she caught her breath at how utterly stunning it made him look. "Apparently," he responded softly.

Their eyes met, his touch on her neck became a grip, and he gently urged her toward him. He made a move to kiss her, and she turned her head away. She couldn't allow him to have this kind of control over her senses. "The first kiss I'll let you get away with, Mitchell, but not the second."

His hand moved down and cupped her chin, turning her back to face him. "You're brave and you're smart, and you've got one hell of a right hook. But you have a lot to learn about negotiations."

He pulled her toward him, closing his mouth over hers. Sparks of electricity shot through her stomach, and of their own free will, her hands slid up and curved around his neck. She parted her lips beneath the pressure of his tongue, and his grip on her back tightened. Groaning, she gave herself up to the kiss, never having experienced anything quite so powerful before.

White-hot flames of desire licked at her very core, taunting her with the knowledge that there could be so much more. The very idea of him covering her with his big strong body was enough to make her want to fall at his feet and beg him to take her, then and there.

Her fingers curved into the bulging muscles of his shoulders, and his hand went up beneath her shirt to touch the silky material of her bra. She arched against his questing fingers, her breasts aching with wanting him, her thighs tightening at the very idea, until she couldn't stand the torture any longer. Another second and she was bound to give in to him, offer him her body on a silver platter. And giving this potent male animal open access to her emotions was one risk she wasn't prepared to take.

With just a subtle flexing of her nerves, she shut herself off. She gathered up her yearnings, as she had so many times before, and tucked them away in that little place at the back of her mind reserved for mistakes, experiences best forgotten, and pointless longings that didn't fit into her neat little life.

Mitchell didn't try to keep her next to him when she broke off the kiss and pushed him away. She was sure, however, that he'd caught a glimpse of the raw feeling in her eyes before she'd had a chance to lock it up and throw away the key.

She touched her fingers to her mouth and moved a safe distance away from him. "So . . . what do we do now?"

His answering look was predatory.

"I mean do we stay here, or bury ourselves even deeper into these mountains?"

"We stay here."

He moved a few steps toward her, and she moved a few steps back. "And in four days you'll take me back to Lincoln."

He gave her that twisted smile of his and took another few steps forward. "Did I say that?"

She froze to the dirt floor. "We had a deal, Mitchell!"

"Like I said, you have a lot to learn about negotiating."

"That's not fair! I helped you!"

"You helped yourself."

"You son of a bitch!" she shouted. Feeling helpless and completely deceived, she stole a glance at the grass hut's open doorway.

"I wouldn't recommend another daring attempt at escape. I doubt the village has forgotten the last white attack, and they might take it personally if they catch you trying to get away from me."

Dear God, she was trapped! Even worse than she was before. Her eyes darted around the bare hut, this time looking for something heavy to throw at Mitchell's head.

"Settle in, Doctor. We could be here for a while."

He walked toward the open doorway and disappeared into the afternoon sunshine. A while? Why did that sound as though he never intended to let her go?

12

"*It is good to see you again,* White-Wolf. To what do we owe the honor of your visit?"

Kurtis entered his grandfather's wickiup and sat down, cross-legged, on a reed mat. "I'm searching for Kyle, Grandfather. Has he been to see you lately?"

"Your brother has not been to the village since his heart was broken by the white shaman's daughter."

"Did you know that he's running with the outlaw Billy the Kid?"

His grandfather nodded seriously. "Two-Thunder's judgment has never been strong. It is good that you search for him. You must find him before the white's justice brings down its heavy hand."

"I've managed to make a deal with the Lincoln County sheriff, Grandfather."

The old man's eyes sharpened. "Pat Garrett?"

Kurtis nodded. "If I help him to capture Billy the Kid, all the charges against Kyle will be dropped."

"It is a dangerous game you play, White-Wolf. The one called El Chavato is protected by very strong spirits, and eludes even the best of scouts."

"The Kid's luck is bound to run out eventually. And helping Sheriff Garrett is the only hope we have of keeping Kyle's neck out of a noose."

His grandfather grunted. "Your brother should stop this wildness and find himself a nice Indian girl to marry."

Kurtis smiled. Ever since he and Kyle were young, their grandfather had been trying to marry them off to "nice Indian girls."

"Kyle fancied himself in love with the preacher's daughter."

"A young man will sometimes mistake the burning in his buckskins for love. He must learn to tell the difference." His grandfather's eyes narrowed, eyes so much like Kurtis's mother's, it almost hurt to look at them. "Wind-in-Leaves tells me you have brought a white woman to camp. You aren't mistaking the burning, are you, White-Wolf?"

The flash of Josie Reed's entrancing blue eyes danced through Kurtis's mind, and he shook his head. "I've been around long enough to know it for what it is, Grandfather."

"Good. It wouldn't do for you to make the same mistake as your brother."

His grandfather was studying him carefully, trying to read the true emotions behind Kurtis's expression. But as far as Kurtis was concerned, there was nothing there to read. White women considered themselves too good for red men, especially a red man with white blood in his veins—Kyle had learned that lesson the hard way. Josie was just a distraction for him, nothing more. A challenge to take his mind off the dangers that lay ahead.

"You need a nice Indian girl, White-Wolf. Dancing-River speaks often of you. She asks me when you will return and claim her as your chosen one."

The image of Dancing-River's lithe young body nudged at Kurtis's mind but lost the battle to replace the image of Josie's eyes, her soft, pliable mouth. "Dancing-River's just a child."

"Your mother was the same age when your father stole her from—"

"Don't."

His grandfather paused, filling the hut with a tense silence. "Forgive me, White-Wolf. At times bitterness is a hard thing for an old man to swallow. Tell me, have you brought the woman doctor along to heal your leg?"

Kurtis looked down at his thigh. The wound still pained him occasionally, but his limp was hardly noticeable.

"Wind-in-Leaves tells me you were shot by men who mistook you for your brother. He tells me about your white doctor. He says she has a mouth that spews scalding air."

Kurtis laughed. "That pretty well sums Josie up."

"She wears her hair like a young boy."

"Which only shows off her beautiful eyes. . . . " Her image was back, stronger than ever, and Kurtis found himself wanting to go to her, to kiss her, to make love to her until neither one of them had the strength to move.

"You have chosen her." His grandfather's words

broke through his daze. "She is haunting you as we speak."

Kurtis shook his head. "No. She's just a distraction for me—"

"Your lips say no, but your heart has already decided, White-Wolf. Sometimes, a man mistakes the burning for merely the burning. It takes a brave man to look deeper."

Kurtis shook his head again, a little more adamantly this time, and his grandfather's wrinkled face broke into a smile. "At times it takes a little while for what is in here"—he nudged a gnarled finger at his head—"to catch up with what is in here." He laid his hand over his buckskin-covered chest.

The two of them sat quietly for a while, eating raspberries from a bowl resting between them on the floor. Kurtis refused to believe what his grandfather was telling him, that he wanted Josie Reed for more than just a few lusty tumbles. The woman was far too stubborn for his tastes. She insisted on total control and threw a fit when she didn't get it. No, she was just a little too independent for his peace of mind.

A shaft of sunlight fell upon the floor, and Kurtis looked up to find the tribe shaman, Soaring-Eagle, standing in the threshold. The old, imposing man didn't wait for an invitation. He shuffled into the grass-and-mud hut and sat down beside Kurtis's grandfather.

Kurtis waited quietly for the man to speak, knowing that a visit from Soaring-Eagle could mean only one thing: a vision.

"Six nights past I had a vision," the old man began in a cracking voice. And Kurtis knew instinctively that it had been about him. "The Great Spirit came down from the sky in the form of an eagle and greeted White-

Wolf's spirit with wings spread wide. White-Wolf went joyously and walked the clouds. But then came forth a small white woman dressed in odd gray clothing with white beads of wisdom strung together like moons around her neck. In the woman's palm she carried a tiny black fox with eyes like the ocean, and the Great Spirit was confused, for he had not expected to see the black fox for many years." Soaring-Eagle paused for a long moment before going on to say, "The black fox leaped onto White-Wolf's shoulder and began to whisper in his ear, and the small woman explained to the Great Spirit White-Wolf's fascination with the creature in a language meant only for the gods. And then . . . the Great Spirit lifted his wings"—Soaring Eagle raised his arms—"and sent the wolf on his way. He sent the wolf to be with the black fox. Back to the form of man."

To date, Kurtis had never been able to decipher any of Soaring-Eagle's visions; however, it was said that he had foreseen the death of the great white Indian hunter Colonel George Armstrong Custer and the imprisonment of the red people on government reservations long before the episodes had even occurred.

"You have been returned to the living to answer the call of your destiny, White-Wolf," the old shaman continued as he rose to his feet. "The black fox will come to you, with secrets gripped in her fists. If you can capture her trust and hold her without ropes, she will bring great joy to your heart. If you fail . . . you will return to the Great Spirit."

Stunned and confused, Kurtis watched as the man stood and left. Then he gave his grandfather an irritated look. "White beads of wisdom? The call of my destiny? Why does he always have to be so goddamn mysterious? Why can't he just come right out and say

'Hey, when you come to a green river, don't drink the water' or 'If you happen across a man whose gun is bigger than yours, run'?"

"Soaring-Eagle is very wise, White-Wolf. You must learn to listen to what he tells you and then search your heart for the truth."

Kurtis snorted. "It sounds to me as if he either wants me to capture a fox or throw myself off a cloud."

His grandfather smiled. "It would be hard indeed to capture the trust of one so stubborn and so independent . . . and even harder to climb to the top of a cloud," the old man added with a smile.

Kurtis smirked. "My luck, he probably ate bad meat the night of the vision."

"Remember, White-Wolf, the images that Soaring-Eagle has spoken of to you are not as important as how you perceive them. You must ask yourself: What do these images mean to me?"

Kurtis settled back on his hands. A woman in gray clothing? He supposed he'd met enough of those in his life. But a black fox? He'd never even heard of an animal like that. And with eyes like the ocean. Blue. . . . Blue eyes like Josie's. . . . And who in the world did he know who was more stubborn or more independent than Josie Reed?

He scampered to his feet, earning himself an odd look from his grandfather. "Excuse me, Grandfather," he said as he stumbled out. "There are a few things I think it's high time I found out the answers to."

Her teeth clenched, her arms crossed, her eyes glued to the doorway of the wickiup, Josie waited for Mitchell to return. And she knew he'd be coming back any minute because he had a little present waiting for him that had already been *generously* unwrapped.

He came striding in moments later, a bowl of nuts and berries in his hand, and she jumped all over his case before he had a chance to take another breath. "If you think I'm going to just sit here and watch, you're out of your mind!"

He paused, gave her a confused look, then shoved the bowl of food at her. She refused to take it. "Keep your damn food—and your damn pants on, for that matter!"

"Josie, if you'd tell me what you're rattling on about, maybe this could be a two-sided conversation."

She crossed her arms. "A little gift arrived for you not long after you left. Oh, and I knew it was for you when the wrapping came off!"

Mitchell's gift giggled from where it lay buried in a pile of furs across the floor. His eyes narrowed. "Dancing-River?"

Josie snorted. "More like Willing-Thighs."

He walked toward the pile of furs and hauled the naked Indian girl up by her arm. She dangled there for a moment, her creamy bronzed skin glistening, her high full breasts bobbing, the whole while giggling and darting looks at Josie. "Put your clothes on, Dancing-River, before I fetch your father."

The young girl's almond-shaped eyes rounded. "Do not be angry with me, White-Wolf. When I hear of pale boy you bring to village, I know you need River now."

Josie clenched her fists as the Indian maiden dribbled narrow fingers down Kurtis's neck and into the V of his open collar.

"She screech at you in front of village. She shameful and loud. Choose me, White-Wolf. Choose me now and I will show you much respect—"

"Put your clothes on," Mitchell reiterated.

The young girl stuck out her bottom lip, and it was all Josie could do not to stride forward and tear it from her face.

"Go back to your father's tent and don't come back unless I call for you."

With smooth seductive motions, her dark almond eyes half-closed in an enticing stare, Dancing-River slipped back into her buckskin dress. Then, with a final glance at Josie and a final skim of fingers down Kurtis's arm, she whispered, "I await your command," and left as gracefully as she'd arrived.

"You command her while I'm here and I'll tear your heart out," Josie snapped.

He turned to her, the bowl of nuts and berries still in his hand. He studied her for what she thought was an awfully long moment and then said, "Where are you from, Doctor?"

His change of topic startled her. She gave him a queer look and snatched the bowl of food away from him. "New York."

"Nice try. No lady from the east dresses like that. Shall we try again? Where are you from?" he said more adamantly.

"Okay. I'm from California." She sat down, Indian style, on a woven mat and started eating.

"Why did you lie to the people in Lincoln about where you were from?"

"Maybe I didn't think it was any of their business."

"And your family?" he persisted.

"Dead."

"All of them?"

"Yes, Mitchell, all of them."

He gave her an intense look. "Why do I get the

feeling you're keeping something from me."

"Keeping secrets isn't a crime."

"No. But it's a damn pain in the ass." He looked away for a moment and then back at her. "Is Josie Reed your real name?"

"Is Mitchell yours?"

He gave her an impatient stare, and she gave him one back. He finally said, "My name's Kurtis Mitchell."

She arched her brows and popped another berry into her mouth. "It's a disaster to meet you, Kurtis Mitchell."

"Why did you leave California?"

"The usual: the crime, the congestion, the smog."

He crouched down in front of her. "Come on, Josie, let's have it straight. No bows. No ribbons. What are you doing in New Mexico?"

He was being far too serious for Josie's peace of mind, and she wondered what had happened to spark this interrogation. She started to tell him that she'd left to find her pot of gold at the end of the rainbow, but then he said, "And save the timeworn story about leaving to seek your fortune."

She shrugged. Why not tell him the truth? she thought. With just enough ribbons and bows to keep herself from being tossed into the nearest asylum. "I was brought to Lincoln by a woman claiming to have my best interests at heart."

His look was steady. "What woman?"

"She didn't tell me her name."

"You traveled hundreds of miles with a woman whose name you didn't know?"

"She claimed she was my godmother or something."

"So this godmother-or-something convinced you to take a trip south?"

"Sort of."

"And you *sort of* hopped on a stage and left your life behind without a backward glance?"

"Sort of."

He let out an impatient sigh and narrowed his eyes to the point where Josie wondered if he could even see out of them. "And you expect me to believe this story?"

Josie laughed. "I don't care what you believe, Mitch—"

His hand snapped out and took her by the chin. "The games are over, Josie. I want the *real* truth . . . and I want it now."

"Breaking my jaw certainly won't speed things along."

His fingers relaxed, but his expression darkened. "Why are you here?"

She wasn't about to say "To find my perfect man, the poor slob." So instead she snapped, "You kidnapped me, remember?"

"Yeah." He grew thoughtful. "And it was a pretty easy thing to do, now that I recall."

"Easy for who?" she said with a short laugh.

"My God," he suddenly whispered. "It's Garrett, isn't it?"

She gave him a baffled scowl as he stood to tower over her.

"It was Garrett's idea all along that I take you with me. . . . He set this whole thing up, didn't he?"

"What?" She rose up in front of him.

"He sent you along to be sure I'd stick to my part of the bargain."

Josie shook her head. "You're out of your—"

"I don't need you chasing after me, lady," he interrupted. "I know my lines. Garrett just better make sure that when this is all over and he has Billy the Kid once and for all, he keeps his part of the deal and lets my brother go free."

"Mitchell, I don't know what in the hell you're talking about, but you've really got my attention. What is all this talk about your brother going free? Free from what?"

His scowl deepened, and he stared, deeply, into her face. Then, as quickly as his interrogation had started, his whole demeanor changed. "Nothing. Forget I said anything."

He turned to leave, but she took hold of the back of his shirt and held him in place. "Oh, no, you don't. So you and Sheriff Garrett struck a bargain? I always thought it was pretty suspicious that he didn't notice your hands were loose when I barged in and found him questioning you. And while we're on the subject, since when do reputable lawmen make deals with bloodthirsty criminals?"

Mitchell's jaw tightened much the way it usually did whenever she referred to his life of crime.

"Come on, Mitchell, no ribbons, no bows. What exactly is it that you're accused of doing?" she persisted.

He gave her a level stare. "I got in the way of a bullet."

"One meant for you?"

"In a roundabout way."

"Now who's fudging on their answers? If you expect me to be honest with you, then there's going to be a little give and take here. Let's have the whole messy story."

He nodded. "All right. The whole messy story. I was looking for my brother. He'd been seen in the company of some pretty bad fellows, and I was intent on catching up with him, talking some sense into his rock-solid head, and then dragging him home if need be."

"Uh-huh."

"I was hot on his trail, practically had him in my

hands, as a matter of fact, when damned if I didn't get blown right out of my saddle."

She blinked. "Your brother shot you?"

"No. The fearless Marshal Riggs of Lincoln City and his faithful dog Deputy Green shot me. It seemed they were following the same trail, intent on catching my brother along with every other man who was riding with the Kid."

"So your brother rides with Billy the Kid, too? Keeping it all in the family, are we?"

"Josie, I do not ride with Billy the Kid."

"Then who do you ride with?"

He laughed. "Nobody. Riggs and Green shot me because they thought I was Kyle."

"Your brother?"

"My brother."

"But . . . but they were going to hang you!" she blurted, suddenly realizing all the implications. At his nod, a sickness settled in her stomach. "What's this deal you've made with Pat Garrett?"

"If I help Garrett catch Billy the Kid, he'll drop the charges against Kyle."

"Catch him? But you can't catch him. You'll just end up getting yourself killed!"

"Thanks for that vote of confidence," he said, smiling ruefully.

Josie blinked. She was seeing her wayward patient in a whole new light. He wasn't a criminal. He was just a loyal brother looking out for his own and obviously willing to risk his life to do it. She hadn't helped an outlaw escape, she'd saved the life of an innocent man.

And she'd be damned if she was going to let him throw it away chasing after a murdering snake like Billy the Kid!

"Listen, Mitchell. You asked me why I was here. . . .
Well, I know this sounds crazy, but the woman who
brought me told me I was seeking out my true destiny,
or something to that effect—"

His face went stone-wash pale. He took a step back
from her. "Then it's true," he whispered.

"What's true? Are you all right? Is it your leg?"

He wasn't speaking, though it looked as though he
were trying to. She moved forward and reached out to
check his pulse against her wristwatch. His heart rate
was fast and still picking up speed.

"Damn it, Mitchell," she said, concern ripping through
her. "What the hell is the matter? Are you having chest
pains?"

She turned for her medical bag, but he took her by
the arm and yanked her back to face him. "What did
she look like?" he demanded in a half whisper.

"Who?"

"The woman."

"I don't know. She's—she's short . . . and she always
wears this gray suit and pearl necklace . . . "

Now he looked even worse than he had before,
with his eyes practically bugging out of his head.

"You're starting to scare me, Mitchell. Either tell
me what this is all about or I'm going to confine you
to bed for a week!"

He stared off into space for a moment longer and
then gave her a direct look. "Does this woman have
anything to do with your need to get back to Lincoln
City?"

Josie blinked, still not sure she should tell him the
whole truth. "She's taking me back home."

"Does she live in Lincoln?"

"Uh . . . not exactly."

"Then exactly where is she from?"

Josie didn't have the courage to speculate on that one. She clamped her lips shut and shrugged.

His eyes narrowed again, and she didn't like the stubborn glint that came into them. "Fine. You keep a tight grip on your secrets, Josie. But you're not going anywhere, especially not back to Lincoln."

He moved toward a pile of clothes in the corner and began stripping off his torn pants. Josie didn't bother to turn her back, but she kept her eyes leveled on the backs of his shoulders. "You can't keep me here against my will, Kurtis. I've told you I have to be back in Lincoln by the fourteenth, and so help me, I will be there!"

"You're not going anywhere, Doctor. Not until . . . "

He paused and turned to her, buttoning a pair of tight buckskin pants with fringe running down the outside of his muscular legs.

"Not until what?" she prodded, hardly capable of tearing her eyes away from the primitive sight of him in those pants.

He gave her a steady look. "Not until I've figured out just why the hell you've stumbled into my life."

Josie dropped her forehead into one hand as he strode from the hut. She wouldn't mind having the answer to that question herself. "Fairy lady," she whispered. "I certainly hope you're enjoying yourself."

13

Josie spent the rest of that afternoon alone in Mitchell's wickiup, trying to come up with an escape plan. Everywhere her thoughts roamed, however, turned out to be a dead end. She just couldn't see any way of sneaking out of a village full of Apaches.

Mitchell returned to the hut just as the brilliant crimson light of the sunset began to glare in through the open doorway. With him was the tall Indian who had insulted her hair earlier.

"Someone is sick," Mitchell said. "And the village medicine man has gone on a raid."

She looked up at them and immediately said, "I'll get my bag."

She retrieved her medical bag and strode out of the wickiup. After she brushed past Mitchell she paused and turned to look back at him. "Things aren't settled between us."

Though he was looking directly at her, he acted as if he hadn't heard a word she'd said. She knew from experience that if Kurtis Mitchell set his mind to ignoring her, he'd do just that.

But Josie considered herself to be even more stubborn than he was. And she wasn't giving up.

Her patient turned out to be a fifteen-month-old baby girl. The child was lying on a bed of blankets inside the tall Indian's wickiup, wailing as if someone were poking her with hot needles. The baby's mother was kneeling over her, silently sobbing, looking desperate and helpless.

Josie knelt beside the Indian woman and placed her hand on her shoulder. "I'm Dr. Reed."

Mitchell, who'd followed her in, quickly translated her words.

Josie looked down at the crying infant and saw three scabbed-over sores on one of her chubby, tear-streaked cheeks. She gently pulled aside the infant's buckskin dress and found more blistering spots on her chest and stomach.

"How long has she been like this?" She set her hand on the child's forehead to gauge her temperature, and the crying increased to a frenzied, frantic pitch.

Mitchell translated and then relayed the answer back to Josie. "She broke out in the spots five days ago. They've been applying a poultice, but the sores have only spread and grown worse."

"She's not feverish."

Josie tried to press down on the baby's tiny chin to look inside her mouth, but the little girl shrieked and turned her head away. Josie would have persisted, but the child's mother pushed her hands away.

Josie looked back at Mitchell. "If you want me to do any good, you're going to have to get the mother out of here."

Kurtis translated her words to the Indian brave, and the man forced the woman to her feet. The pair left the hut, and with her mother gone, the child's eyes grew round with fear, its cries now hiccups and squeaks.

"It's okay, sweetie," Josie cooed. "It's all right. Your mama tells me you haven't been feeling well. Is that right? You haven't been feeling well?"

The child's panic seemed to dissipate a bit at Josie's high tone of voice. She gave the baby a warm smile. "You don't have to be afraid of me, sweetheart. I promise I won't hurt you."

She slowly reached out a finger and touched the baby's rounded nose. "Boop," she said playfully. "Boop, boop." The little girl broke into a gap-toothed smile.

"Those are some nasty-looking sores you've got there, honey. Got yourself a case of the chicken pox, don'tcha? Well, that's not a problem. No, it's not." She set her finger on the child's chin and gently opened her mouth. "I don't see any on your tongue. Don't feel a fever. . . . " The little girl let out a giggle, and Josie grinned. "No, I don't. But I bet you're itchin' like the devil, aren'tcha, sweetie? Well, I got somethin' for that."

Josie reached behind her for her medical bag and took out a bottle of children's antihistamine. Mitchell shuffled closer as she unscrewed the childproof cap and poured a small amount of medicine into the dosage cup.

"How would you like a drink of something sweet?"

She reached the cup toward the little girl's mouth and smacked her own lips together. "Mmmm. You're gonna love this."

The medicine went down in one swallow, and the child's eyes went round as she noisily licked the remaining drops from her tiny lips.

Kurtis let out a soft laugh from behind her, and Josie smiled. "I told you you'd like that. Now I need to listen to your chest, sweetie. Just gotta make sure those little lungs of yours are clear." She lifted her stethoscope out of her bag, and the child looked wary again. "You wanna have a look at this?"

The little girl reached out a cautious hand and touched the black tubing. Josie put the chest piece to the end of her nose and made a funny face. The girl giggled.

"You want to put it on your nose? Here." She held out the instrument and touched it to the baby's nose. The little girl blinked and pulled back. "It's cold, isn't it?" Josie said with a laugh.

After the child played with the stethoscope for another minute, Josie was able to listen to her heartbeat and then to her lungs. "Everything checks out, sweetie. You got yourself a case of the chicken pox. Not a very bad one at that. You tell your mama to stop worrying so much."

The little girl didn't want to give up the stethoscope, so Josie gave her a piece of tourniquet tubing in its place. "I'll check back with you tomorrow, little patient. Until then, get lots of bed rest, don't scratch, and stay away from chickens," she said, giving the child a quick tickle in the ribs.

She stood and watched the little girl play with the rubber tubing for a moment. Then she turned for the door. Mitchell was standing in her way, and his expression was one she'd never seen him wear before. "I need you to help me talk to the parents," she said, taking a step toward him to get to the door. He didn't budge.

"You do know that the baby didn't understand a single word you said."

"She knew my intentions were good."

"They're always good."

She searched his face, wondering what he was expecting of her and at the same time afraid to find out. "I'm a doctor, Mitchell. It's my job to—"

"No. Primrose is just a doctor. You're a healer, Josie. Someone who's dedicated her life to helping people. What you just did wasn't only amazing, it was poetic."

She swallowed and looked down at the floor, not knowing how to respond to such raw admiration. "Like I said, I'm just doing my job. Now, will you help me speak with the baby's parents?"

He nodded and stepped out of her way. Josie left the hut and approached the baby's parents who were standing by another wickiup in the distance, but her mind was on the man following behind her. She'd finally gained his respect, and now she didn't know what to do with it.

When they reached the child's parents Kurtis made the introductions. "Dr. Reed, this is Wind-in-Leaves and his wife, Singing-Bird."

Josie held out her hand, but the two just stared at it, apparently not sure what to do. She lowered her hand to her side and said, "Your daughter has the chicken pox—"

"Pox!" the woman cried.

"No, no, the *chicken* pox. It's a very common child-hood illness." Mitchell was translating as fast as Josie could talk. "It very rarely ever causes serious damage to the infected, and your child has a very mild case. I suspect she's crying so much because it tends to be very itchy, like a bad case of mosquito bites."

The mother had calmed down enough to under-stand what Mitchell was telling her. She looked at Josie and nodded, although still visibly shaken.

"I've given her some medicine that should help with the itching, but you need to put some mittens or something on her hands so she can't scratch. The sores can become infected and cause scarring."

The woman nodded again. "As for the rest of you, the chicken pox can be very contagious, and it tends to be a little harder on adults. I suggest you limit your exposure to her."

"When will she be well?" Mitchell asked on behalf of the parents.

"I'd say in another three to five days. Tell them to watch her for fever, and to come to me if they have any concerns at all."

The couple began talking rapidly to Kurtis. "They want me to thank you," he translated, "and offer you the hospitality of their home."

Josie saw tears pooling in Singing-Bird's eyes and reached out to take the woman's hands. "She's going to be all right." She smiled. "Really."

By the time they returned to Mitchell's wickiup, crickets were chirping in the warm night air, and wolves were sporadically howling at the rising moon. Josie went immediately to the back of the hut for a fur to sleep on during the night. She decided on a heavy buffalo skin and spread it out on the ground. From the corner of her eye she could see Mitchell still standing by the door, watching her.

"Have I amazed you so much that you've decided to change your mind?" she asked as she curled up in the center of the rug.

He finally moved toward the pile of furs to choose one for himself. "Change my mind about what?"

"About keeping me for your private pet."

"I haven't changed my mind." He spread out his pallet not two feet from hers and settled on top of it. "By the way, sentries are posted at night. They kill anything that moves outside camp after dark."

"Then maybe after you fall asleep, I'll drag you out past the foul line."

His laugh was a soft, deep rumble. "I wouldn't put it past you, Josie."

"You're not going to win this round, Mitchell. I think you should know that I'm notorious for getting what I want."

"Then we have a lot in common."

There was a moment of silence, and then Kurtis said, "So, what did she say it was?"

"What did who say what was?"

"This godmother of yours. You said she claimed you were here to meet your true destiny. What did she say it was?"

Josie hesitated. For the first time, she actually considered her purpose in 1881. Supposedly there was some poor fool out there, waiting for her to show up on his doorstep, not knowing she'd been detained by some so-called outlaw who needed her to inject him with penicillin every twelve hours so he could go chasing after Billy the Kid.

She and this dream man would probably never

even meet, and, actually, she was glad for that. What if they'd met and fallen madly in love? Then she'd be stuck with the decision of either staying in the land of the lost or enduring a solitary life in the twentieth century, knowing what she'd given up. No, she was glad she wouldn't be forced to make that kind of choice.

"Well?" Kurtis persisted. "Did she tell you your destiny or not?"

"Something about love and happiness. Nothing to take too seriously."

He laughed in the darkness. "A woman? Not taking love and happiness seriously?"

"Yeah, well, I've never been the fairy-tale type."

"Fairy tale?"

"You know, you spend your life looking for the perfect handsome prince, get married, and live happily ever after? That kind of story is for frustrated stepdaughters, for the most part. And women who are so desperate they go around kissing frogs."

"And you don't consider yourself that type of woman?"

"Nah."

"Well, that's a relief."

"What?"

"That you apparently don't consider me a frog."

She smiled. "Fishing for a compliment, are we, Mitchell?"

"And if you were to give me one, Josie, what would it be?"

She thought for a moment, letting herself smile because she knew he couldn't see her. "You have nice hair."

"Nice hair?" he repeated with a definite note of astonishment.

"It's silky and it's thick. Any woman would admire it."

"Nice hair," he grumbled.

"It goes well with that devastating face," she mumbled to herself. "And those broad shoulders. And that great butt—"

"What was that?"

"Nothing."

"I guess it was the wind," he said in a knowing tone.

"Go to sleep, Mitchell. How can I escape from you if you never shut your damn eyes?"

There was another soft laugh, and then he said, "Josie Reed, the day you escape from me will be the day a man reaches the moon."

Josie rolled her eyes. The way she figured it, she had eighty-eight years to go.

The sound of frantic voices pulled Josie back from the peaceful void of sleep. Someone was shaking her, and she lifted her head to find Kurtis crouched down beside her. "What is it?" she whispered.

She looked to the doorway, where a shaft of moonlight was being blocked by a tall silhouette. It was Wind-in-Leaves, the little girl's father. The physician in Josie kicked in, and she reached for her medical bag.

"The baby has the heat sickness," Mitchell said.

Josie climbed to her feet. "What's the heat sickness?"

"Fever that makes her whole body shake."

Josie raced to Wind-in-Leaves' wickiup, pausing only long enough to snatch a stick from the woodpile. Kurtis and the Indian brave were not far behind as she charged inside and found Singing-Bird in tears once again, trying to hold down her convulsing infant.

Josie didn't have to set hands on the child to know her fever had spiked. The little girl's face was a brilliant shade of raspberry, her tiny dark head was covered in a thick sweat, and she was bundled in layers upon layers of fur and buckskin.

Without hesitating, Josie raced forward and shoved the mother aside. She pried open the child's mouth and put the stick between her clamping teeth to prevent her from biting her tongue. Then she picked up the little girl and dashed toward the stream that ran along the eastern side of the village.

Once she reached the rocky bank, Josie fell to her knees and immersed the child in the cool mountain water. Mitchell dropped down beside her and helped to peel the layers of sodden blankets and clothing from the little girl. "Are you sure you know what you're doing?" he asked.

"We have to cool her off." She tossed aside fur and buckskin. "She's having a grand mal."

"A what?"

"It's a seizure, Kurtis! Her brain is too hot!" She poured cool water over the baby's head, and gradually the little body began to relax. After a few minutes more the little girl's brown eyes were wide and her tiny bare feet were beginning to slap at the water. By this time the entire village had gathered around to watch them in the glow of the full moon.

Josie turned to Mitchell. "Get my medical bag. I dropped it in Wind-in-Leaves' hut."

He returned in seconds, and Josie retrieved a bottle of Tylenol and shook out a tablet. She halved it and set a piece on the child's tongue. "This, I'm afraid," she told the little girl, "isn't going to be quite as tasty as the last medicine I gave you."

The child made an awful face and shuddered, but Josie made sure that all the medicine went down.

She continued to bathe the little girl for another ten minutes, talking to her, waiting until the Tylenol had accomplished its purpose and brought down the fever. Then she stood and handed the dripping little girl back to her mother. "Tell her not to bundle the child," she said to Mitchell. "Tell her to lay the baby out with only a comfortable amount of covering, and that if she notices the fever rising again to bring her back to the stream. I'll be back in four hours to give her another dose of medicine."

Mitchell repeated all of this and then listened while Singing-Bird spoke. "Singing-Bird would like to know which holds the magic, the water or you."

Josie sighed, suddenly feeling the fatigue of an arduous week. "Tell her the magic is in simply knowing what to do."

She stumbled back to Kurtis's hut and set the alarm on her watch. It was after one o'clock in the morning. She dropped down onto the soft fur and promptly fell asleep.

Her watch alarm went off just after five A.M., and it wasn't so much the nagging, high-pitched *beep beep beep* that woke her as Kurtis's reaction to the sound. Two hundred pounds of man landed on top of her, knocking the wind out of her lungs in a *whoosh*. Despite her cry of protest, Kurtis pulled the watch off her wrist, banged it, hard, on the floor, and threw it across the room, where she heard it smash against a pole. Then he fell down beside her, his breath coming fast and hard, and Josie propped herself up on her elbows.

She stared at the direction her watch had gone and

then looked up at Kurtis. He still looked wary and completely disoriented with his hair crumpled and hanging in his eyes. "My hero," she remarked.

"What the hell was that thing!"

"My watch. And by the way, killer, it's trained to stay on my wrist."

"But it was screaming— Christ, it scared the hell out of me!"

"No kidding." She couldn't help it, she broke into laughter. "But you really showed it. I'm sure it'll never scream again." She pictured her Timex mangled and broken, lying in a pile of shattered pieces across the room. "Yep, I'm pretty sure."

"Very funny, Miss Reed. You got any other strange devices on you that I should know about?"

"No, you killed the only one." She rose up from her makeshift bed. "It's time for Little-Sparrow's medicine."

He continued to stare at her, though, as if she'd risen from the bowels of hell. She laughed again and picked up her medical bag. "I should have brought my beeper."

The baby was sleeping, cool and peaceful, beside her mother in Wind-in-Leaves' hut. This time she took her medicine without a protest.

Josie barely noted the sun creeping up over the horizon as she stumbled back to Mitchell's wickiup. And she certainly didn't notice his sleepy look of surprise when she grumbled good night and fell down next to him on his fur.

14

Josie woke the next morning to the sound of female giggling. She opened her eyes and stared up at the grassy ceiling above her, a vivid picture of Dancing-River, naked, racing through her mind. She lurched upright.

The giggling stopped as Josie confronted Mitchell and Singing-Bird, who were standing and talking by the hut entrance. Singing-Bird broke into a smile.

"Singing-Bird says Little-Sparrow is doing much better this morning," Mitchell said. "She has no new spots, and the old ones are disappearing."

Josie rubbed her eyes, trying to make sense of the fury she'd felt upon first waking. "Glad to hear it."

Mitchell continued to stare at her, an odd smirk tugging his mouth. And then Josie realized she wasn't sleeping in the same spot she'd chosen the night before. She looked down at the fur she was resting on, then over at the fur she was supposed to be resting on, and gave Mitchell an accusing glare.

He ignored it. "Singing-Bird would like to give you a gift."

Josie didn't accept gifts for simply doing her job. But the dainty Indian woman stepped forward and held out the most beautiful dress she'd ever seen. It was made of pale, creamy buckskin. Bright tiny beads of red and green were sewn into the bodice in an intricate geometrical pattern, and the entire neckline and hem were edged in snowy white rabbit's fur.

"Really, I couldn't possibly—"

"Don't insult her by not accepting it," Mitchell said.

She sat forward and reached out to let her fingers glide over the fur at the hem. "It's the most beautiful thing I've ever seen."

Mitchell translated, and Singing-Bird's smile widened. Then the woman said something that made Mitchell laugh.

"What did she say?" Josie asked.

"She said that if you think the dress is lovely, you need to bathe more often and study your own reflection in the water."

Josie frowned. It seemed she'd been insulted and complimented in the same breath.

Singing-Bird draped the buckskin dress over one arm and then held out her other hand to Josie. Josie gave Mitchell a questioning look.

"She wants you to come and participate in the women's morning bath," he explained.

Josie's eyes rounded. "A bath?" Even the words had the ability to make her feel just a little more clean.

"She won't force you if you don't—"

Josie jumped to her feet and took the woman's hand. "You just lead the way, Singing-Bird."

The path to the bathing hole wound through dense brush and picturesque views. They followed along the edge of the stream for well over five minutes before coming to the base of a cliff, where water fell from twenty feet over their heads and into a clear pond.

Naked women frolicked in the water, giggling and splashing each other, while their bronzed bodies glistened in the morning sun. Josie had never been too uptight about these sorts of things, but she actually felt a little uncomfortable standing there watching. It was like a scene from the Playboy mansion, and she felt like a voyeur.

She averted her eyes as Singing-Bird pealed her buckskin dress from her golden body and waded into the water. Josie chewed her lip and fidgeted with the hem of her dirty T-shirt while she stood on the bank, feeling like the kid who wasn't allowed to get wet.

Suddenly the giggling and splashing stopped, and Josie found herself the center of everyone's attention. There was a palpable silence, and then they all started to call to her. She couldn't understand a single word they were saying, but there was no mistaking the enticing lilt of their voices as they beckoned to her.

Josie had never gone skinny-dipping, although the idea had always held a sort of wicked fascination for her. She took one final look around at the concealing foliage and began to take off her shirt. The women laughed and started splashing her. She was drenched before she'd ever made it into the water.

As she eased into the pond she found it surprisingly refreshing. It wasn't as cold as the water by the cabin, and she assumed there was some sort of underwater hot spring feeding it. The water lapped at her thighs, her hips, her waist, and then her breasts as she sunk farther and farther into the first bath she'd had in over a week. If this wasn't heaven, it was pretty damn close.

Keeping his head down, Kurtis crawled up the hillside on his belly until he'd reached the crumbly rocks at the edge of the cliff. Bear-Claw, lying stretched out beside him, turned and gave him a wicked leer.

Kurtis dropped his face into the musty moss beneath him to catch his breath. "I can't believe I let you talk me into this, Bear-Claw."

"Come now, brother, it's a tradition," Bear-Claw said over the roar of the waterfall.

"A tradition between children, not full-grown men."

The man laughed. "It takes a bit more energy for you to climb this cliff these days, does it, White-Wolf?"

"Not as much as it'll take for me to throw you over the edge."

Bear-Claw lifted his head to see down over the waterfall. "Ah, Stepping-Deer is still magnificent. She filled my dreams as a child, made this boy feel like a man—"

"I'm sure your wife will be pleased to know that."

Bear-Claw glanced back at him and grinned. "Sitting-Cat would geld me like a stallion." His attention returned to the spectacle below them. "Ah, but wait. I see something unusual down there. Something pale and white instead of dark and bronze. Something remarkable—"

Kurtis took hold of Bear-Claw's buckskin shirt and pulled him down beside him. Just the thought of Josie

Reed standing not twenty feet below him wearing nothing but water and sunshine made him hard and aching, and he didn't appreciate the idea of sharing the sight with anyone, not even his best friend.

Bear-Claw gave him a knowing smile. "I only saw her back, brother. Perhaps you'd like to take a look and describe the other side?"

Kurtis licked his lips, his mouth suddenly gone dry. It wasn't right spying on her this way—if she ever found out, he'd be the one gelded—but the temptation was just too great.

He lifted his head and peered over the edge.

She was standing in the center of the pool with her back to him, talking with a group of three other women, moving her hands around as if trying very hard to make them understand her. He could just see the indentation of her bottom where the water was lapping at her hips, caressing her skin with each gentle motion. He'd never envied a liquid so much in his life.

He swallowed, waiting with bated breath as Josie slowly turned.

Kurtis could have sworn that time actually stood still at that moment. Nothing around him moved or sounded as he took in the beauty of her gentling swelling hips, her narrow waist, and her full, pearly breasts. There was no doubt about it; he had to have this woman.

The weight of Bear-Claw's hand came down upon his shoulder, but Kurtis shrugged him off. He wasn't ready to give up his position yet—doubted if he'd ever be ready.

"White-Wolf!" Bear-Claw said in an urgent whisper. "It is Horse-Woman! She is coming!"

With reflexes born of experience, Kurtis dropped his head and began scrambling backward down the hill. Passion and desire had been quickly replaced with panic.

Horse-Woman, all three hundred pounds of her, had retained the duty of standing guard over the bathing women ever since time began, or at least as long as Kurtis and Bear-Claw could remember. It was said that if a boy were caught spying, the women would strip him and parade him in front of the whole village.

That terrifying threat alone was enough to keep most adolescent males away, but never Kurtis and Bear-Claw. They'd been spying ever since they'd discovered that girls were different and if a boy thought about that fact and touched himself just right, he could feel pretty damn good about life.

Now, even though Kurtis was a grown man, he was scrambling down that hill like a gun-chased rattler, just like old times. He was too damn old for this. And as he landed at the bottom of the hill, his buckskin pants filled with dry grass and dirt, his hands skinned, his chin scraped, he hoped that Horse-Woman would take that fact into consideration.

She was waiting for them, with her beefy fists planted on her even beefier hips and her eyebrows arched in smug victory. "Boys," she said in smooth Apache as they stared up at her in openmouthed horror.

Kurtis felt like a ten-year-old again, which was understandable, he supposed, since he'd been acting like one. He sat up and picked the dirt from his mouth as Bear-Claw started stammering excuses of why they'd felt the need to have a conversation on the very cliff that overlooked the bathing hole.

Horse-Woman wasn't buying a word of it. And as Kurtis listened to his friend's pitiful attempts to seek mercy, he knew that the time had come. They were about to pay for each and every transgression they'd ever committed against the women of his late mother's village.

15

Horse-Woman took Kurtis by the ear and dragged him to his grandfather's wickiup, just as if he were a ten-year-old boy. It was probably one of the most humiliating moments of Kurtis's life, especially since his grandfather couldn't seem to stop smiling, but at least the punishment that Kurtis had so dreaded as a boy didn't come to pass. Because he and Bear-Claw were grown men, his grandfather said, the incident was best swept under the rug. Punishing the two transgressors wasn't worth the wrath of angry husbands and Bear-Claw's temperamental wife.

But that didn't mean that rumor wouldn't spread quickly through the village, and that Josie Reed wouldn't somehow catch wind of what Kurtis had done.

She returned to his wickiup a few minutes after he did, and his eyes almost popped out of his head. She was wearing the creamy buckskin dress Singing-Bird had made and knee-high moccasins to match. The soft material hugged her body from hips to shoulders and only reminded Kurtis of exactly what he'd been trying to forget for the past hour. His desire for his little doctor sprang to life all over again.

As she draped her wet shirt and denims on a stick by the door, he waited, his heart racing, to find out if she'd heard anything of what he'd been doing while she'd been in the bathing hole.

She turned back to him, brushed a swatch of her gleaming black hair from her blue, blue eyes, and crossed her arms in a stance Kurtis must have seen a hundred times in the past week. "And what have you been doing this morning?" she asked, her tone less than congenial.

Kurtis's pride rose up to lodge somewhere between his heart and his throat. "Why"—he cleared his throat—"why do you ask?"

She narrowed her eyes and then reached down to where he'd thrown his dirty, scraped-up pair of buckskins. "Haven't I told you to give your leg a break, Mitchell? It might be healing a lot faster than I'd anticipated, but crawling around in the dirt, or whatever the hell you did to mess up these pants, isn't going to do it one bit of good."

Or whatever he'd done? *She doesn't know. She doesn't know!* his mind began to chant.

He scowled and took the pants from her hand. "Bear-Claw and I were . . . catching gophers."

She arched a brow. "For lunch?"

"For the hell of it."

She walked away from him, across the dirt floor, and his eyes invariably glued themselves to the curves of her swaying backside. "Did you catch any?" she asked.

"Any what?"

She looked back over her shoulder at him, and he quickly adjusted the level of his gaze. "Any gophers."

"Uh . . . no. We—we didn't catch anything."

That silky black eyebrow arched up again. "Not much of a hunter, are you?"

When she bent forward to set her odd white shoes against the hut wall, Kurtis craned his neck, trying to see up her dress. The backs of her knees were like beckoning little notches where his tongue longed to roam. Her knees? Hell, he'd like to lay her out flat and lick every tasty, luscious inch of her!

"I'm going to head over to—" She'd turned back to find him out of breath and completely pale. "Mitchell? Are you having another one of those attacks like you had yesterday?"

He shook his head, but that didn't stop her from dashing toward him. She sat him down on the old stump he sometimes used as a chair, then moved in between his legs. He stared at her chin while she checked his pulse and his skin temperature, and he tried to keep himself from grabbing her.

His best efforts failed. When she peered into his eyes he came completely undone. He took hold of her small waist and pulled her, hard, against him.

"Mitch—"

That's the farthest she got with his name before he smothered the word with his mouth.

Josie was taken completely off guard by Mitchell's impassioned kiss, and before her mind could even consider resisting, her body was melting into his, begging him for more. He was an inferno racing through her blood as no other man had ever been, and she couldn't seem to resist playing with his particular brand of fire.

His tongue slipped into her mouth, making her feel weak and aroused, and she clutched the back of his neck where his silken hair teased her fingers. His hands roamed down her back to cup her bottom through the soft material of her buckskin dress, and she moaned as a primal burst of lust shot through her. The pleasure was overwhelming, despite her impulse to deny it.

"Ah, Josie," he murmured, and a surge of warmth swept through her. "Your mouth is so damn sweet."

His breath was a rasp in her ear as he gently sank his teeth into the sensitive flesh of her lower neck. She could feel his hands tugging up the hem of her dress and knew that he intended to have her. The idea was so appealing, so dangerously tempting, that Josie almost let herself give in. Almost.

With all the willpower she could muster, she set her hands against his chest and shoved back. She broke from his arms and fell to the dirt floor.

Looking bewildered, Mitchell remained where he was while she got her breathing under control, but he continued to stare at her with impassioned eyes.

"I . . . I don't want to make love with you," she said raggedly.

She could tell by the way his expression changed that he took that bit of news personally. "Tell that to your body," he responded with a hard edge to his voice. "It, apparently, wouldn't mind the experience."

She adjusted the fur neckline of her dress and sat forward. "You're a seductive bastard, I'll say that much for you, Mitchell, but I'm afraid I'm not interested."

"Is that why your nipples are hard?"

Her mouth dropped open, and she resisted the urge to check his claim for herself.

He sat forward and gave her a stare that could have melted metal. "Is that why you go hot with just a look from me?"

She stiffened her jaw and rose to her feet, tugging down the hem of her dress. "Sorry. I don't go for King Kong types who roar and pound their chests."

"King who?"

"And for that matter, men who give their word and then take it back don't sit well with me either!"

"Oh, now, what the hell is that supposed to mean?"

"I'm referring to that daring escape we pulled off yesterday morning, in which I promised to help get you away from the posse and in return you would get me back to Lincoln by the fourteenth!"

"I never said—"

"You led me to believe that we had an agreement!" She took a stride toward him. "You know, I've done everything I can to help you, only to have you spin full circle on me each and every time and stab me right in the back! I can't trust you at all, and, frankly, I'd feel a whole lot better if you'd just stay the hell away from me!"

His eyes were dark and fathomless. "I had no idea you felt that strongly."

"Then you haven't been paying attention!"

He didn't speak for a few moments, and Josie began wondering if she might be finally getting through to him.

"What will happen if I send you back to Lincoln?" he finally asked.

Her heart leaped at the thought, but she gave him a suspicious look. "What do you mean?"

"I want to know *exactly* what will happen."

"I'll leave," she responded softly.

He stood and walked toward her. Soon her only view was the broad span of his shoulders and the magnetic draw of his deep brown eyes. He lifted his hand and, with just the lightest skimming of his fingers, sent trickles of electricity down the back of her neck. She looked up into his face.

"Where would you go?" he whispered.

Their gazes met across the span of over one hundred years, and suddenly the thought of leaving him caused an ache inside her that she couldn't explain. "Home," she whispered back.

"Home?" He moved his hand over her left breast, resting it against the rapid beating in her chest. "Home is here, where your heart is."

That's right, she wanted to say. *And my heart's planted firmly in my chest, exactly where it belongs.* But with every passing second that his gaze held hers, she could feel it easing away from her, little by little. Her mother had once told her that love was blind, and, like an earthquake, it usually hit with great force and no advance warning. Now, looking up into Kurtis Mitchell's warm, inviting gaze, Josie was beginning to understand exactly what her mother had meant.

She couldn't let it happen.

"Stay here with me, Josie," he said softly. The offer sent a wave of warmth surging through her. He moved his hand to caress her cheek. "I'll keep you safe, and happy."

She flinched. *I'll keep you,* her mind echoed. *I'll keep you.*

Fear like nothing she'd ever felt before swept through her. A vision of her mother, her once dignified features haggard, her once unquenchable spirit battered, flashed through her mind, and Josie shoved Mitchell's hand away. "*Kept!* I don't need to be kept!" she shouted into his face. "As a matter of fact, I don't *need* anything from you!"

He blinked, startled. And suddenly his handsome face became the disapproving countenance of her father. Josie didn't pause to sort through fantasy and reality. She pulled herself up straight and lashed out with all the venom she could muster.

"Just because I happen to be afflicted with the unfortunate birth defect of being born female doesn't mean I need a man taking care of me and telling me what to do! I was born without a penis, not without a brain, and I damn well can take care of myself!"

He pulled back from her as if she were brandishing a knife, and Josie swallowed as hot tears scalded her eyes. "You men are all alike," she said, her voice choked. "You lure us in with pretty words and promises. 'I'll take care of you, I'll take care of everything.' And once you've got us dependent on you for all our basic needs, you strip us of our dignity, take away everything in our lives that doesn't pertain to you—no matter how much it means to us. Just so that we can focus all our attention on serving your every goddamn whim!"

She brushed at her tears and turned away so he wouldn't see her pride disappearing from her face. "I told you once before, Mitchell. I don't do submissive. You want somebody to push around, go find your damn dog!"

He remained silent behind her, but she sensed the moment he left the hut. Then she covered her face with her hands and did her best to regain control. She hadn't thought of her dead father in so long that it felt as if she'd torn the stitches of an inflamed wound. She always did her best to keep the memories tucked back in that secret compartment along with everything else better left alone, but Kurtis's unexpected plea for her to stay had brought all the old painful memories of her parents back to the surface.

She slipped down into the pile of furs at her feet and did something she hadn't done in a very long time: she cried until she was numb.

Kurtis sank down into the water up to his chin. He hadn't enjoyed a real bath in almost two weeks. He was trying to relax, but thoughts of Josie, sweet and willing in his arms, kept nagging at him. Josie, kissing him back with equal passion. Josie, clinging to him and pressing herself against his aching body. She was the closest thing to heaven he'd ever known.

"What are you mooning about, brother?"

Kurtis looked to where Bear-Claw was floating on his back in the water a few feet away. As a mild punishment for their childish action that morning, Kurtis's grandfather had decided that the two of them would do the hunting for the day by themselves. As a result they were both covered with sweat and dirt, and completely exhausted.

He ignored Bear-Claw's question and reached down to rub the ache out of his thigh. Though his wound was healed and covered with a fresh pink scar, it still caused him pain whenever he overexerted himself.

"If your scowl were any darker, you would turn the water to mud," Bear-Claw said as he splashed water onto his chest.

"I was thinking about how to get even with you for talking me into spying this morning."

Bear-Claw laughed, and Kurtis was struck by how much his friend reminded him of his brother Kyle. But that wasn't so surprising considering the three of them had practically grown up together. The Mitchell ranch was only fifteen miles away from the Indian village.

"It is the first thing I have *ever* been able to talk you into, my brother," Bear-Claw said with a smile still in his voice. "Tell me. Did you purposely make it easy on me this time? Was there, perhaps, a certain white maiden you were interested in seeing wet and naked?"

That image alone made Kurtis go hard beneath the water. "Tell me, Bear Claw, has your wife *Spitting-Bat* found out about your actions this morning?"

Bear-Claw broke into unbridled laughter. "If Sitting-Cat had heard the faintest peep, I would be knee deep in my own grave. No, it seems we worried as youths for nothing. We have seen the best our village has to offer, and our male dignity is still intact. What about your white doctor? Has she heard anything?"

"Considering a fair number of women in this village speak some English, I must admit I was a little . . . "

"Terrified?"

"Concerned for my own safety," Kurtis finished pointedly.

"And?"

Kurtis shrugged. "Not a peep."

"You see! It is as we suspected all along as boys. They *want* us to spy! They just don't want us to *know* they want us to spy!"

As Kurtis tried to follow that logic, Bear-Claw

began wading to the shore. "Mark my words, brother," Bear-Claw continued. "They probably *all* know, and are hoping that our meager punishment won't deter us, come tomorrow morning."

Kurtis rose out of the water and joined his friend on the rocky bank. The sun was low in the sky, casting red-and-purple shadows throughout the scattered clouds.

Bear-Claw turned to clap him on the back. "Take my advice and have your doctor tonight, brother. While the image of you spying on her is still fresh in her—"

Suddenly they heard a great commotion coming from the cliff overhead, and Kurtis and Bear-Claw looked up to find the entire female population of the village standing above them, clapping their hands and shouting.

For a moment, Kurtis and Bear-Claw were both too stunned to move, but then reality returned and they spun around simultaneously to get the clothes they'd discarded earlier.

They both froze. Standing on top of their clothing was Horse-Woman, a wide grin of triumph on her face.

Kurtis and Bear-Claw exchanged a chagrined look; they would have to run for the water like cowards or try casually to cover themselves and take their just desserts. In the end, they both decided to tough it out like men.

For five minutes they stood quietly while Indian women of every age, shape, and size whistled, shouted, and threw taunts down at them. Finally, after more critiques on his manhood than Kurtis cared to have, the women began to lose interest and wander away.

When Horse-Woman finally left them with their clothes, Bear-Claw snatched up his buckskins and headed for the dense brush. Kurtis chose to sit on a fallen log and slip on his pants with dignity, all the while thinking that justice with women certainly was a strange thing.

Was it justice that his father, a powerful white rancher, had fallen helplessly in love with an Apache squaw? Was it justice that his brother had had his heart broken so badly that he'd chosen a life of crime to help him forget? Was it justice that Kurtis now found himself captivated with a woman who kissed like an angel and then struck out like the devil himself?

"Learned your lesson, have you?"

He looked over his shoulder to find the woman of his thoughts coming up behind him. "In what?" He returned his attention to the bathing hole and wished his feelings toward her could be as clear and calm as the water. "In spying, or in venturing to think that there might be something between us?" he asked.

There was no response, and he wondered if she'd turned and left. But then he felt the prickle of her gaze on his back and knew she was still there, fighting with herself as she always did whenever he was concerned. She was probably wondering if it was safe to advance and move closer to him, or if she should lash out as she had in his wickiup. How such a courageous woman could be so frightened where he was concerned baffled him. And it infuriated him that she refused to give him one iota of her trust.

"There is no us, Mitchell," she said quietly, still at a distance. "There's only a patient and his doctor."

Denial. That was the game she'd chosen to play.

Well, Kurtis Mitchell had never in his life made the offer he'd made to her that morning, and he'd be damned if he'd fall down on his knees and *beg* her to stay with him.

"You're right," he finally said. "I guess it's just some misplaced sense of gratitude."

There was a pause, and then, "It's at least nice to know you're finally feeling some."

He was feeling plenty of something, but gratitude didn't even come close to describing it. "You were right earlier," he admitted. "I did break our agreement. I won't be able to take you back to Lincoln myself, but I'll talk to a friend of mine and see if he'll agree to the trip."

"That . . . that would be very nice of him."

Was that hesitation he heard catching in her voice?

"Then it's settled," he said, his voice as raw as his wounded pride. "The day after tomorrow we go our separate ways."

16

Josie spent that night alone. She had no idea where Mitchell had chosen to sleep, and she refused to let herself care, even if it was with that sleazy little Dancing-River. But after convincing herself that she was glad to have the small hut to herself, that she was more than happy to have Mitchell out of her hair, she ended up tossing and turning the entire night.

By the time she woke late the next morning, grumpy as a bear and dressed in her freshly washed, modern clothing, the women had already finished their morning bathing. She had given Mitchell his final shot of penicillin before dawn that morning, then he and most of the men had left on a hunting expedition and weren't expected to return until sunset.

Josie had felt a flash of disappointment at that bit of news. She had to admit, she'd actually been hoping to spend a little time with Kurits smoothing matters

over on their last day together. But it seemed a recon-
ciliation wasn't to be. Maybe it was for the best. Considering how well she and Kurtis had gotten along in
the past, she doubted the tension between them could
be wiped away with just one day of civility. They'd
probably wind up in another argument and only make
things worse.

Intent on checking in on Little-Sparrow, she walked
through the village and found mother and child playing in the center of a mat on their wickiup floor.
Standing unnoticed at the entrance, Josie watched the
tender scene for a moment before deciding not to
interrupt. The little girl was obviously recovering well
and didn't need her doctor interfering.

She headed back across the compound, skirting a
group of frolicking children, and wondered how she'd
occupy herself for the day. Suddenly a tall Indian
stepped into her path and looked down his long nose
at her. "White-Wolf tell me you leave next sunrise."

Josie nodded, taking in his fringed buckskin shirt
and breechcloth. He had long, smooth, muscular legs,
and she had the most incredible urge to ask him if he
ever caught a chill in that flimsy piece of nothing. For
God's sake, the man's pants consisted of a strip of
buckskin tied around his waist that held in place two
measly, strategically placed panels: one in the front
and one in the back. A good strong draft and, va-va-
va-voom, moon over New Mexico!

The image of how Mitchell might look in one of
those garments skipped into her mind, and quick as a
wink, she stomped the thought to death; it wouldn't
help matters to start fantasizing about him now.

She wasn't sure of this particular Indian's name,
but she could remember seeing Mitchell talk to him a

few times. The man was the "Magic Johnson" of the village, standing at least six and a half feet tall, and she guessed him to be in his late thirties by the few strands of gray hair she could see weaving through his long, thick braids.

"White-Wolf say you want go back to city," he said in the broken English that a handful of the people in the village spoke.

"White-Wolf?" she responded.

"Kurtis Mitchell."

She nodded. "Yes, that's right. I'd like to be taken back to Lincoln City."

"Why?" the man asked, his expression stern.

"Because I have business there."

"What kind business?"

Josie didn't feel she had any obligation to explain herself to this man, but in the end his stoic stare convinced her to answer. "I'm meeting a woman who will take me back to my home, back where I belong."

The man studied her for a long, uncomfortable moment, then said, "White-Wolf say you not know horse from own ass."

Josie smirked. "Sounds like something he'd say."

"He say you not know gun from own foot, rifle from own arm—"

"I get the picture."

"He ask me take you to city."

She blinked. "You?" She took another long look at the man. He was lean, but clearly powerful, with long gleaming hair and bronzed leathery skin—that would probably crack at the first hint of a smile. The idea of riding through the mountains with him made her a little uneasy.

"How you get anywhere, you not ride horse?"

"I . . . well . . . I walk, I suppose." She didn't think he was ready to hear about the Mazda she had sitting in her driveway at home.

"Lincoln too far walk." He looked down at her legs, and she curled her toes inside her Nikes. She couldn't get over the feeling that he was studying her—and finding her lacking. "Legs too skinny walk that far."

She refused to get angry. He obviously had no real concept of common courtesy, and he *had* agreed to return her to Lincoln . . . hadn't he?

"Then I suppose I'll have to ride a horse," she said.

"Suppose," he replied.

She waited and then said, "Is there one I might borrow?"

His frown turned into a full-blown scowl. "Indian no lend horse. Horse mean honor, importance, wealth."

"Then I guess I'll have to catch my own." It was hard to keep her irritation from her voice, but the man didn't seem to notice. Or maybe he just didn't care.

"White-Wolf say you have buckskin. She good mare. Gentle. Not kick or bite, you sit on wrong end. He say you ride with saddle, tie strong rope around waist so you not fall off."

Josie gritted her teeth. No wonder the Indian kept looking at her with such disdain; Mitchell had made her out to be a bumbling fool. "I'm sure, with a little practice, I'll do just fine. Where is this mare?"

He pointed toward a group of horses in the distance, corraled together with just a rope encircling them. Josie nodded. "Thank you."

She turned on her heel and started toward the animals. "You not break neck," the man called out to her.

"No," Josie grumbled to herself as she crossed the compound. "I break White-Wolf's neck."

This time, when she fell, she tucked her head in but still landed hard on her shoulder.

Josie groaned and climbed unsteadily to her feet. She'd fallen off the mare ten times now, and if the stoic-faced Indian hadn't followed her to watch, she would have given up nine times ago. He wasn't just watching her, he was measuring her, and she'd be damned if she was going to come up short.

She took another handful of the buckskin's mane and swung herself up onto its back. In the past hour she'd gotten fairly good at mounting, she just wasn't very good at staying that way.

"You need sap from tree," the Indian finally said from his place beneath a giant pine.

Josie frowned at him. "What for?"

"For keeping ass stuck to horse."

She held back a biting retort, knowing that he was enjoying each of her attempts as they ended in failure. She wrapped the fingers of both hands securely in the horse's golden mane and gave the animal a nudge with her heels.

The mare was gentle, Josie could tell that by its unending patience with her, but that little fact did nothing for her when she started slipping to the side once again.

She let out a frustrated screech as she slid to the left. She clung to the horse, refusing to fall this time. But then she finally either had to let go or have her arms torn from their sockets.

She rose from the ground and slapped the dust from her jeans. "Okay, Tonto. What's the secret?"

The man pulled away from the pine tree and walked toward her, the fringe on his shirt and the back panel of his breechcloth blowing in the warm breeze. Though Josie assumed he'd enjoyed watching her defeat, there wasn't a hint of pleasure on his face. This man had only one expression: stone.

"You need saddle."

"I need to know how all the rest of you stay on."

He looked down at her jeans. "You no stay mounted with twigs."

"Twigs?"

"Legs too puny."

Josie clenched her jaw. "First they're too skinny to walk, and now they're too puny to ride? Maybe I'm taking my life in my hands just standing here, *Lurch!*"

"Name Walks-Tall. Not Tonto. Not . . . Lurch."

"Well, Mr. Tall. Don't let these skinny, puny legs fool you. I happen to be the only woman on my street who can crack a walnut between her knees."

His eyes flickered with what she almost thought might be humor. "You very strange."

She set her fists on her hips. "You very annoying. How do I stay on?"

"Use saddle."

"I want to learn *this* way."

"Stubbornness good in man. Stubbornness not good in woman. Get man killed."

"That's man's problem." She walked toward the mare, which turned skittish for a moment before letting Josie swing up on board yet again.

Josie tangled her fingers in the horse's mane and prepared to hold on for dear life. Then Walks-Tall reached up, pulled her hands out of the horse's mane, and set them on her thighs.

"You not use arms," he said. He slapped the side of her knee. "You use skinny, puny legs."

He gave the horse a pat on the rump and sent it into motion. Josie felt herself slipping, but she knew that Walks-Tall was watching, and she had too much pride to steady herself with her hands. Instead she tightened her legs around the horse's middle and tried to keep her balance.

"You look like tree," Walks-Tall said. "Tree no ride horse."

"Thanks for the encouragement," Josie grumbled, doing her best to concentrate as the horse took slow, measured steps.

"Bend. Like leaf."

She glanced over at him. "Bend like what?"

He saw her confusion, and then he did the funniest thing: he started rolling his back and bobbing his head like a break dancer with arthritis. "Like leaf," he called again.

Josie pursed her lips to keep from laughing, and then she attempted to imitate what Walks-Tall was trying to show her. And it worked. She began rocking in motion with the horse. Her legs were tight, her body loose, and damn if she wasn't riding that mare!

She made one full circle in the makeshift corral and came back to where Walks-Tall was standing. "I did it!" she shouted.

"Legs not too very skinny."

She slipped to the ground feeling very proud of herself. "Now, where's that saddle?" He gave her a confused frown, and Josie smiled. "You didn't think I'd keep riding bareback, did you? Why, I'd probably break my neck."

He gave her one final look, and then walked off,

shaking his head, grumbling something about how women "change mind more often than clothing."

Once the mare was saddled, it was short work for Josie to master riding. By the end of the day she'd spent over four hours on horseback. She was stiff and sore, but she could control the animal at every pace, including a gallop.

There was still an hour left before the men were expected to return from hunting, so she decided to stretch out on a fur in Mitchell's hut, wearing nothing but her white Calvin Klein underwear and her "I Don't Give a Damn" T-shirt. Feeling comfortable and cool for the first time all day, she closed her eyes and took a nap.

She slept peacefully for a while, but then began having the most vivid dream. Someone was rubbing her bare feet, making her sigh in her sleep. Then the backs of her calves were being caressed, massaged with strong hands, and she emitted a soft moan. Hot, scalding lips began kissing the backs of her knees, making her heart pound and her stomach clench, and suddenly her eyes flew open.

The sun had gone down, leaving the interior of the wickiup dark. Josie couldn't see her own hands, which were folded beneath her cheek, but she could feel the heat of those other hands and that other mouth making their way upward from her feet.

This was no dream.

The pressure of firm fingers slid up the backs of her legs, and soft, firm lips followed. She felt the tantalizing scrape of a tongue as it dipped down around the inside of her thigh, and she had to bite the back of her hand to hold in a moan.

Strong hands shifted and came to rest enticingly upon the slope of her bottom, while those same hot lips moved to the V between her legs. She pulled in a sharp breath, not able to move—only to feel—as hot, moist breath fluttered where she was already growing damp and musky.

Fingers curved around her hips and arched her upward, moving that sultry mouth into better position, and Josie's entire world slipped out of focus. With only the faintest sound of surrender, she willingly parted her thighs.

He pressed against her underpants, bringing the gauzy material to rub at just the right spot. She felt his tongue, his teeth, heard the deep inhale as he sampled her scent, and soon wasn't sure whether her panties were damp from his kiss or from her own growing passion.

With deft fingers he pressed the leg seam of her underwear aside and slipped his tongue just inside the edge. Josie bucked, her hips and stomach rising up off the floor. He settled one big hand into the small of her back and held her in place for him to taste.

The pleasure was more than she could stand. And his own heavy breathing and faint groans only made the sensuous torture more intense. She began to squirm, fighting not to beg for more.

Finally he eased her underwear down and slipped it from her legs. When he returned to her, she felt his warm, uneven breath in the small of her back where her T-shirt had ridden up. As he kissed her there, his hands, large and warm, cupped her bare bottom and his thumbs began to trace the cleft downward, to the place he'd been, the place that, before, had been so meagerly guarded by her panties.

His fingers curved around the tops of her thighs, and with maddening slowness his thumbs continued tracing their path, until she felt them slip inside her.

She cried out, unable to help herself as she sensed him lowering his mouth to have his first full taste. The muscles in her back contracted, and she arched with the help of his strong hands, bringing herself completely against his lips. His tongue pressed deeply against her, savoring her as if she were his first drink in a long, long while, and she felt the first faint tremors of her climax.

He must have felt them, too, because he gave one slow, broad stroke of his tongue—and she lost control. Her body shuddered, and she let go with an animal groan as each frantic flutter produced another, and then another.

When her body had finally quieted, he rose above her and sent her T-shirt the way of her underwear. Then he slowly eased up and over her body until they lay together, front to back, like two pieces of a primitive jigsaw puzzle.

His lips were at the base of her neck, his hands braced on the ground beneath her arms. His breath was a moist, hot rasp in her ear, and his weight was pressing his racing heart against her back.

His thighs pressed hers even farther apart, until she could feel him, hard and insistent, against the ache that he alone had built deep within her. And with just a nudge he was inside.

They both let out a sharp gasp, and he paused in his efforts. Then he pressed in a little farther, his teeth grazing the back of her neck, and the sensation was incredible. All Josie wanted in the world was to have this man buried inside her till the day she died.

She tried to arch against the sweet pressure, but he gently sank his teeth into her shoulder and forced her back down to the ground with his hips. It was clear that he intended to do this very long and very slow.

He was incredibly large, almost more than her body could manage, but he worked above her like a master, his lips and hands creating magic where they wandered, his sensuous gyrations forcing her to dig her nails into the soft fur beneath her until she'd stretched to accommodate his size. Finally, when he had her writhing with desire beneath him, he pulled back and slipped all the way inside her on the return.

Through it all neither of them said a word. Their mating was a mixture of ragged breathing and impassioned groans, even when he finally climaxed and once again pulled her past the edge of torturous pleasure and into the realm of fulfillment.

When it was finished, he collapsed over her, the sweat from their bodies melding them together as surely as their passion had moments before. Josie pushed her face into the soft fur beneath her to wait for her heartbeat to return to normal.

Still he lingered inside her. She felt his mouth between her shoulder blades, the rough graze of his tongue against her damp skin. He moved one hand between her body and the rug and tantalized a nipple through the sheer silk of her bra.

She closed her eyes against the pleasure, willing it away, but he was kissing her neck, fondling her breasts, taking her back to the desire she'd barely left behind.

"You're the most beautiful thing on earth," he whispered in her ear.

He gently pinched her sensitive nipple, and she let

out a faint, impassioned cry. "You men will . . . will say anything to get what you want," she whispered back, her voice as hoarse as his.

He flexed, deep within her, reminding her body of what it had just shared with his. "But I already got what I wanted," he replied with a soft laugh.

His hand slipped beneath her bra and cupped her breast, his thumb flicking back and forth over its rigid center. Josie let out a groan and tried to arch back against him, but his body kept her firmly in place on the rug.

His mouth covered her ear. "Tell me what you did today."

"I . . . I . . . " Her mind had shut down—she couldn't think past the feel of him growing hard once again inside her.

His teeth worked at her earlobe. "Did you think of me?"

"I learned to ride."

His laugh was soft and seductive and acted like fine wine on her already drugged senses. With a final tug on her ear, he slipped out of her and rolled to the side. He took her by the hips and lifted her to straddle him.

As Josie looked down into Kurtis Mitchell's gleaming eyes, his dark, dangerous stare glowed up at her through the dimness, and she felt passion flare once again. She leaned forward and braced her hands on his powerful shoulders. "You're a naughty boy, Mitchell."

"Is that the way you like it, Josie? Naughty?"

She bent forward and kissed him, wet and deep, the way she'd always wanted to.

"Show me what you learned today," he whispered. When she looked at him in confusion, he smiled lecherously. "I promise you a ride you'll never forget."

She hesitated only a moment before closing her eyes and easing herself back. Finding the broad tip of him, she relished in the glide of her body as she covered him from end to end. Then she went still, savoring the hard, tight feel of him fully embedded inside her.

He took her hips in his hands and eased her forward. Their mouths met in the stillness, nothing around them but the night and the beating of their own hearts. She kissed him as she'd never kissed before, with all of her being, and felt the effect in the very depths of her soul. And then he pressed her back, back to envelop him, back to impale her not only on his flesh, but on all the desire that came with it.

And she let herself go. She gave in to the call of his strong, powerful body as it flexed and strained beneath her own. There was no contest of wills here, no battles to be won. Neither of them was in control of anything—neither emotions nor actions.

He brought his knees up and rose to a sitting position. Then he found her breasts and quickly pulled her bra up and over her head. After wrapping her legs around his waist, he leaned her back against his muscular thighs and took one tiny bud in his mouth.

Josie sighed, basking in each quiver of her body. She pushed her fingers through his long hair, thinking she could sit here forever with him inside her and his incredible mouth suckling her like this. His tongue swirled around her nipple, and she let out a wicked giggle.

"Ummm," he said, and then pulled back from her. "Ticklish?" he whispered.

"Here and there," she teased back, and stole a lingering taste of the lips she knew were so close to her own.

"Where else?"

"Why don't you discover that for yourself?"

His answering laugh was low and seductive, and he flexed inside her, making her moan and clench her muscles around him.

"Ohhhh," he said, half laughing, half groaning. "That was a very sweet thing you just did."

She smiled and clenched again, harder this time, and he threw back his head and let out a low growl. "You want it, then?" he asked her, his voice weak and strained.

Josie had been close to the edge of her own climax for some time now, and just the sound of his deep, impassioned voice in the darkness was enough to nudge her perilously closer. "Yes," she whispered, rocking her hips in a sensual dance. "Yes, Mitchell, I want it."

He thrust upward with a liberated shout, feeding Josie's need. Her own body followed the path of his, shattering into a thousand tiny pieces, scattering like stars, and then drifting back to earth after a few glorious moments in heaven.

Afterward, once their breathing and body temperatures were back under control, he curled his hands up over her shoulders and pulled her down to lie beside him. She stretched out on the rug, her left leg still hitched over his hip, and relaxed as his hands worked magic through her hair and down the curve of her naked back.

And before too long, she'd closed her eyes and fallen fast asleep in the security of his strong embrace.

17

When Josie woke late the next morning Kurtis had already left the wickiup. Smiling, she rolled to her back, stared up at the grass-and-mud ceiling, and remembered the night they'd shared.

A sound in the doorway caught her attention, and expecting to see Kurtis, she looked over and saw Dancing-River standing there with a burlap sack in her hands. Josie grabbed the edge of the fur she was lying on and covered herself as the wily Indian girl walked into the hut.

"Good morning, Black-Fox," Dancing-River said. "I bring food for your trip."

Josie's eyes narrowed. Not only was she suspicious of Dancing-River bringing her *anything*, but she didn't appreciate the girl reminding her that she would be leaving that day. She couldn't help but wonder if, after she left, Kurtis would turn his attentions to this pert young thing. Would he show River the wondrous kinds of pleasure she had found in his arms the night before?

"Black-Fox look angry with Dancing-River."

Josie clenched her teeth in aggravation. "Why do you keep calling me Black-Fox?"

The girl strode forward and dropped the sack she carried onto the floor beside Josie. "Black-Fox is name Soaring-Eagle has given boyish woman doctor."

"I'm more woman than you'll ever be, sister!" Josie snapped without thinking. The young woman pulled back in surprise, and Josie cleared her throat. "I'm sorry," she said. "I'm not exactly a morning person. . . . Who is Soaring-Eagle?"

"He village shaman. He have vision about White-Wolf and Black-Fox. That why White-Wolf make you his chosen one."

"His what?"

"He chose you for wife."

"He *what!*" Josie was on her feet in an instant. She snatched up the bear rug and wrapped it around herself. "I think you're mistake—"

"The vision say you brought to White-Wolf by goddess."

"What goddess?"

"Goddess with beads of wisdom around neck."

"Beads of . . . " A thin sheen of perspiration broke out on Josie's forehead. The pearls, she thought.

"Soaring-Eagle have vision before you come to village with White-Wolf. Soaring-Eagle say you are Black-Fox. One who has come to fulfill destiny. You are White-Wolf's chosen one."

"Breakfast is ser—"

Her heart racing, Josie glanced to the doorway and

saw Mitchell standing there with a large wooden bowl in his hand. "River," he said in a warning voice. "What are you doing here?"

Josie could barely remain standing as she considered everything she'd just learned. Most important, she realized that Kurtis must have intentionally set out to seduce her so that she, *his chosen one,* would find it harder to leave him. She had no doubt that that was the reasoning behind their passionate night together.

"Tell me about the vision, Mitchell," Josie demanded.

He went still and looked down at the bowl of food he had in his hands. "Leave us, Dancing-River."

"I do something wrong?"

"Leave," he growled at the Indian maiden.

Dancing-River looked coyly at Josie and then left the hut.

"Josie, this is nothing to get—"

"I want to know if you believe it."

"Believe what?"

"All this crap about visions and destiny!"

"How can you say it's *crap* when you yourself told me about the exact same woman from Soaring-Eagle's vision?"

Holding the fur tightly to her chest, she stepped toward him. "Then you do believe it! Which means this has all been a sneaky, underhanded way to keep me from leaving!"

"I don't know what the hell you're talking about!"

"Don't you dare get angry with me! I'm the one who's been used here, pal, not you! You slept with me last night hoping that I'd fall for you and stay!"

He stared at her and shook his head. "You're out of your mind."

"Am I?" Her whole world seemed to be crumbling around her. "It had to be you, didn't it. It had to be you I was sent here to be with." A man who actually had the power to steal her heart.

Mitchell's expression hardened, and he threw the bowl of food to the floor. "And what the hell's wrong with me? This breed's good enough to share your bed, but not your life!"

She was wounding his pride, but she couldn't afford to care. If this was the man the fairy meant her to spend eternity with, then she had to get away from him— fast! Before he gained enough power over her to convince her to stay. "You slept with me last night just to keep me here, didn't you? Admit it, damn it!"

"It sounds like you're going to believe whatever you want no matter what I say," he responded tightly.

"Well, it didn't work, Mitchell! I am *not* staying! And there isn't any trick you can perform in my bed that will make me change my mind!"

His eyes turned as black as a stormy sky. "I got my fill last night, lady. You're free to do whatever you like."

She lifted her chin. "Good. Then I'll be leaving this morning as planned."

"Good. You have yourself a nice little life."

Kurtis spun on his heel and walked out, leaving Josie feeling dazed and overwrought. She watched his back until he was out of sight, then wiped the wayward tear drizzling down the side of her nose. If she'd only known who he really was before they'd made love, maybe she could have stopped him from creeping so dangerously close to her heart.

*　　　*　　　*

Josie steadied the horse beneath her, her eyes focused on the horizon. She had borrowed one of Kurtis's big shirts to keep warm on this brisk mid-July morning, and she was holding the front edges of it together over her T-shirt. But it couldn't warm her on the inside, where she still felt empty and chilled.

She was leaving. And although the idea of finally going home filled her with a definite sense of relief, the knowledge that after today she would never see Kurtis again put her in a mood she couldn't shake off. After almost two weeks together, through thick and thin, they were about to ride off in opposite directions.

He was sitting on his horse a few feet away, speaking with Walks-Tall. "Take her to Sheriff Garrett in Lincoln. Garrett will see to it that any suspicions about her are laid to rest."

He was still refusing to look at her, in fact hadn't said a single word to her since their argument two hours ago.

"Where you go?" Walks-Tall asked him.

"Toward San Patricio. It's one of the Kid's favorite haunts."

Josie straightened in the saddle. "You're going to get yourself killed. Billy the Kid is nobody to play with, Mitchell. You've already been shot once trying to catch up to him."

Kurtis finally focused on her, and Josie had to swallow a surge of fresh emotion at his baleful stare. He hadn't looked at her with so much hostility since that first day in the Lincoln City Hospital. "My health isn't your concern anymore."

Josie gripped the reins of her horse and returned her attention to the horizon, deciding that Kurtis Mitchell could fall off the face of the earth for all she cared.

"You sure you want me take woman?" Walks-Tall asked softly. "Bear-Claw say he can tie her up and keep her until White-Wolf return."

Josie stiffened. There were those words again: *Keep her.* She wondered what, if anything, she could possibly do if Kurtis even considered such an idea.

"The lady wants to go home," Kurtis replied. "You can't tie a fox to a tree and expect it to go tame."

Josie refused to look at him, although she could sense he was watching her now. A cold gust of wind blew through her hair and made her ears ache, but she kept her mind focused on her home, her friends, her life that had become a faint and distant memory during the past few days.

"The lady no look happy," Walks-Tall said.

"I'm sure she's just anxious to be on her way. . . . Isn't that right, Doctor?" Kurtis said a little more loudly.

Josie nodded stiffly, knowing that if she spoke, her voice would fail her. Why was it that this seemed to be the hardest thing she'd ever done?

Walks-Tall looked back and forth between the two of them and shook his head. He nudged his horse in front of Josie's and turned back to Kurtis one final time. "May we live to see each other again," he said, and began leading Josie through the village.

The sun was a big orange ball hanging midway in the sky, painting the sandstone ridges of the plateau a glistening purple and pink, as Josie and Walks-Tall rode out. Singing-Bird stood in her wickiup doorway, smiling, cuddling Little-Sparrow, waving as they passed. Josie smiled and waved back, remembering the pale buckskin dress that was now tucked neatly in her saddlebags. It would be her only memento of this place.

One by one people stepped out of their simple huts to wave good-bye, making her feel like a member of the family striking out on her own. A member of Kurtis Mitchell's family.

She turned in her saddle to look back at him and found he was still in the same place, sitting tall and proud on his horse. His hat was tipped low over his eyes, keeping her from seeing whatever emotion, if any, was on his handsome face, but she knew he was watching her, perhaps brooding over her departure. If she was causing him grief, she regretted it.

Then she was struck with the overwhelming urge to shout out that she cared, that despite everything, he'd come to mean something very special to her. But the words got caught between her emotions and her pride, and the moment was gone in one beat of her heart.

Don't look back, she told herself. *Life's too short for regrets.*

Her eyes burned with tears, and she twisted back around to hide them as they began to fall like hot brands down her cheeks. Damn it, she was going to miss him; he'd accomplished that much. Her mornings wouldn't be the same without Kurtis there to irritate her and challenge her every move. And after today . . . there was no chance of her ever seeing him again.

She spun back around for one final look. But this time Kurtis Mitchell was gone.

18

"Wolf mates for life."

"What?" Josie responded distractedly. She and Walks-Tall were riding through a thick outcropping of saplings, and it was all she could do to keep from getting slapped in the face with the whiplike branches he was pushing aside ahead of her.

"Many animals have many dens. Wolf chose one."

"Look, Walks, I've got news for you"—she caught a branch before it hit her in the face—"Kurtis Mitchell isn't a virgin sitting around waiting for the right woman to come along."

"Virgin heart," Walks-Tall replied.

Josie rolled her eyes. "Please. The man's probably fallen in love a half a dozen times."

"Boy *consider* himself in love. Man know when destiny calls."

"I am *not* the man's destiny!" Josie said to him for about the twentieth time that day.

"You are the Black-Fox."

"I am the Josie Reed! Besides, destiny is a crock. A word used by people who are afraid of taking control of their own lives."

"Not true."

"Then show me an example of destiny."

He looked up through the trees at the brilliant blue sky. "It is destiny that sun will set. Destiny that sun will rise."

"That's nature."

He glanced back at her. "What is difference? It is destiny that snow falls. Destiny that snow melts. Destiny that man lives. Destiny that man dies. Mother Earth covers herself in mystery like child beneath warm blanket. Why can it not be truth that destiny has brought you here?"

"Look, I'm not sure who or what brought me here, Walks, but I'm damn straight going back home."

"Home not in this direction."

She pushed back a branch and followed him into a golden meadow. Wildflowers poured over the waving hillside in a sea of red and yellow. They paused beside each other to take in the beauty before them, and Josie couldn't help but envision what this peaceful hillside would look like in one hundred years: asphalt roads, speeding cars, dull buildings, airplanes roaring overhead.

"You're right, Walks," she said softly. "Home is a long, long way from here."

"Your home with Wolf. He carries your heart."

She gave him a sharp look. "My heart is here"—she thumped her chest—"exactly where it belongs!"

"That is only shadow. Black-Fox know this to be true." He nudged his horse forward, to wade through the high, golden grass and colorful flowers. "You must learn to trust yourself."

"I trust myself!" She nudged her horse after him. "In fact, I'm the only one I can trust!"

"You fear your desires."

"I do not! And there's nothing wrong with being cautious. I'm certainly not about to give my heart to just any Joe who might stomp all over it and grind it into dust."

Walks-Tall paused to wait for her before moving down a path that led through a copse of dense pine trees. "Some . . . Joe . . . will keep heart of Black-Fox safe and not fear her strength as much as glory in her spirit."

"You're starting to talk in riddles, Walks, just like that damn fairy."

"Some Joe," he went on, "like White-Wolf."

"White-Wolf?" Josie gripped her saddle horn as her horse stepped, high, over a fallen tree. "I've got news for you, pal, he's the most controlling human being I've ever met."

"You talk of Black-Fox."

"Excuse me? *I* am not controlling. I am forceful and determined—highly admired qualities in a man, I might point out."

For the first time since she'd met him the day before, Josie heard the soft, deep sounds of Walks-Tall's laughter. She gritted her teeth. "This conversation is over. I'm just glad your White-Wolf finally saw reason and let me go."

"White-Wolf like his father. He believe in freedom for all things."

"Hah! The man kidnapped me!"

"You tell him he die without your medicine."

Josie grew quiet. Walks-Tall was right, she had told Kurtis that. And if she'd been in his shoes, doomed to hang for a crime she hadn't committed, wouldn't she have done anything she could have to get away?

"He will come for you."

She blinked. "No, no, he won't." She felt sure that she'd successfully driven Kurtis Mitchell away, just as she had every other man who'd shown a genuine interest in her.

"You have his heart."

The impact of those words hit her like a swift kick in the stomach, and Josie looked back in the direction they'd come, as if expecting Kurtis to be charging toward her. The path was empty except for a squirrel, and she took a steadying breath.

"I don't have his heart."

"And he has yours."

"No." She refused to believe it. She felt sure that she'd gotten away before he'd had a chance to pull her toward that depth of emotional caring.

"He does love you, Doctor."

Josie's eyes widened at the sound of the little woman's voice. She yanked her horse to a halt and twisted around to find the fairy woman standing directly behind her. She stared at the woman for a moment and then said, "Don't you have any other clothes besides that gray suit and pearls?"

Walks-Tall stopped his horse and turned to stare back at her. "To whom do you speak, Black-Fox?"

"Admit that you love him," the little woman demanded.

"Sorry, lady, your plan to throw us together didn't

work. Now, would you like to explain to me just how the hell you found me out here in the middle of nowhere?"

The woman gave her a tiny smile, her pearls glistening in the sunlight. "I always know exactly where you are."

Josie glared at her. "Then why did you insist I meet you in Lincoln? Do you have any idea what I've gone through, worrying about whether or not I could get back to that damn city in time!"

"Lincoln was your idea, my dear, and don't lose that temper of yours on me. I won't stand for being shouted at."

Josie knew that little threat meant that if she didn't simmer down, the woman would vanish in the blink of an eye. "Just tell me if you're here to finally take me home."

"Things are still not ready for you to return yet. And before you blow your proverbial top, I think I should tell you that your Indian friend is right. You're headed in the wrong direction."

"I'm headed back to Lincoln. That's where we agreed to meet."

"But you're going there against your better judgment."

It was true that Josie had felt uneasy about leaving Kurtis, but she wasn't about to let her emotions rule her head. "Lincoln is where you said you'd meet me six days from now. *That* is where I'm going."

"He's going to die, you know."

Josie's heart nearly stopped. "Who?" she managed to get past her tightening throat, though she knew exactly whom the woman was talking about.

"Without you beside him, he's going to die."

Josie looked up at the sky to gather her composure before asking, "When?"

"In three days."

Three days? her heart cried. "How?"

"I can't say."

"Can't . . . or won't?"

"You're the only one who can save him, Dr. Reed."

"Now, isn't that convenient. How do I know this isn't just another ploy of yours to get us together?"

"Would it matter? If I manage to keep the two of you together for a year, maybe more, would it matter, Doctor? Would you ever come to love him enough to want to stay?"

Josie struggled with her answer. The real question was, did she have enough strength to resist the strong pull that existed between herself and Kurtis Mitchell? An image of her mother, cowering at her father's feet, drinking herself into oblivion so she wouldn't feel the pain of her broken spirit, flashed through Josie's mind. "No," she finally said. "I will never stay."

The woman nodded, though she was clearly disappointed. "Then what would it matter if you went after him and saved his life a final time?"

"And what about going home?"

The woman sighed impatiently. "Yes, yes, I'll still send you back home on the appointed date. We wouldn't want to forget that, now, would we. Will you help him or not?"

Though terrified of what might happen to her resolve if she faced Kurtis again, Josie knew she couldn't just let him die. "Yes. I'll help him. But when I'm finished, *you* will come to find *me*."

"Agreed."

The woman looked over Josie's shoulder, and Josie

turned to find Walks-Tall sitting rigid on his horse a few feet away, looking like the statue she sometimes thought he was. "Who is there, Black-Fox?" he whispered.

It was plain that he couldn't see the little woman who was standing not ten feet in front of his nose. "Uh . . . I'm just having a little conversation with God. You know, praying. Be done in a second."

"You must go after Mr. Mitchell alone, Doctor," the little woman said. "It will only endanger the Indian's life if you take him with you."

"But how will I ever find Kurtis on my own?"

The woman smiled. "Trust yourself. For once in your life, Josie Reed, have a little faith."

And then she was gone, in the blink of an eye.

Josie turned to the Indian beside her. His sharp eyes were scanning the very air in front of him. She sighed. How in the world was she going to ditch a full-blooded Apache?

Josie had been riding in no particular direction for most of the afternoon. She'd managed to sneak away from Walks-Tall when he'd gone off hunting for their dinner. And now she was wondering if leaving him behind had been such a grand idea. She had no clue where she was. Every tree looked the same, along with every ravine. For all she knew, any minute now she'd ride straight off a cliff.

"So where's the golden arrow to point my way?" she called out. "Where's *my* burning bush, fairy lady?"

Despite her frustration, the last thing Josie expected was for someone to answer her. "You go and get yourself lost, little fella?"

She looked up, and her heart nearly stopped in her chest. Marshal Riggs and Deputy Green were sitting on horses not ten feet away. "Well, lookee here, Deputy. It appears as if we've found ourselves half of the Mitchell gang. We've been looking for you, Doctor."

Josie stared at the marshal's eager gaze and then at the stupid grin spreading on Deputy Green's dirty, round face. "I'm not a part of any gang."

"Where's Mitchell?" the marshal demanded. "He's to be shot on sight."

She clenched her free hand into a fist. "I have no idea," she replied. "And I wouldn't tell you if I did."

"You're already in a heap of trouble as it is, Doctor. Don't add obstructing justice to the list."

"Justice?" she said with a cold laugh. "You wouldn't know justice if it climbed up your pant leg and took you by the balls."

"Still got that attitude," Deputy Green said. "If ya ask me, she's more man than woman."

"I'd ask a snake before I asked you anything, Deputy," Josie sneered.

The marshal wouldn't give up. "Is he with you?"

"Who?"

He let out an impatient sigh and settled back in his saddle. "You know very well who, Doctor. Kyle Mitchell."

"Now, Marshal," Josie replied with a confident smile, "I wouldn't know that, considering I've never met the man. He could be you as far as I'm concerned."

Deputy Green snorted. "You ain't gonna get nothin' outta her, Marshal. She was an injun lover the second she hit town. She burst in on Doc and me, took one look at Kyle Mitchell, and—"

"He wasn't Kyle Mitchell, you idiot!" she shouted. "You shot the wrong man! The man you tried to kill was *Kurtis* Mitchell! Kyle Mitchell's older brother!"

"We didn't try to kill—"

"And you almost succeeded, Deputy. You almost killed him. In fact, you were all set to execute him, probably even had his spot picked out in the local cemetery!" She placed both hands on her pommel and leaned toward them. "Tell me something, gentlemen—and I use that term loosely—if someone had come forward with proof of exactly who Kurtis Mitchell was, would you have still hanged him just for the hell of it?"

"You don't know what ye're talkin' about, lady!" Green replied. "That there *was* Kyle Mitchell! Plain as the nose on the end of my face! And *you* helped him escape!"

"Twice, as I recall," the marshal interjected calmly.

Josie took a tight grip on her reins. She'd tried reason, but how did one reason with men who lacked consciences? "You two bastards aren't fit to carry your own brains, let alone loaded weapons."

The marshal drew his pistol, and Josie found herself staring down the long barrel of his gun. "Would you like me to run, Marshal?" she asked through her drying throat. "Just to make this murder more sporting?"

"We're taking you in to stand trial for aiding and abetting a known outlaw."

"Kurtis Mitchell isn't an outlaw," she found the courage to reply. "Ask Sheriff Garrett."

"Garrett?" Green said.

"Sheriff Garrett made a deal with Kurtis. If Kurtis helps him get Billy the Kid, his brother, Kyle, goes free."

There was a brief moment of silence, and then Deputy Green broke into laughter. "Sheriff Garrett don't cut deals with criminals. He'd rather eat his own foot! Ain't that right, Marshal?"

"Just take me to him in Lincoln," Josie said. "Garrett will straighten this whole mess out."

The marshal shook his head. "Sorry. The sheriff's back at his home in White Oaks. Said he doesn't want to hear another word about Billy the Kid as long as he lives."

Josie felt her heart drop. "I don't believe that."

"It's true, ma'am," Green responded. "Been in all the papers. Garrett's finally given up on the Kid."

Josie couldn't believe what she was hearing. It was no wonder the little woman had claimed that Kurtis's life was in danger. Kurtis was counting on his deal with Garrett to save both him and his brother, and Garrett was backing out on them.

"Dr. Reed," the marshal said, "it is my duty as the marshal of Lincoln City to bring you in to face justice."

Without a second thought, Josie wheeled her horse around and made a dash for the thick foliage. The marshal shouted after her, and she could hear him and his deputy pursuing her at a frantic pace, but she refused to stop. Kurtis had to be warned that Garrett was double-crossing him.

She doubted she had any chance of outrunning the two experienced riders, but she kept her face tucked down against her horse's neck and pounded against its flanks with her heels with all her might as branches tore at her face and arms and slapped at her legs. She prayed harder than she had in her life.

It seemed that hours went by as she raced onward, but finally the marshal's shouts became faint and distant, until Josie could no longer hear him above the sounds of her own ragged breathing and her horse's pounding hooves. She reined in beneath a thick piñon tree to check her pursuers' positions and listened as their voices moved farther and farther away.

By some strange miracle, she'd lost them.

She sat back to catch her breath, to look around at a woods so dense, the pink of the sunset barely filtered through.

And then a new fear took hold.

It was growing dark. And here she was, in the middle of the wilderness, with no food, no water, and absolutely no way of knowing what lay in wait for her behind the next tree.

19

She had no matches to build a fire. Good news for Smokey the Bear, bad news for her. She buttoned up the front of Kurtis's shirt and huddled into a tighter ball.

Right now what was worrying Josie more than the cold, however, were those pairs of golden eyes that kept staring at her periodically through the darkness. She could hear the animals circling, their heavy feet padding on fallen pine needles, their panting like a soft chant in her ears. She was backed up against the truck of a tree, and with each passing second the desire to move to higher ground was becoming stronger.

"So, wolves mate for life," she whispered. "But can they climb trees?"

A mournful howl raced through the night and sent chills skipping down her spine. "Go eat Bambi!" she shouted, and listened to them scurry at the sudden sound of her voice. "Or Snow White! I hear she's got seven tasty little friends!"

She tugged the shirt tighter around her shoulders, mindful of the tiny tears that had occurred during her mad dash from the marshal and his deputy. "And if you're not partial to fairy tales, I know a *fairy* you could gnaw on for a while. Yeah, a nice, bite-sized, fleshy fairy."

As she envisioned the sly little woman who'd put her in this predicament of being eaten by ravenous beasts, she wondered how many other people had been screwed up by the woman's oh so charitable efforts. How many other people had been plucked from their perfectly okay lives only to be dumped in the middle of a bad late night movie? Josie figured they should form an angry mob, hunt the woman down, tie her up in a gunnysack, and toss her into the middle of the Atlantic!

A low growl sounded in front of her, and she pressed back harder against the tree. "My sentiments exactly," she whispered.

A pair of brilliant yellow eyes seemed to float not ten feet away from her, and she swallowed a scream. She slowly edged her knees up to her chest, instinctively protecting her vital organs, and decided to try prayer since she'd tried everything else.

"Oh, please—please—please don't let it eat me. I don't wanna be dinner. Make it go away and I'll be nice to the fairy. I'll give more to charity. Be more considerate—" A large form sprang past her with a menacing roar. Her whole body clenched, and she let out a terrified scream.

A vicious combination of snarling and snapping went on in front of her, and she squeezed her eyes shut, preparing herself for a horrible death . . . but nothing touched her. And then there was no sound at all.

After a moment, Josie opened her eyes to stare into the darkness. She wondered briefly if she'd actually been killed and was now waiting for someone to shine that bright light down on her. Then she saw a pair of blue eyes staring at her from a few feet away. She froze, afraid to move. A gust of putrid breath blasted into her face, and the moonlight flickered briefly through the trees above to glint down on golden fur. Josie gasped, hardly daring to hope. Then a long wet tongue went sliding over her hand.

"Bart?"

A low whine came from the animal, and Josie lurched forward and threw her arms around his massive, shaggy neck. She burst into tears. She'd never been so happy to see anyone, man or dog, in her entire life.

The dog sat in front of her and let her lean against his big body. He was warm and soft and familiar, and she mentally took back every bad thing she'd ever said about him.

"You didn't just save me so you could eat me yourself, did you, Cujo?" she said, laughing now through her tears. "I think I'd take great exception to that."

He licked her chin, and she didn't mind, not even when he moved closer and plopped himself down across her legs like a two-ton furry blanket.

"I thought I'd seen the last of you when you ran off from that posse at the cabin," she said, rubbing his gnarled ears. "That was a pretty chicken thing to do, Bart. . . . Wish I'd thought of it at the time."

He whined and yawned.

"And your breath hasn't improved much. . . . I—I don't suppose you brought Kurtis with you?" She peered into the inky darkness but somehow sensed that Kurtis was nowhere near.

The dog stared up at her, seeming to listen to her talk. When it appeared as though she were through speaking, he laid his head down on her legs and shut his blue eyes.

Josie leaned back against the tree. "I guess sleep is the best thing for both of us at the moment. Who knows, maybe in the morning I'll get that big golden arrow telling me which way to go. Yeah, and maybe in the morning a big herd of pink elephants will give us a ride to the nearest truck stop."

She settled in, feeling reasonably comfortable beneath Bart's warmth. She couldn't quite close her eyes, though, knowing that pack of wolves was still out there. But after a little while she found that she was too worn out to wonder if Bart would leave her unprotected during the night. She simply had to close her eyes and trust that he would stay.

There was a river of spit trailing down her pant leg to rival the "Mighty Mississip."

The dog rose from Josie's lap, where he'd slept away the entire night, and let out a huge, toothy yawn. Josie grimaced as his bad breath filled the air around her. "You really have to do something about this leakage problem, Bart." She used a handful of pine needles to wipe the sticky saliva off her pants.

The dog whined and sat in front of her. He looked much the same as he had the week before, maybe a little dirtier, but Josie's opinion of him had changed drastically. He'd saved her life the night before, whether intentionally or not, and she planned to keep him close at hand until she'd found her way back to Kurtis.

"We need to stick together—"

Just as the words came out of her mouth, Bart rose and trotted off. Panicked, Josie hurried after him. She lost him for a moment behind a thick bush, then found him squatted down behind it. He looked up at her in a way that clearly stated she was invading his privacy, and she quickly turned her back. Dog or not, he deserved a certain amount of solitude at a time like this.

She took the opportunity to follow suit behind a tree close by, and then the two of them walked back to her horse. She was starving—and a drink of water would have been a very welcome sight. But hunting was out of the question, considering she couldn't catch a snack, let alone a whole meal, and she hadn't seen water since leaving the village stream behind the day before.

"So where do we go from here?" she asked the dog. He pricked his ears, tilted his head, and stared at her.

Josie gave him a discouraged smirk and glanced around the small clearing, hoping for that mysterious golden arrow she so longed for, but there wasn't even any sign of a trail through the trees. She glanced up to where the sun was filtering through the forest canopy, and wondered if the place Kurtis was headed was east or west.

And would Riggs and Green be east or west? That was an important question. But what if she rode north or south and stumbled right into their camp?

Bart let out a low bark. She glanced down at him to find him looking back over his shoulder at her. In Lassie language that usually meant "Follow me." But this was Bart, the dog who ran at the slightest hint of a posse. Then again, he'd found and saved her, hadn't he? Maybe, just maybe, he could help her find Kurtis.

She decided to follow the dog, considering that even if he had no idea where Kurtis was, his way was just as good as any she might have chosen at random.

Despite being the greenest greenhorn on the face of the planet, Josie knew enough to be aware that her and Bart's trek through the forest would have to be slow and careful. If they moved too fast, they might walk right into a trap laid by Marshal Riggs and his deputy. But Bart kept racing on ahead of her, and Josie kept having to call him back.

The damn animal wouldn't quit chasing rabbits! Every time she turned around, he was barreling off into the woods, barking up a storm, pursuing some poor rodent until it made it back to its hole or its little lungs gave out. And during each episode, Josie would stop and wait, call to him as gently and kindly as she could, and then firmly but calmly tell him to knock it the hell off!

By the time the sun started sinking low in the sky, however, her patience with Bart's games was wearing pretty thin. "Get back here, you goddamned dog from hell!"

She stared after Bart's tail end as he bounded over a fallen tree in the distance. "Man's best friend, my ass!" He didn't even hesitate at her shout, and she let out a frustrated groan. A deaf man in India could have heard all the noise she and Bart had been making throughout the long day.

A few minutes later Bart came lumbering back, his tongue hanging out of his mouth, leaving a trail of spit to mark his path. Josie gave him a cold stare. "Next time, I go on without you!"

That threat obviously scared the dog to death. He sat down to scratch himself and then wandered out in front to lead the way again.

"I'm being saved by Lassie's evil twin!" she shouted at the sky. They'd spent the entire day wading through thick, insect-infested trees, and she didn't think they were any closer to finding Kurtis than they had been that morning. For all she knew, Bart was leading her around in circles. And somehow she wouldn't have put that past the mutant beast.

Finally, just before sunset, they broke through the thick forest. Josie's relief didn't last long, however, when she came face to face with a wall of sandstone Spiderman couldn't climb.

She stopped and stared at the pink-and-orange cliffs, glowing in the sun. "Great. Now what?" She looked down at the dog, who didn't appear fazed in the slightest. "Remind me to never recommend you as a Seeing Eye—"

"What the hell are you doing here!"

Josie's head came up at the shout, and she stared in shock at a man standing on a ledge ten feet above the ground.

It was Kurtis. His hands were planted on his hips. His hat was tipped low over his forehead, much like the last time she'd seen him, but his stance alone said he was mad enough to skin her alive.

After she got over her shock of suddenly finding him standing in front of her. she scrambled off her horse and ran for him. He dropped down from the ledge and was there to catch her as she ran into his arms.

He felt solid and comfortable, and she gripped the front of his shirt to make doubly sure he was real. "I can't believe we found you," she said breathlessly.

He took her by the shoulders and shoved her back so he could look into her face. "I asked you a question, Doctor. What the hell are you doing here?"

The flash of his eyes told Josie that he wasn't quite as happy to see her as she was to see him, and the realization brought up her defenses. "Trying to keep you alive, that's what I'm doing here."

He narrowed his eyes, then looked past the top of her head. "Where's Walks-Tall?"

"I ditched him."

"You *what?*"

She swallowed, suddenly not so sure that Kurtis was going to take her arrival in the charitable way it was meant. "I ran off when he was hunting for our dinner."

He gave her a look that said, clearly, he thought she was half-mad. "You ran off? When he was gathering your dinner? You ran off into the wilderness by yourself! Are you out of your mind!" He gave her a hard shake that rattled her teeth.

She glared at him and wiggled out of the tight grip he had on her shoulders. "More than you'll ever know!" she shouted back at him.

"Why the hell aren't you in a hotel room in Lincoln by now, for God's sake!"

"I told you!" she screeched, raising up on her toes. "I'm here to save your life! *Again,* I might add! Jesus, Kurtis, can't you keep yourself out of trouble for more than five straight minutes!"

His lips thinned to a tight line, and he took hold of her arm. "I want you back on that horse now, Doctor. You head straight into the sun and you'll reach the village in a few hours."

"And ride right into Marshal Riggs and Deputy

Green?" She shook him off. "Not on your life. They're out hunting those woods for me as we speak."

His hard expression changed to one of shock. "You saw Riggs and Green?"

"They tried to arrest me and cart me off to jail. Do you see the mess you've gotten me into?"

"Tell me what happened?"

"They threw me some threats, but I managed to get away from them."

He shook his head and laughed, that glow of admiration coming back up in his eyes. "How in the hell did you manage to find me?"

She glanced back at where Bart was still sitting by her horse. "Your dog isn't as brainless as he looks."

"He's got a good nose. And he can lead you back to the village."

"I'm not leaving, Kurtis. Your life—"

"What I've got planned is dangerous, Josie, and I don't need you underfoot."

She scowled up at him. "I thought we'd agreed a long time ago that I could take care of myself."

"Not this time."

"Why?" she demanded. "Because I'm a woman? Because this is a man's world and a man's business, and my two breasts will only get in your way?"

He gave her a steady look, but she could have sworn she saw a smile hovering in the depths of his eyes. "Because you can't shoot, you can barely ride, and I doubt you could kill a man. Any more questions?"

Josie hesitated. He was right. If his life was in danger, what kind of help could she possibly be? She supposed the fairy lady hadn't thought of her inexperience with the Wild West before endowing her with this mission. Chances were, if something did happen, she'd end up getting them *both* killed.

"I suppose you're right," she said in a soft voice. "I suppose the best I can do is warn you to be careful, and hope that you will be. So"—she looked up into his liquid brown eyes—"be careful, Kurtis."

She turned for her horse, but he caught her by the arm. She looked back at him in confusion, until he pulled her to his chest.

"There's just one more thing," he whispered. And then he was kissing her, hard and lustily, sliding his tongue into her mouth and pressing her against him. Within seconds the only thought on Josie's mind was how interesting it might be to make love with him under an open sky.

The rumble of racing horses pulled the two of them apart. Kurtis listened and then let out a heated curse. He left her there and hurried to the ledge he'd been standing on to peer off into the distance. With another curse, he jumped back down and returned to her.

"What?" She searched his face. "Is it Riggs and—"

Without a word he slammed his hat onto her head and buttoned the front of the blue shirt she was still wearing over her T-shirt. "Keep your mouth shut and do as I say."

Before Josie could respond to this outrageous order, four men rode up and reined to a stop in front of them. They were the dirtiest, scruffiest looking young men Josie had ever seen.

The one in the center, a reddish blond man with a tall dark hat, edged out in front of the rest. His lower face was shadowed by a thin, patchy, reddish beard, and his narrow lips were compressed in a tight line over slightly protruding front teeth. "Who the hell are you?" he demanded of the two of them.

Josie held her breath. The distinct, crawling feeling that she was about to die came over her, but Kurtis didn't seem interested in giving the dangerous-looking man an answer.

She started to respond, but Kurtis cut her off by saying, "Who the hell are you?"

The man's blue eyes narrowed for a moment, then he glanced back at his companions and broke into an evil grin. "The name's Garrett. Pat Garrett."

Josie blinked. This certainly didn't look like the Pat Garrett she knew.

"And I'm Abraham Lincoln," Kurtis responded coolly.

"Well, that can't be right," the young man responded, still smiling. "Abraham Lincoln's dead. Ain't that right, boys?"

Kurtis stared, that same frigid stare Josie had become so well acquainted with in the beginning of their relationship. "And Pat Garrett will be joining him soon enough."

The young man broke into laughter. "A man after my own heart. You got a real name, mister?"

"The name's Kurtis Mitchell."

"Mitchell? Why, I believe I know your brother, Mr. Mitchell."

"Do you now?" Kurtis replied casually.

"Yes. Yes, I believe I do."

The young man held out his hand, and Josie watched, nervously, as Kurtis walked forward to take it. "The name's Billy Bonney, Kurtis Mitchell. I believe you've heard of me."

The last wasn't a question, it was a statement, as if

all of mankind had heard of Billy Bonney. And in fact they had. Josie was standing in front of none other than Billy the Kid. And he didn't look like much more than a sixteen-year-old boy.

His sharp blue eyes turned on her. "And who might this be?" he asked.

Josie cleared her throat. "Jos—"

"Joe," Kurtis interrupted. "He's what you might call my right-hand man."

Josie gave Kurtis a disbelieving stare, then held her breath as Billy Bonney gave her the once-over. "Joe, huh? Well, Joe. Kurtis. You two gentlemen look as though you could use a place to sleep for the night." He turned and called to one of the men behind him. "Dave? We got enough hard ground to go around at our place?"

"S'pose," came the gruff reply.

"Then it's settled. Clean the house, boys, we got company!"

20

The "house" of Billy the Kid was nothing but a campfire built beneath the shelter of a large rock overhang. The six of them—Kurtis, Josie, Billy, and his three men—rode up as the sun was setting over the mountaintops to the west.

That was when Josie finally came face to face with Kyle Mitchell. He was just as handsome as his brother, though more youthful and carefree, it seemed. His smile was easy as he and Kurtis embraced and slapped each other on the back.

As the two stood together, Josie could see why Kurtis had been mistaken for his brother. Though Kurtis wore his dark blond hair longer than Kyle's, they both had the same Apache coloring and the same strong features.

"What the hell are you doing here, Kurtis?" Kyle asked, still smiling. "I would have figured you to be home, fence buildin' and brandin' your way through the summer."

"Jessica insisted. Said she wouldn't sleep at night until I checked up on you."

Kyle looked down at his dusty, worn boots. "I suppose she's not very happy with me, running off the way I did."

"Nope. And I understand she's got a skillet with a picture of the back of your head on it in honor of your return."

"She been giving Richardson hell?"

"He's been sleeping on the sofa."

"Shit. So basically you've come to tell me that my sister's itching to chase me around with wrought iron, and that her husband's bound to finish the job with his shotgun?"

"They miss you, Kyle. We've all been worried."

Kyle sniffed, as if they were heading for a subject he wasn't interested in visiting. He looked over to where Josie still sat on her horse. "Who's that with you?"

Josie stole a quick peek at Billy the Kid. He was feeding his horse a handful of oats just out of hearing range. Things between Billy and Kurtis had seemed amicable enough on the short ride to camp, but the little woman's warnings about Kurtis being killed still weighed heavily on Josie's mind. Billy made her nervous. He was too confident for his own good—and everybody else's as well.

"That's Joe Reed," Kurtis replied to Kyle's question. "He's a hand we hired on about a month ago. Real good with medicine. I thought I'd bring him along just in case. . . . "

Kyle laughed, a deep, warm sound. "Big brother, you know hot lead avoids this body like a finicky

mosquito." He walked forward and held up his hand
to Josie. "Pleased to meet you, Joe."

Josie shook it and tried to avoid meeting his dark
gaze, which was almost as magnetic as his brother's. He
smiled up at her and then stepped back toward Kurtis.

"I heard about the trouble you had in Lincoln, Kurtis,
because of me. I'm sorry about that. By the time I'd
gotten word, you'd already escaped, or I would have
come running."

"Don't worry about it. Things worked out in the
end."

"Don't worry about it!" Josie blurted. "They almost
chopped off his leg and hanged him!"

Kyle raised a brow at her, and she pressed her lips
together. She hadn't meant to say anything, but she
couldn't stand the idea of Kyle getting off easy after
all the trouble he'd caused his older brother.

"My, my, Joe," Kurtis said. "Is that a *cold* you're
picking up?"

Josie took the hint and cleared her throat. "Yeah,"
she said in a deeper voice. "I—I've been feeling it
comin' on for a few days now."

"I heard about the hanging part," Kyle said, "but
what's this about chopping off your leg, Kurtis?"

"Joe is exaggerating," Kurtis responded. Josie snorted
derisively, and he gave her another warning look. "The
important thing is, I'm just fine now," he added.

"How the hell *did* you get out of there, Mitchell?"
They all turned to find Billy had finished with his horse
and had joined their circle. "Hell, I hear they even had
a guard posted outside your door day and night."

"They figured I was too weak to pay much attention
to. The one guard was easy enough to take care of."

"And I hear a lady doctor gave you a fine spot a'

help," Billy continued, his smile growing. "Is that right, Joe?"

Josie's heart nearly stopped. She wondered what the notoriously unpredictable Billy the Kid would do if he found out he'd been duped and *she* was that lady doctor.

"A smile and a wink always did the Mitchell men well with the ladies," Kyle said proudly.

Kurtis smiled, his casual attitude serving only to intensify Josie's bout of nerves. He seemed to be taking all this danger in stride.

"She must have been pretty desperate to fall for a line from an accused outlaw," Billy said with a laugh. "She a big ugly thing, Mitchell?"

"She heal you up?" Kyle asked.

"She did an adequate job."

Adequate! Josie was outraged.

"And what else did she do for ya, Mitchell?" Billy asked slyly.

Josie arched a brow at Kurtis, and his lips twitched as he stared up at her. Billy was waiting for his answer, and Kurtis didn't miss a beat. "She taught me a thing or two about women."

"And where is she now?" Kyle asked.

"I left her with Grandfather."

"Mother's village? How'd the relatives feel about that?"

"They took her in like one of their own."

While Kyle seemed to ponder this bit of information, Billy said, "You best watch it, Mitchell. That woman's liable to be gettin' all kinds of pretty ideas about you now."

Kurtis's eyes met Josie's before settling on Billy Bonney. "She prefers to go it alone."

Kyle grinned. "Independent women can be so difficult."

"And pretty damn fascinating all the same," Kurtis added.

Josie could feel color rising up her neck. She felt as if she were eavesdropping on a private conversation—except it was about her.

"Well," Billy said. "Now that we've all gotten acquainted . . . Dave, why don't you show our newest Mitchell brother and his right-hand man, Joe, here, where they can bed down for the night?" Billy laughed again. "Show 'em to the spare room, Dave."

Josie slipped down from her horse, making sure to keep Kurtis's hat pulled low to shield her eyes, even though the sun was now only a reddish glow above the mountain peaks. She followed Kurtis's suit and untied her bedroll from the back of her saddle, then trailed along as Dave led them up a steep path to a place where they could look down and see the campsite twenty feet below.

"I figure up there," Billy called to them, "you can keep a real close eye on your brother! You wouldn't want any lawmen sneakin' in and puttin' a bullet in his head, now, would ya?"

Dave Rudabaugh smiled, but the action didn't quite reach his eyes. Josie instinctively disliked the man. She could tell he was suspicious of her and Kurtis by the piercing way he kept looking at them. If they were going to get out of this alive, they couldn't afford to raise anyone's suspicions.

She made a hacking sound in her throat, pulled together a mouthful of saliva, and spit it five feet. When she looked back at Dave, he didn't appear quite so interested in her. "You can bed down here for the night," he said. "Up here's guard duty, though, so one of you keep your eyes open all the time."

The outlaw left them for the campfire and his cohorts below.

Kurtis dropped his bedroll to the ground. "Remind me to have a talk with you about expectorating in public."

"He was looking at me far too closely," she whispered.

"You keep that hat low on your head and that shirt hanging loose and you'll be fine. And don't get too close to any of them. I don't want them touching you."

She arched a brow. "Feeling a little proprietary, Kurtis?"

"They touch you, and there'll be no doubt of your gender. They find out you're a woman and we're all dead."

She pursed her lips and then whispered furiously, "Well, why did you tell them I was *Joe* in the first place?"

"What do you think a group of lawless men on the run for their lives would do with a pretty woman, Josie? Force her to tuck them in and sing lullabies?"

She swallowed, not interested in discussing the possibilities further. "So what do we do now?"

"We wait for the opportunity to tell Kyle what's going on. Then we make some serious plans."

"Wait a minute, Kurtis. There's something I still have to tell you about—"

"You two come on down here, Mitchell," Billy called. "We're starting a game of poker and are figurin' on takin' you and that wet-nose for all you got." Billy laughed, and the others joined in. "Come on, now. It's a tradition. If you don't enter inta my gang broke, then I'll surely make ya that way."

As Kurtis rubbed the back of his neck and gave her a dubious look, Josie realized that her explanations about Pat Garrett were going to have to wait. She smiled at him. "Don't worry, *boss*. This is one wet-nose who can definitely hold her own with an ace of spades."

She'd lost every single hand.

And about thirty-five of Kurtis's hard-earned dollars, at his last count. They'd been playing five-card stud for hours, and Kurtis was still waiting for a glimmer of the poker genius Josie claimed to be. Two of the men had long since fallen asleep, but Dave Rudabaugh and Billy Bonney were having too much fun robbing "Joe" blind to end the game just yet.

Kyle wasn't doing so bad, either. Every time Josie chewed her bottom lip, a sure sign she had a lousy hand, he'd grin like an idiot and bet even higher.

Kurtis, however, had seen enough of the slaughter, and as Billy began dealing out the cards for another round, he announced that it would be his and "Joe's" last hand. His dark, moody tone didn't allow for questioning, not from any of the men or from Josie herself.

The betting began, and as sure as daylight, Josie started chewing the hell out of her bottom lip. Kurtis rolled his eyes. "It's your bet, Joe."

Josie studied her down card, then the card she had showing. She chomped on her bottom lip and tossed in two-bits.

Kurtis couldn't stand it any longer. He threw down his cards. "I'm out."

Billy Bonney grinned at him through the firelight

and then looked at Kyle. "What about you?"

Kyle called and raised, and Rudabaugh did the same. Billy followed suit and then dealt them all another card. All eyes turned to Josie once again.

"You in, Joe?" Billy asked, obviously fighting not to laugh at this pigeon he had in the hand.

Josie nodded and threw in her four dollars to call and an extra dollar to raise the stakes.

Kurtis shook his head. Why in the hell did the woman always insist on staying in the game?!

The bets went around, more cards were dealt, until, finally, Josie looked up at Kurtis and said, "This is the last hand, right?"

He nodded stoically and then almost fainted when she tossed in the rest of the money he'd loaned her to play with, close to fifteen dollars in all. "I think I've got a pretty good hand this time," she said with a smile.

Hell, they all knew better. Her bottom lip was practically corn mush—the woman couldn't bluff her way out of a gentle breeze!

Dave looked at Billy, grinned, and matched what Josie had thrown in. Kyle did the same.

Billy added a fistful of money to the pot. "I'll call ya, Joe," he said, not bothering to suppress his laughter this time. "Let's see what ya got."

Josie looked around the campfire at the men who were watching her with blatant amusement. And then, slowly, her hesitant smile curved into a grin. Kurtis sat up a little straighter, sensing that something unexpected was about to happen.

She laid down her cards in the firelight. "Straight flush to the queen." She smiled up at Billy. "Care to beat that, Bonney?"

Every jaw around the fire dropped. She'd duped them! She'd been setting them up for the big fall all night long! "Damn!" Billy shouted. "I can't believe this! Can you believe this, Dave?"

"Nope," Dave Rudabaugh replied with narrowing eyes. "I cain't."

"You been foolin' with us all night, haven't ya, boy?"

Josie shrugged, but they all knew the truth, and Kurtis felt a solid streak of pride and admiration for the woman sitting beside him as she reached out and scooped up the almost sixty-dollar pot. Josie Reed never ceased to amaze him.

"Who'da thought you had that kinda brain beneath that hat, boy?" Billy said, clearly impressed.

"It's probably all swelled up," Dave said in his usual slow way of talking. "That's why he never takes the damn thing off."

"Shit, boy, you could make some money down in old Mexico. Them dealers don't know a cardsharp from their asses. We could bleed 'em dry!"

Josie was still smiling, humbly now. She shuffled the cards and set them in a neat stack in front of Billy. "Cards are just a hobby I picked up in medical school. I don't really like to gamble."

"Medical school?" Billy spat out. "You tellin' me you're a doctor!"

"Uh, yeah," she responded. Kurtis remained calm, hoping Josie would do the same as she flashed him a look of desperation. "I'm—I'm a doctor."

Billy held his flask of whiskey out to her for the third time that night. "Well, damn," he said. "I'll drink to that!"

Josie held up her hand and declined Bonney's offer. She'd refused anything but water with her supper, even though a strong shot of alcohol would have made the inedible mess they'd been fed go down a whole lot easier.

"And you don't drink, neither," Billy said, amazed.

"That stuff'll kill you," she replied.

Billy snickered and tucked the flask back into his inside jacket pocket. "Life'll kill you, Joseph."

Kurtis tensed as Billy flopped his arm over Josie's shoulders. The outlaw had been paying her an awful lot of attention all night long, and Kurtis had to keep reminding himself that Billy thought she was a young man, someone the Kid could take under his wing. Jealousy was a hard thing to kill once it took hold of you, however, and at the moment it was eating away at Kurtis's insides. He was fighting not to scoop Josie up and put a bullet between Billy Bonney's eyes.

"Where the hell d'you find this boy, Mitchell?" Billy asked him.

"Joe sorta found me," he answered.

"Well, tell him to lighten the hell up. You only live once, Joe. Better grab excitement while you can." Billy removed his arm from her shoulders but gave her a good-natured jab with his elbow. "Take some advice from me, boy. Small fellas like us, we don't get no respect. You wanna be treated like a man, ya gotta act like *three* men. Understand?"

Josie nodded.

"You know, boy, I got the perfect opportunity for you to grab yourself a name. Tomorrow, at noon, we're robbing ourselves a bank. I was gonna let Dave go in with me, but now I think I'll take you. Whaddaya say, boy? You wanna be famous like me? You wanna be like Billy the Kid?"

Kurtis held his breath as Josie hesitated. She

glanced over at him, a question in her eyes, and he felt his heart jump in his chest. That she'd been looking to him all night for guidance could only mean she was beginning to trust him.

"Answer up, boy," Billy persisted. "You wanna be an outlaw or not?"

"Sure—sure, Billy," Josie finally answered. "That would be great. Just great."

Josie looked back at Kurtis, and he held her eyes for one long moment. Over my dead body, he thought to himself. Or better yet, over Billy's.

21

Josie sat on her bedroll beneath a starry sky, her arms crossed and her determination riding high. "I refuse to stroll into a bank tomorrow, gun in hand, and stand beside Billy the Kid."

Kurtis was sitting across from her on his bedroll, and he held a finger to his lips to remind her that her voice might be overheard in the camp below.

Josie gritted her teeth and whispered, "You certainly don't seem very concerned about Joe becoming an outlaw. Damn it, Kurtis, I am *not* robbing a bank!"

"Of course you're not. Now stop worrying about it."

"Stop worrying about it? This is happening tomorrow, and I doubt a 'Gee, I don't think so, Mr. Bonney, but thanks for the offer' is going to cut it!"

"Don't get so—"

"Wait a minute. I've got it. I'll tell him I can't shoot!"

Kurtis shook his head, and the moonlight reflected off his golden hair. "He won't believe you."

"Why not?"

"Folks around here normally learn to shoot before the age of twenty-five, Josie."

"Actually, I'm twenty-eight, but I'm flattered. Then how about if I fall off my horse and pretend I've broken my leg?"

He shook his head again, and she rolled her eyes. "Then I'll slam myself over the head with a rock and claim the sky is falling!"

He gave her a direct look. "You'll relax . . . and trust me."

"Do you have an idea?"

"I'm getting one."

She sighed in frustration and leaned back on her hands. "I'd feel better if you had one handy, Kurtis."

"Do you trust me?" he said softly.

She gave him a baffled look. "Of course I trust you. After all, you know men like Billy better that I— What's that smile for?" The man was grinning as though he'd just won the California lottery.

"I was just admiring your newfound faith in me."

"Yeah, well"—she suddenly felt flustered—"make sure you don't abuse it. I can be a great ally but a lousy enemy."

He snorted. "Don't I know it." She gave him a cutting look in response. "Look, Josie, there's no way I'd let you walk into that bank and risk your life. Even if you wanted to."

"If I *wanted* to, I hope you'd wrap me up in a tight white jacket and toss me in a padded cell."

"No," he whispered, leaning toward her. "I'd just take a moment to fill your head up with better ideas."

His attention settled on her mouth, and her stomach did the two-step. Desire was blatant in his eyes, and she found she wanted the kiss as badly as he did, maybe even more. He leaned closer, until the tips of their noses were touching, their breath mingling as their bodies longed to do, and then opened his mouth over hers.

The thought of resisting never occurred to Josie. She wanted his touch. Wanted to feel his strength blend with her own and give her the added reassurance she so desperately needed at that moment.

He slowly teased her lips, once . . . twice . . . three times, until she clutched her fingers in his thick hair and kept him in place for a long, deep embrace.

The world, her home, Billy the Kid, slipped from her mind. There was only Kurtis, the man who could ignite her passion like no other and melt away her resistance with just a look.

After a few moments he pulled back, and she buried her face against his chest, listening to the ragged beating of his heart. "Why did it have to be you, Kurtis? Why you?" she whispered.

"My father once said the same thing to my mother."

She eased away and looked into his face.

"She was a full-blooded Apache squaw, and when they married they were shunned by both his kind and hers. It was a hard life for them both."

"Then why did they bother, knowing they faced so much adversity?"

"Because they were in love. When they looked at each other they didn't see color. They saw forever."

The poetry of what he'd said made her smile, and he gazed down at her in such a way that she felt as if he were seeking out her deepest emotions and pulling them to the surface.

"You always speak of your parents in the past tense, Kurtis. Are they both gone, then?"

"Yes."

A look of sadness crossed his face, and she chose to press him no further on the subject. She dropped her gaze to his chest and mumbled, "Mine, too."

She felt his hand on the back of her hair and looked up at him. "Did they go together?" he asked her.

"No. My father drank and smoked himself to death about five years ago, and my mother . . . " Josie hadn't spoken about them in so long. Why, then, did the memory still leave a rock the size of Rhode Island in her chest? "My . . . my mother killed herself not long after that."

Kurtis went still. "I'm sorry."

"Yeah, well, the only person who should be sorry is my father. He was her lord and master. When he died, she just didn't know what to do with herself." She let out a bitter laugh. "The woman couldn't even drive a car."

He gave her a confused look, and Josie shook her head. "Never mind."

He slipped his hand along her jawline to the back of her neck and tipped her face up with his thumb. "Some men believe that it's their job to dominate everything and everyone. . . . I'm not one of those men, Josie."

Her chin trembled, and she felt tears well up in her eyes. Her mother had been so terrified of being alone that she'd taken her own life, but Josie's fear had always centered around being controlled, upon being driven to an existence and an end not unlike her mother's. And that fear was a live thing that constantly sent her running from commitment.

"Damn it, Josie. You have to believe me. I no more want to hold you down than I want to tear out my own heart." He cupped her face in his hands. "You have such strength and courage. It's something to be admired, not stifled."

There was a long moment when they both just sat there, staring into each other's eyes, and finally Josie had to laugh to break the tension. "My God, from where you're standing, I must seem to be a very strange human being."

He smiled. "You definitely keep my life interesting."

"I'm sure you've wanted to strangle me more times than once."

His expression darkened a little, and she thought she understood. "You're still angry with me for leaving you yesterday, aren't you?"

"And I'm still angry with you for returning."

"I'm sorry," she replied. "I came back because I was worried about you."

"Well"—he tipped her face up toward him again—"like you've said to me many times, I can take care of myself."

He kissed her deeply, tenderly, and she moved closer, once again leaving the rest of the world behind as she lost herself in his embrace.

"You two keep your eyes open up there!"

She and Kurtis both jumped to their feet at the sound of Billy's shout.

"Don't be gettin' into any distracting conversations during your watch!"

Josie placed her hand over her racing heart and took a steadying breath. Kurtis smiled at her and wiped his lips. "I'll stand watch," he said. "You get some rest."

Josie settled back down on her bedroll. "Wake me when it's my turn for guard duty."

He looked down at her with smoldering eyes. "I'll have to weigh the consequences of that. Now close your eyes and go to sleep."

"What about Billy, and the bank robbery tomorrow?"

"Everything's going to be fine, Josie. Trust me, remember?"

She yawned and stretched. "Yeah. I remember. Trust you. . . . " *But don't let you anywhere near my heart.*

When Kurtis finally nudged Josie, the morning sun was glaring in the eastern sky. He'd apparently decided not to wake her the night before, and instead of feeling unneeded, she appreciated his kindness. There was, however, no time for her to thank him, because Billy and the rest of the men were already mounting up, getting ready to ride for the unsuspecting bank.

Where was the grand plan that Kurtis had spoken of? She gave him a questioning look as she jammed his hat onto her head, but he barely acknowledged the action. As she mounted her mare she began to suspect that Kurtis hadn't been able to come up with anything to get her out of this bank robbery.

They all had their horses in a circle, and Billy was giving them some final words of encouragement, when, suddenly, Kyle Mitchell let out a groan and fell from his horse.

At that point Josie forgot about her personal concerns and scrambled to Kyle's side. He was doubled over on the ground, moaning incessantly.

"I think I ate somethin' that didn't agree with me," he said with a weak whisper.

Josie felt his forehead. His skin was cool and dry to the touch, but then one could never be too careful with salmonella.

"What's the matter with him?" Billy demanded.

Josie helped Kyle to a sitting position. "I'm not sure. It could be food poisoning."

"How kin a person git poisoned by food?" one of the other men asked.

"If it's gone bad, the bacteria can cause vomiting, diarrhea, even worse," Josie answered.

All four members of Billy's gang scrunched their faces in disgust at her description.

"Well, he sure the hell ain't coming with us if he's gonna be barfin' and shittin' all over the place," Billy said. He was the only one smiling, and at that moment Josie came to the conclusion that the entire world was one big joke to Billy Bonney.

She glanced at Kurtis, interested to see how he was taking his brother's sudden illness. He looked worried, but not as concerned as Josie would have expected. That was when she began to get the idea that maybe he *had* come up with a plan and had somehow gotten Kyle involved.

"Somebody will have to stay here with him," she announced. "He'll be on his back most of the day, and he'll need to be looked after, kept clean and hydrated."

Billy looked over his shoulder at his men. "Dave?"

"Uh-uh, don't be lookin' at me, Billy. The only man's ass I wipe is my own."

"I'm a doctor, Billy," Josie spoke up. "The logical choice to stay would be me."

The outlaw leaned forward on his saddle horn and looked down at Josie with sharp blue eyes. "Looks like the only answer, Joe. Sorry 'bout that. We'll have to grab you a name some other time. Say, maybe I'll call Dave, here, 'Joe' just to get the ball rollin'." He broke into laughter, but Dave didn't appear to appreciate the joke.

Josie gave Kyle a mean look. "I hope you realize what you've just cost me, Mitchell. *My* name in the annals right beside Billy the Kid's."

"Gee, Joe." Kyle was still clutching his stomach. "I'm real sorry."

"Fine." She kicked at a clump of weeds and walked over to unsaddle her horse. "You men just go on without me. But the next time"—she pointed at Billy—"the next time I get to go."

Billy broke into a wide grin. "Hot damn, you got some spunk, Joe! And don't you worry. I'll see to it you get your moment in the sun."

The five men rode off.

Relief flooded through Josie as she watched until they'd disappeared over a hill. Then she began to worry about Kurtis. She wished she'd had an opportunity to warn him to take no chances where his life was concerned, but she supposed she was just going to have to trust him to take care of himself, as he'd said the night before.

Kyle sprang to his feet and dusted himself off. "Whaddaya say we go swimming in the watering hole to while away the day?"

Josie turned her back to him. She wasn't sure what Kurtis had told Kyle to get him to go along with this charade, but she felt sure that he would have informed her if he'd let his brother in on exactly who she was.

She cleared her throat and responded in a deepened voice, "I hate water. Listen, I hope you don't think I'm a coward, Mr. Mitchell. It's just that I can't shoot a gun—"

"A coward? Why no, Joe." She felt his presence directly at her back. "Frankly, I think you've got more guts than a lot of men."

She wasn't about to argue with that. "I'm assuming Kurtis told you why I wouldn't be going along with the Kid?"

"He said he refused to be a party to your downfall at such a tender age."

Josie nodded. That was as good an excuse as any. "Then I can assume your stomach is feeling fine?"

"No danger of me losing breakfast on your shoes."

"Good." She uncinched her saddle and tried to pull it off her horse, and Kyle moved forward to help. She gave him a hard stare, trying her best to act like a disgruntled young man. "I can do this by myself, you know. I'm a lot stronger than I look."

He gazed into her eyes and smiled, a handsome smile that undoubtedly had the power to drive young girls wild. "I imagine so," he said in a soft voice.

He was staring at her strangely, so Josie asked, "Are you sure you're feeling all right, Mr. Mitchell?"

"Well"—he edged a little closer—"now that you mention it, I do have this nasty case of butterflies. But maybe"—he snatched her hat off her head before she could stop him—"maybe that has something to do with those huge blue eyes of yours."

Josie grabbed for her hat, but he tossed it aside and gave her a mischievous grin. By the way he was looking at her, Kyle Mitchell was either a *different* sort of man or he knew beyond a doubt that "Joe" wasn't actually a member of his gender.

She backed up a step, but he pursued her. "Now,

Kyle." She held out her hands. "I'm not sure you know what you're dealing with here."

"Oh, I believe I do, *Joe*. And I have a feeling that once I get those clothes off you, all my suspicions will be confirmed."

He reached for one of her hands and yanked her up, hard, against him. Josie hated to use force, but when Kyle clamped his fingers around one of her breasts, he left her with no other choice.

As he let out a hoot of discovery, she let out a screech of indignation, and Kyle Mitchell found himself with a serious pain between his legs where her knee had connected with his privates.

"Did Kurtis tell you!" she shouted down at him. He was on one knee, moaning as if he really did have salmonella.

"Tell me what?" he replied through a clamped jaw.

"That I was a woman!"

"Hell no! I figured it out yesterday when I shook your hand. I've touched enough women to know the difference between a male and a female, *Joe*."

"Does he *know* you know?"

"Not likely." Kyle was regaining his composure and rising back to his feet. "I doubt he would have left me here alone with you if that was the case."

"Why? Are you some kind of rapist along with all your other talents?"

He smiled. "Yeah. I'm a real lady-killer. They all fall at my feet."

"Really."

He reached out and tugged a short lock of hair lying against her neck. "And you are one fascinating woman, Joe."

"Josie," she corrected, and moved back a step.

"Josie," he drawled. "I suspect you're the woman who healed my brother and then helped him escape?"

"I didn't help him escape. I only unlocked his manacles so he'd be more comfortable. That was when he kidnapped me and forced me on the run with him."

"No kiddin'? I always pictured Kurtis to be too lawful to steal himself a woman."

"He stole himself a doctor"—she slapped his reaching hand away—"and he's damn well going to see that she's put back!" Kyle was standing in front of her, his hands on his cocked hips, his constant grin unnerving her. "I stayed behind to help you, Kyle," she said in a warning voice. "Don't make me regret my charity."

"I'll give you one little kiss if you ask me nice."

She looked at him, stunned. "And if I ask you mean?"

"I'll probably give you one anyway."

Josie should have gotten angry at that point, but she couldn't help but laugh. The man was actually serious. He really believed she wanted to kiss him. "Look, Kyle. I'm sure I'm very flattered, but I think I'm a little too old for you."

"Hell no." He reached out and brushed his finger over her lips. "A woman is never too old for love. You know, your daddy must have been a thief."

"I beg your pardon?"

"He stole the stars from the skies and put them in your eyes."

She groaned. "Does this stuff actually get you women?"

His smile was quick, devilish. "Invariably."

"And they're in complete control of all their faculties at the time?" she asked.

He threw back his head and laughed. "Good God, Jessica's gonna love you."

"Jessica?"

"My older sister. She's been trying to marry Kurtis off for years. She appreciates a quick mind."

"Unfortunately, I probably won't have the pleasure of meeting your sister. If I had any sense at all, in fact, I'd climb up on my horse and leave right now."

"Yeah, Kurtis said something about Joe wanting to run off and visit his godmother. Said I should make sure *Joe* doesn't go anywhere while he's gone."

Josie fumed. She hadn't told Kurtis that it was no longer important for her to return to Lincoln, that the woman could pop up anywhere and anytime, but it really galled her that he had gone to the trouble of making sure she *couldn't* leave if she'd wanted to.

"You're loyal, Josie. You'll make my brother a good wife."

"I—," she sputtered. "I am not marrying your brother."

"Oh, yes, you are."

"Oh—no—I—am—not!"

Kyle blanched at her shout, but then his grin was back. "Well, then maybe I can talk you into having me."

She gritted her teeth. "Not if you were the last man on earth." She jabbed him in the chest. "Not if your very life depended on it—not if *my* very life depended on it! I am not getting married! Ever!"

Kyle pursed his lips, and Josie thought that she might have finally gotten through to a Mitchell man. But then he leaned toward her and said gently, "Don't worry, Josie. He'll ask you soon enough."

Josie checked the sun's position for the third time in as many minutes. It had to be after two o'clock in the afternoon. Where were they?

"A watched hen never lays."

She glanced over her shoulder to see Kyle climbing the cliff toward her. "A watched pot never boils," she corrected, and returned her attention to the distant horizon.

"That too." He sat down beside her on the ground. "You really are worried about him, aren't you?"

"Aren't you? I mean, the man rode off with Billy the Kid."

He scrunched his chin. "Kurtis has always been pretty good at taking care of himself."

"Not from what I've seen."

"You've just caught him in a bad spell."

She gave him a direct look. "What I've done, is caught him at a time when he's almost been killed—twice—trying to save your skin. And you don't seem the least bit contrite about that."

He shrugged. "That's what big brothers are for."

"Is that right? Well, then I'm glad I'm an only child."

"An only child? Ah, that's just plain sad."

He reached his hand over to pat her leg, and she slapped it away. "Would you stop touching me!"

"You like it better when Kurtis touches you?"

Her glare was intense enough to defrost a polar ice-cap. "Would you just go away and leave me alone?"

She scooted away, but he only scooted up next to her again. "Well, yes or no, which is it?"

"Kurtis left you here to torment me, didn't he? He knew that a man like you would drive me stark raving mad."

"A man like me?"

"A smiling, laughing, *conceited* pickup artist like yourself, Mr. Kyle Mitchell."

"Pickup artist?" he said with a grin. "What the hell is that, exactly?"

"That, exactly, is a person who spends all of his spare time thinking up ways to hit on unsuspecting women."

"I've never hit a woman in my life."

She directed her impatient scowl to the sky. "That's not what I meant."

"Then what, exactly, did you mean?"

"That I would appreciate it if you would keep your remarks—and your hands—to yourself."

He folded his hands over his bent knees. "I suppose I just like touching pretty women. Haven't had a complaint yet."

"Well, you have now."

He grew quiet, and she looked over to find him grinning at her. And damn if his boyish smile wasn't contagious. She rolled her eyes and shook her head. "What in the world are you doing out here, Kyle? You should be busy breaking hearts, not hanging out with Billy the Kid."

His smile faded, and he looked down at his hands. Josie had seen that same moon-eyed look before on a number of her friends, and she nodded in understanding. "Got your own heart broken, did you?"

He cast her a sideways look.

"And so you ran off and ended up here?"

He laughed. "Out of the frying pan and right into the fire."

She turned back to the horizon, feeling a spurt of compassion for the young man beside her. "I'm sorry she hurt you."

"My father always said, 'Life is a constant challenge. If it doesn't hurt some of the time, you're not doing it right.'"

She smiled. "I like that. It sounds like your father was a very wise man."

"Yeah. He was killed in a fire along with my mother four years ago. . . . Kurtis is a lot like him, you know."

"Your brother is very special."

"I think he'd like to hear you say that."

She laughed a little. "I think he's fresh out of luck on that score."

"I assume that means you don't plan to tell him how you feel. Why, Josie? You got a problem being honest?"

She clenched her fingers together. "Here's honesty for you, Kyle. Your brother scares the bejesus out of me." She looked over at him, to judge his reaction to that statement, and found him staring at the horizon, nodding his head.

"My father also used to say that running never solved a thing."

"And I guess we're both guilty of that, aren't we."

"I suppose we are. But," he added, "I now plan to turn and face my problems." He met her eyes. "What about you?"

Josie sighed, suddenly feeling very tired. "In my case, I think it's a little too late for that. Old habits die hard."

"A wise man once told me that it's never too late to start over."

"Your father again?"

"No. Kurtis. Just last night." Kyle paused. "He's in love with you."

Her heart seized in her chest, and she had to remind herself to breathe. "Now, how would you know that?" she asked playfully.

"I've been watching him with you."

"The whole time we've been here he's been treating me like a boy, Kyle."

"Not by my standards, he hasn't." Kyle was grinning again. "He sits too close to you, for one thing. And he's always staring at you when he thinks nobody's looking. If I hadn't known you were a woman, I'da thought my brother had gone light in his shoes."

Josie laughed, imagining what Kurtis might say to that.

"I know he loves you simply by the way he puts up with you."

"Puts up with me?"

"Kurtis has never had a whole lot of patience when it comes to women. They normally don't have a hell of a lot to say that interests him."

She arched a brow.

"Well, they don't. It's always, 'Oooh, look at my new dress.' Or 'Oooh, doesn't my hair look divine—'"

"Maybe that's because all they're allowed to do is shop and primp in the mirror."

He grinned again. "Maybe. Now, I want to know what your intentions are toward my brother."

"My intentions?" she repeated with a laugh.

"Yeah. Do you intend to marry him when he asks, or do you plan to run off and break his heart?"

Josie swallowed and looked off toward the distant mountains. "You don't understand. My life is a lot more complicated—"

"'Will you marry me?' It's a very simple question, Josie. Will you say yes? Or will you say no?"

Josie hesitated. She had to admit that she did feel something for Kurtis Mitchell that she'd never felt for any other man. But marriage? What about her home, what about her career?

What about her freedom?

Kyle was still waiting for her answer when Billy, Kurtis, and the rest of the gang rode into view. Josie stood and counted out all five of them, to be sure no one, namely Kurtis, was missing. They were moving at an easy pace, so she assumed everything had gone as planned during the robbery.

She put Kurtis's hat back on just as they reined up at the base of the ridge she and Kyle were on. Kurtis stared up at her, and Josie met his eyes. He looked all right—in fact, he looked terrific.

And then Kyle's question came back to her mind and nudged her conscience. Would her answer be yes . . . or no?

She could only hope that Kurtis would never ask.

22

"I had me this woman once, she was with a circus from China. She could bend in *the* most unique ways...."*

The circle around the campfire erupted into laughter at Dave's story, and Josie stole a quick glance at Kurtis and Kyle. The bank robbery had gone off without a hitch. Apparently there weren't many who wanted to tangle with Billy the Kid. The men had ridden back to camp feeling empowered, and they had spent the rest of the day in the watering hole, fooling around like a bunch of children.

Kurtis had apparently been accepted as one of them, although Josie was afraid to ask just what he'd had to do to accomplish that. The two of them hadn't had more than three seconds alone together to discuss a single thing.

Now they were all sitting around the fire, having just finished a pretty disgusting stew of wild onions and gamy rabbit. And unlike last night's quiet poker game, the topic of the evening was women. Neither Kurtis nor Kyle appeared inclined to join in, which was clearly bothering the other four men—including Billy the Kid.

Josie imagined the two men's reluctance had something to do with the fact that she was sitting there. She supposed they'd found time enough alone for Kyle to admit to Kurtis that he knew Joe was in fact Josie. Now they both looked like shamed monks, huddled together on the sidelines, and if they didn't lighten up quick, they were going to grievously offend their host. Josie guessed it was up to her to pave their way.

"What about you, Kurtis?" she asked.

He glanced over at her with wary eyes, and she almost burst out laughing. "What about me?" he said.

"Tell us about the women you've had."

The look he gave her told her he thought she'd lost her mind, and she almost took pity on him and told him to forget the whole idea.

But then Billy jumped in. "Yeah, Mitchell. I'm sure the two of you have something to share with the class. Y'ever plow one together?"

The two brothers exchanged a faint, horrified glance.

Josie couldn't hide her smile this time. "Yeah. Come on, Mitchell brothers, tell us all about all your women."

Kurtis gave her a dark, warning look, and then Kyle said, "Go on, Kurtis. . . . Why don't you tell Joe about that chesty brunette from New York."

Chesty brunette? Josie suddenly felt her heart drop

to her stomach. Maybe this wasn't such a good idea after all, she told herself.

Kurtis nodded. "You mean the one interested in horsemanship?"

"Ooh-wee, tell us about that one, Mitchell," Billy shouted. "I bet she was quite a ride!"

Kurtis gave Josie a pointed look. She was getting the distinct impression that he was going to make her regret bringing him into this conversation.

"Well, she was about five foot five . . . legs to her chin . . . "

"And tits clear to Canada," Kyle added.

Everyone's eyes rounded. As a group, they all leaned forward to catch every word, everyone except Josie, that is, who suddenly found herself wishing she could crawl under the nearest rock.

"Was she hot?" one of the men asked.

Kurtis smiled. "Like a stick of dynamite."

"And?" Dave prompted.

Josie wanted to plug her ears, stick her fingers so far in that she couldn't hear her own heart beating.

"Her skin was like silk. And she tasted like lemonade on a hot summer day."

Against her will, Josie pictured Kurtis sampling the charms of a leggy brunette while lying in a field of tall wildflowers. She gritted her teeth.

"And I bet you had yourself a good long drink," Billy said with a lecherous laugh.

"Was it in broad daylight?" somebody asked.

"Nah," Kurtis answered. "But the sweat was dripping from our bodies like rain."

"Ahhh, man," Dave whispered.

"Did she holler?" someone asked.

"She wiggled and shouted my name right alongside God's for close to thirty minutes."

"So then"—Dave swallowed visibly—"you made her . . . you know?"

Kyle leaned forward. "Probably three or four times, my friend. Right, Kurtis?"

The men all let out a collective sigh and sat back. "No way," Billy said. "Three times?"

Kyle slapped his brother on the shoulder. "This man bangs like a stallion. It runs in the family."

Josie's throat had gone painfully dry. She desperately needed a drink, but she didn't have the courage to get up from where she sat in front of the fire. It hadn't bothered her listening to the other men's exploits; in fact, she'd found it all sort of interesting. But the very thought of Kurtis Mitchell with some woman wrapped around his hips made her want to pummel the life from somebody—namely, Kurtis.

"You have her, too, Kyle?" Billy asked.

"Naw. Kurtis and I don't share. It's either one brother or the other. What was her name, anyway, Kurtis?"

Josie closed her eyes. She didn't want to hear it. A name would only make the woman more real.

"Her name was Josie," Kurtis answered.

Josie's head shot up, and she stared at him, hard.

"Josie, huh?" Billy said. "I'll have to remember that."

Kurtis wasn't looking at her, and Josie couldn't decide whether he was being serious or if this had all been just a joke.

"Yeah, Josie," he said wistfully. "I sure do miss her."

"You plan to see her again?" Kyle asked with a great big smile.

Kurtis pursed his lips and looked down at the

ground. "I sure the hell hope so. But from what I understand, she's just not herself these days."

Josie wanted to reach out and slug him. Nobody else seemed to notice, but the damn man's lips were twitching like a pair of bumblebees! He angled her a look that was full of mischief, and she didn't know whether to laugh or scream. Unbeknownst to him, not only had he gotten even with her for egging him into the conversation, he'd made her stark raving jealous—and of herself, no less!

"Yeah. I plan to remember that name, too," Dave said. "A big-titted brunette named Josie ever crosses my path, I'm gonna be at her like ticks on a hound."

"And with the same size dick," one of the men said, making the others laugh.

"She'll probably scratch you right off like a tick, Rudabaugh," another added.

While Dave jostled with the two men, Josie composed herself and rose to her feet. "I believe I'll get some sleep."

Billy scowled at her. "It's barely ten o'clock. I was hopin' you'd give me a lesson on bluffin' at poker."

"Ah, let the boy go to bed, Billy," Dave said. "He didn't get a nap today. 'Sides, he probably wants to take himself firmly in hand and recall all the stories he's heard tonight."

The four outlaws erupted into laughter, and although Josie wasn't quite capable of what they were making fun of, she still felt the sting of the insult on poor young "Joe."

"Good night, Mr. Mitchell," she said to Kurtis.

"'Night, Joe," Kurtis answered.

"Be sure to tuck those blankets around you nice and tight or something might crawl in with you in the middle of the night," Kyle said, grinning.

Josie stole another quick look at Kurtis, and his smile broadened. She was surprised to feel a blush climbing up her neck as she hiked up the steep trail to the lookout spot. He'd said that he missed her.

She stretched out on her bedroll and stared up at the starry sky. Home seemed like a million lifetimes away—not just three or four. But, surprisingly enough, she wasn't missing it as much as she had before. What had she actually left behind, anyway, besides a handful of friends who didn't need her now that they had their own families? She still had her profession, which she'd practiced quite a bit since arriving, and she still had herself—despite the fact that she'd spent practically every waking moment in the presence of a very strong minded man. She was still the same opinionated Josie Reed.

And Kurtis Mitchell didn't seem to mind that fact one bit.

Josie woke during the night to the sound of Kurtis and Kyle talking beside her. The moon was full and hanging low in the sky overhead. She stirred, rolled to her side, and looked up at the two men.

"The fair Joe awakens," Kyle whispered, nodding toward Josie.

Kurtis turned to her and brushed the hair from her eyes. "Go back to sleep," he said softly.

She reached out her hand and set it on his hard thigh. The gesture appeared to startle him, but she didn't pull back. "Tell me what the two of you are talking about."

Kyle grinned. "You mean after we stopped talking about you?"

Josie looked up at Kurtis, who quickly looked away. "I hope it was all nice," she said.

"Nice?" Kyle said with a laugh. "In my life, I've never heard my brother ramble—"

"Shut up, Kyle."

Josie bit her lip to keep from smiling. "So I assume Kyle has told you that he knows who I really am."

Kurtis gave his brother an irritated look. "He let me in on that when I got back this afternoon."

Kyle only grinned in the face of his brother's irritation.

"So now you two are making plans to coincide with your arrangement with Garrett?"

"We're working on something," Kurtis replied.

"Well, before you go designing the H bomb, I think there's something you two should know. When Riggs and Green found me in the woods, they told me Pat Garrett is back at his home in White Oaks. That he's not looking for Billy the Kid anymore, that he's not even interested in hearing another word about him as long as he lives."

"The H bomb?" Kyle repeated with an odd look.

Kurtis shook his head. "Never mind. She talks like that all the time."

Kyle nodded.

"Didn't you two hear what I just said?" Josie persisted. "Garrett has backed out on you."

"That's part of the plan, Josie," Kurtis replied. "He's laying low so Billy will let down his guard."

"But they said it's been in all the papers. What if he really has—"

"What better way for Billy to hear about it than to make sure it hits the press?" Kyle said.

"So you don't think he's backing out on you?"

"Nope," Kurtis replied.

"You're sure?"

"I'm sure."

"Then you're still planning on going through with this crazy plan?"

"Josie," Kurtis said impatiently.

"Why can't you and Kyle just leave, go back to your ranch—move to Tasmania or something?"

"It doesn't work that way. We would be outlaws, wanted men, for the rest of our lives."

Kyle was grinning. "I think it's sort of sweet that she's worried about us, Kurtis."

"I'm a doctor, Kyle. It's my job to worry. And if I had a stick, I'd take it to your rear for putting us through this in the first place."

"Oooh, whip me, woman."

"Knock it off, Kyle," Kurtis said in a low voice.

"Just playin' around."

Josie smiled too sweetly. "Like you were playing around this morning when you offered me that kiss?" She wasn't sure what had made her say that, spite or maybe just curiosity, but she found that she loved the reaction it got out of Kurtis.

His head snapped around, and he pinned his brother with a glare. "Did we enjoy ourselves this morning, Kyle?"

Kyle was still smiling, even when Kurtis reached out, took a handful of his shirt, and hauled his brother toward him.

"Come on now, Kurtis. I was just tryin' to figure out exactly what you meant to the lady. If she'd taken me up on the offer, *then* I could see you being so pissed."

Kurtis glared at his brother, then finally let him go.

"You keep your lips to yourself, or I'll blacken both your eyes."

Josie had never had a man stand up for her like that, especially against his own brother, and she found the experience very . . . exhilarating. "So what's the big plan?" she said after a moment.

Kyle's charming grin turned placating. "Don't you worry your little head—"

"We're going to lure Billy to Fort Sumner," Kurtis replied.

Kyle gave him a hard look. "I don't know if it's such a good idea to tell the whole world about this, Kurtis."

"Josie's not the whole world. And she can be a big help if we need it."

Josie scooted closer to Kurtis and replaced the hand she had on his thigh with her chin. "How do you plan to lure him there?"

"By telling him that the best and sweetest way to get even with Garrett is to kill him." He set his hand on the back of her neck and caressed her, lightly, sending tingles down her spine. "And that I happen to know Sheriff Garrett will be leaving the security of his home for Fort Sumner very soon, because he plans to collect a prisoner from the jail there day after tomorrow."

Kyle smiled. "Billy won't be able to resist. The rumor that Garrett has called it quits on him has been almost more than he can stand. What glory is there in stealing when nobody's going to chase you for it?"

"Then you think he'll be interested in taking Garrett out?" Kurtis said.

Kyle snorted. "You plant the idea in Billy's head that killing Lincoln City's pride and joy will give him all the fame he could ever use, and he'll do it in a heartbeat. With a wink and a smile."

Josie felt a chill race through her. "This whole thing makes me nervous."

Kurtis slipped his fingers beneath the neckline of her T-shirt and took away her chill with the warmth of his hand. "I could find an excuse to send Joe back to the ranch tomorrow."

She shook her head. "I'd only worry more if I weren't here to help you."

"I won't let anything happen to you, Josie. You know that, don't you?"

She looked up at him, and their eyes met in the moonlight. "I know you won't."

Kyle cleared his throat. "Listen. I'm not exactly tired at the moment. I'll keep watch if you'd like to steal a quick bath, Josie. I know you didn't get to take one with the boys earlier."

"You want a bath?" Kurtis asked her.

"Out here? With four ruthless outlaws sleeping fifty yards away?"

He stood and then pulled her up beside him. "I'll stand guard in case one of them wakes up and gets curious. You'll have all the privacy you want."

Kyle was grinning again. "And I'll be sure to keep my eyes on 'em, too, big brother. Just in case you get distracted."

23

Josie sank into the water and reemerged on the other side of the clear pool. It was a warm night. The coyotes were working overtime, and the crickets were a constant rhythm in her ears. Kurtis stood on the bank, somewhere close by. She couldn't see him in the darkness, but she knew he was there, standing guard.

She could imagine his stare, his dark seductive eyes, the way the moonlight shimmered in his hair and shadowed his handsome, intense features. She knew that as long as she lived, she'd never be able to forget the feel of him, the smell of him, the taste of his kiss on her lips.

She ran her fingers through her wet hair and looked toward the bank. Instead of his silhouette she saw nothing but rocks and trees breaking the starry, black, horizon.

"Kurtis?" she called softly.

He emerged from the shadows, and her heart skipped.

"I thought maybe you'd left."

He didn't respond, and goose bumps raised on her arms, whether from cold or tension she wasn't sure.

"Just waiting for you to finish," he finally said quietly.

She noticed the comforting, deep timbre of his voice, and the water suddenly didn't seem so cold anymore.

"Are you finished bathing?" he asked.

She wrapped her arms around her naked body and nodded.

"I've got a blanket here for you." Something wide and dark unfolded in front of him. "I'll keep my eyes closed."

She smiled. "Yeah, I believe that."

"Come out of there before you catch a chill."

She swam toward him but sank to her knees in the final three feet of water. "You're peeking, aren't you?"

"I said I wouldn't."

"You were lying, Mitchell."

"Of course I was."

"Then why not just admit that you're going to take a good long look, and I'll do my best to pose pretty?"

"Would you throw your arms up over your head and arch your back for me?"

She scowled. "Hell, this isn't a *Playboy* shoot, Mitchell. Next you'll have me riding your horse naked and listing all my pet peeves."

He laughed softly and tossed the blanket to the ground. "Naw. I think it would take too long for you to explain just what the hell a pet peeve is." He was fumbling with something at his chest, and in the next few seconds Josie realized he was taking off his shirt.

"What are you doing?" she asked, unable to keep a thread of excitement from her voice.

"Making love to you."

Her heart bounded, and she moved backward in the water. "The least you could do is wait for an invitation, Mr. Mitchell," she said.

He pulled off his boots, and then his pants, and then strode into the water, the moonlight glinting off his body. Josie wanted him more than anything in the world, but in a moment of sudden anxiety, she turned and swam for the opposite bank. When she looked back, Kurtis was standing where she had been, his arms crossed over his broad chest.

"You're going to make this difficult for me, aren't you, Josie?"

"I've heard every man loves a challenge," she said, out of breath. "Are you up for it, Mitchell?"

His laugh was low and wicked. "Oh, yeah. I'm up for it."

Heat raced through her stomach, and adrenaline sang through her veins. "Then let's see if a wolf can outsmart a fox."

He lowered his head and began swimming toward her. He looked so animal, so completely virile, that Josie had a small impulse to let him catch her, but at the last moment she darted to his right and out of his reach. "You failed to tell me you were part frog and fish," he said behind her.

"I was on the swim team in college."

He was moving toward her again, and she was warming up to the game. This time she dove to his left but felt the brush of his hand on her ankle as he came very close to catching her.

She emerged a few feet away from him. "You're not

trying very hard, Kurtis, and I'm beginning to feel very unwanted."

He was quiet for a moment, then slowly began to approach her again. "Have you ever wondered what the allure of a kiss is?" he asked in a low voice. "Is it the warmth of another person pressed up against you? Or their hot breath mingling with yours? . . . For me, I think it's the way your mouth melts beneath mine, the way you open for my tongue—the way you feel, the way you taste—"

Josie let out a cry and jumped into his arms. She slammed her mouth over his and wrapped her legs high around his hips, aching to be filled with him, to be covered by him again.

"Make love to me, Kurtis," she whispered into his mouth. "Pretend like it'll never end for us."

He held her tightly to him with his forearms. "It doesn't have to end, Josie. It can always be like this. Forever."

He kissed her again and again, long and deep, and she let herself believe him. Believe that, for them, the passion would never die.

He slid his hands down her back, beneath the water, to cup the round curves of her bottom and lift her high against him. She arched and felt the hard tip of him slide between her legs. "Promise you'll never hurt me, Kurtis."

"Never."

"Swear you'll respect me and listen to me—"

"Always."

A sob caught in her throat. "You'll always love me."

"I will," he whispered against her mouth. "I'll always love you."

At that moment, Josie realized they had all been right. Walks-Tall, the fairy woman, Kyle. Kurtis did love her. And the knowledge sent a peaceful surge of warmth through her heart.

She was wet and ready for him when he pushed inside, and she let go with a tiny gasp and arched for more. But he took hold of her hips and held her back.

"Patience, Josie," he whispered. "Slow and easy." She trailed kisses down his neck, over his broad shoulders. God, how she loved the feel of him against her. And just when she thought he might fill her, he lifted her off him and tasted the water dripping from one of her rigid nipples. The sensation sent shock waves of pleasure surging through her, and she cried out his name.

"Shhh, you'll wake the children," he whispered in a playful voice.

The way he loved her was pure, sweet torture. And when he finally set her back over him with a slow, smooth glide, she instantly fell over the edge and into the magical world of fulfillment. He covered her mouth with his as she cried out his name, her body racked with pleasure so intense it overshadowed any sense of caution. And when her body had finally quieted, he kissed her one sweet, lingering time and began the torture all over again.

When they'd loved each other so intensely that they could no longer stand, they moved to the shore, where they stretched out on the discarded blanket and held hands while gazing up at the stars.

"If I asked you where you're really from, would you tell me the truth, Josie?"

She went still. The night had been so magical, the idea of ruining it by talking about reality didn't sit well with her. But after what they'd just shared, she knew she could never lie to him.

"Yes," she finally answered. "I'd tell you the truth."

"It's not California, is it."

"It is California. I didn't lie to you. I just . . . I just held a few things back."

"Like?

She glanced over at him and found him still staring up at the stars. "Like the year I was born, maybe."

He smiled. "You could be fifty for all I care—"

"What about minus eighty-four?"

He turned his head to give her a confused look. She squeezed his hand, hoping that what she was about to tell him wouldn't put a tarnish on the closeness they had just shared. "I was born in the year 1966."

His bewildered expression slipped into a scowl.

"The woman who brought me here . . . well, she took me back in time. That's why I'm so strange, Kurtis," she rushed on. "That's why I wear weird clothes, and have magical medicines. Why I wear my hair short, and have a watch that beeps. I came here from the year 1994."

He looked away from her, back up at the midnight sky, and she was grateful for that, not wanting to face the condemnation that she'd seen suddenly flicker in his eyes. She kept hold of his hand, though, determined that he would be the first to let go.

When he slipped his hand from hers, it felt as though he'd ripped her heart in two. He sat up, his back bare and reflecting the moonlight, and began pulling on his pants.

"I'm sorry, Kurtis," she found the courage to whisper.

"All I asked for was the truth, Josie. After everything we've shared, I would think trusting me would be a little easier by now."

"But I'm telling you the—"

He held up his hand. "Save it. I don't have the energy or the desire to sift through this load of shit."

Tears slid down her cheeks as he stood and walked away from her. She looked up at the stars, wishing she could fly far away from this place, from the misery and regrets she was feeling. Was this love? This wrenching, tearing inside? Because if it was, she wanted nothing more to do with it.

"You heading on over to the *watering hole*, Billy!"

Josie cracked open her eyes and stared up at the bright blue sky, knowing she'd managed to sleep only a few hours.

She sat up and saw Kurtis staring at her from his place against a pine tree a few feet away.

"Is that where you're going, Billy? To the *watering hole?*"

"Would you stop shoutin' at me, Kyle!" Billy responded. "I ain't deaf!"

Josie looked at Kurtis. They both knew that Kyle was trying to warn them about Billy's approach. He obviously assumed that the two of them were about to be caught in a compromising position.

Kyle couldn't have been farther from the truth. Kurtis hadn't spoken a word to her since he'd walked away from their blanket the night before, but no matter how hard she tried, Josie couldn't bring herself to blame him for not believing her. She wouldn't have believed him, had their roles been reversed.

When Billy Bonney broke through the thick brush that surrounded the watering hole, he found Kurtis rinsing off his face and Josie, with a hat pulled low over her eyes, fiddling with a long brown weed.

"You two sure got up early," Billy said as he dropped to his knees and splashed water over his face.

"I need to get an early start," Kurtis replied.

Josie's eyes snapped in his direction.

Billy asked the question on her own mind. "An early start to where?"

"I hear Garrett's coming out of hiding to escort a prisoner to Santa Fe tomorrow morning. I've got a bone to pick with the lawman."

Billy straightened, a smile quirking his mouth. "You figurin' on puttin' a plug in Garrett, Mitchell?"

"I figure me and my brother owe him one, yeah."

Billy sat back on his heels and looked up at the sky. "Well, now. That's a mighty high goal you've set for yourself. Garrett's a fine shot with a rifle."

"So I've heard," Kurtis responded. "But there's not a lot of defense against a bullet in the back."

Billy burst out laughing. "No, sir, there sure ain't. But there's gonna be all kinds of lawmen comin' after you if you do somethin' like that."

"There's all kinds of lawmen coming after me now. Me being written up in every city paper from here to New York won't make a hell of a lot of difference, now, will it?"

Even from Josie's angle, she could see Billy's eyes light up. The Kid was a real glory hound, no doubt about it.

"You're a brave man, Mitchell. The kind of man I like to have in my gang. Say, you wouldn't want a little company for the ride, would ya?" He broke into laughter. "I'd love to see the look on Garrett's face when he drops."

Kurtis ran his gun along his arm, checking the cylinder. "Why not? I don't mind sharing."

"You say he's leaving White Oaks today?" Billy asked.

"All I know is, he's scheduled to pick up his prisoner at Fort Sumner first light tomorrow morning."

"And how do you know all this?"

Kurtis dropped the pistol back into his holster. "Because the prisoner happens to be a friend of mine, Bonney. A close friend."

Billy nodded, studying Kurtis for one long moment. Then he shouted, "Dave!"

"Yeah," came Rudabaugh's distant reply.

"Saddle up the horses! We're goin' huntin'!"

It was a bright, clear blue day as the seven of them rode through the hills toward Fort Sumner. Billy and his three men rode a ways out front, and Kyle, Kurtis, and Josie trailed behind.

Something wasn't right. Josie could feel it like an early spring frost. They'd been on the trail for almost an hour, and Billy Bonney hadn't said a single word to them. Not even to turn around and laugh at something not worth laughing at.

"I'm telling you guys," Josie said softly, "Billy's suspicious about something."

Kurtis narrowed his eyes on the Kid. "I don't know. Seems to me, if he suspected us of setting him up, he'd be laughing with his buddies about how he planned to kill us."

Kyle edged his horse closer to them. "Maybe he's just daydreaming about killing Pat Garrett."

Josie smiled cynically. "Maybe he's envisioning his picture in every city newspaper from here to New York."

"Maybe he's thinking about that winsome Josie we told him about last night," Kyle said with a snicker.

Josie scowled. "Don't remind me."

"That story perk your interest, *Joe?*"

"I'm not sure I understood it, Kyle. Was there a

moral in there somewhere? Oh, I'm sorry. With you there's no such thing as morals, is there."

Kyle let his jaw drop playfully. "Did you hear that, Kurtis? Joe, here, thinks I'm depraved."

"Shut up, Kyle," Kurtis replied.

"What the hell is wrong with you this morning?" Kyle leaned closer to his brother and went on softly, "One would think that, after last night, you'd be happy as a pig in a poke." Kyle looked over at Josie, and she quickly looked away. "Aw, now, don't tell me you two had a spat. Okay, kiss and make up. Come on. It's not good for an impressionable boy like myself to see his elders angry at each other."

"Leave it alone, Kyle," Kurtis said in a dark voice.

Kyle broke into laughter. "Kurtis, you know I can never leave well enough alone—"

"Care to share the joke with the rest of us?"

The three of them looked up to see Billy and his men stopped in a line in front of them. And Billy had his gun drawn.

"What the hell is this?" Kurtis demanded.

Josie was glad that he sounded so brave, because she felt as though she were about to wet her pants.

"There's been a little change in plans, Mitchell," Billy said. He smiled faintly. "You see, I don't think killin' Garrett should be a sharin' experience. Ain't that right, Dave?"

Rudabaugh nodded once.

"I think the three of you should stay behind," Billy continued.

Kurtis and Kyle both leaned forward on the pommels of their saddles, but Josie leaned back. Was she the only one feeling threatened here?

"This whole idea was mine," Kurtis responded.

Josie swallowed. "Kur—"

"Keep your mouth shut, Joe," Kyle interrupted her.

"It's an idea I'm stealin'," Billy said with a smile. "You see, stealin's what I do. I'm an outlaw."

"Ah, what difference does it make, Kurtis," Kyle said. "If Garrett's dead, he's dead. What does it matter who does the killing, right?"

Billy raised his brows. "Your brother's got a point, Mitchell. I think perhaps you should listen closely to what he's sayin'."

Josie couldn't take her eyes off the bore of that gun. How many men had Billy Bonney killed in cold blood?

"You cut me out, Bonney, and maybe I'll just ride off to the nearest telegraph service and wire Garrett a warning," Kurtis said.

Billy's eyes narrowed, and Josie got the distinct impression that Kurtis had said the wrong thing.

"I don't think so," Billy said with a smile. "Oh, and before I shoot Garrett, I'll be sure to let him know that I killed you first."

Josie's heart stopped, and then everything happened as if in slow motion. Billy aimed his gun, she let out a scream, and Kyle dove for his brother. The loudest bang Josie had ever heard echoed through the still air.

She brought her hands to her ears and stared in shock at Kyle, who lay, bloody, over the saddle in front of Kurtis. Kyle had returned the favor and taken a bullet meant for his brother.

She saw Kurtis reach for his gun. "No!" she screamed.

Billy's three cohorts already had their guns in hand, and Kurtis realized this as he looked up at them. Had he touched his gun, he would have been dead for sure.

"Damn fool idiot," Billy said, staring at Kyle. "Ah, well. That oughta teach you a lesson, Mitchell. Don't *ever* mess with Billy the Kid."

Josie reached out and set her hand on Kurtis's arm to steady him. Billy's pale blue eyes fixed on her, and he smiled. "Sorry about that moment in the sun I promised you, Joe. Maybe next time."

With that, he spun his horse around and rode off, his laughter floating back to them like a bitter wind.

Josie climbed down from her horse and scrambled to Kurtis's side. "Lower him down so I can get a better look at him."

Kurtis was still staring off in the direction Billy had ridden, his arms tight around his unconscious brother. There was a murderous look in his eyes.

"Kurtis! Lower him down here so I can help him!"

He glanced down at her, as if he didn't quite understand what she'd said. Then he looked down at his brother and carefully did as she'd asked.

When Kyle reached the ground, Josie yanked open his shirt and probed at the bullet wound in his lower shoulder. "The bullet's still in there. We're going to have to take him somewhere where I can get it out. . . . Kurtis, are you listening to me?"

"I'm going after them."

She surged to her feet. "No, you're not! I need you to help me! He's not dead yet, damn it! For God's sake, help me save him!"

He finally looked at her, and she saw the tears in his eyes. "He's not dead?"

"He's not dead," she said more gently.

There was an expression of such pain and regret on his face that Josie's heart nearly broke in two. "The ranch is only about three miles from here," he told her.

"Then let's get Kyle up over his horse and go there. Fast!" She glanced off in the direction Billy had ridden, marked by nothing but a dust trail and a half-dead man. "Kyle's all that matters now. But Billy the Kid will have his day."

24

The first thing Josie saw when she and Kurtis reached the wooden gate of the Mitchell ranch was Bart, stretched out in the sunshine on the porch of the two-story, red brick house. The big dog pricked his ears, sat up, and loped toward them.

A small woman with flowing black hair stepped out onto the porch and raised her hand to shield her eyes. She smiled and began walking toward them. But as they rode closer, her honey-colored skin went deathly pale. "Kyle!" she screamed, and dashed toward them. "Oh, Kurtis, what on earth has happened!"

They'd draped Kyle over his saddle and ridden as fast as they could, hoping he wouldn't bleed to death before they reached the ranch. Josie had packed his wound with gauze and strips torn from the shirt Kurtis had loaned her, but she knew such meager bandages wouldn't last long.

"What happened?" Tears were streaming down the woman's face.

"He was shot, Jess," Kurtis replied. He had been silent during their fifteen-minute ride, and Josie had wondered what was going through his mind.

He lifted his brother from the horse and over his shoulder. Josie retrieved her medical supplies from her saddlebag and quickly followed Kurtis up across the porch and into the house, where he gently laid Kyle out on a gold overstuffed couch in the large front room.

Josie tried to get close to Kyle, but the dark-haired woman, still sobbing, was glued to his side. "Is he going to be all right?" the woman asked Kurtis. "Is he going to live?"

"We don't know, Jessica, now move out of the way and let the doctor work."

Jessica looked over her shoulder at Josie and blinked her wide brown eyes. Then she let Kurtis pull her away from their brother. Josie quickly sank to her knees beside the sofa and began her examination.

She pulled off Kyle's shirt and listened to his airways. If the bullet had punctured a lung, she wasn't sure what she'd be able to do. She was relieved to note that everything sounded clear.

Next she began to probe his injury. There was no exit wound, leaving little doubt that the slug was still in his shoulder.

"I'm going to need some whiskey, Kurtis, and a bowl of hot water and some towels."

"I'll—I'll get the hot water," Jessica said, and dashed from the room.

Kurtis went to a cabinet at the back of the room and returned with a crystal decanter full of reddish alcohol. "Is he going to make it?"

She looked up at him and gave him a reassuring smile. "I think so. I need to get the bullet out of him, though, and after my experience with you, I'd appreciate it if you could hold him down while I work."

He knelt beside her. "Just tell me what to do."

"Lie over him as best you can, and even if he wakes up and yells his head off, don't let him up. Okay?"

Kurtis nodded and stretched his upper body out over his brother.

Josie took a small scalpel from her bag, doused it in alcohol, and then set to work on removing the bullet. It was lodged in a tricky place, just beneath the left clavicle bone, and she had to do a bit of digging to get at it.

By the time Jessica had returned with the bowl of hot water, Josie was showing the slug to Kurtis.

"I've brought the hot water and towels."

Kurtis gazed down at his brother as Josie used the towels soaked in hot water to clean around the wound. "He hasn't moved," Kurtis said, sounding worried.

"That's not so strange." She picked up the decanter. "But this will wake him up for sure. Hold him down."

Kurtis did as she told him, and, holding her breath, Josie dumped a generous amount of the alcohol into the open wound. Sure enough, Kyle Mitchell let out a deafening bellow. In fact, if Kurtis hadn't been holding him down, Josie had no doubt her neck would have been gripped tightly in Kyle's fists.

"Jesus Christ!" Kyle shouted.

Kurtis was smiling. "Time to wake up, little brother."

Kyle stared at him, then at Josie, then at his sister, who was hovering over the back of the couch, wringing her hands. "Hey, Jess," he said in weak greeting before falling back to the couch.

"Don't you 'Hey, Jess' me, Kyle Mitchell! Where

the devil have you been? You've had us all worried half to death—and then you dare to come home with a bullet in your shoulder!"

Kyle gave his brother a sarcastic look. "How insensitive of me."

Smiling, Josie broke out the morphine and gave Kyle a quick shot of it.

"Am I gonna be all right, Doctor Josie?"

"You just go back to sleep, and I'll take care of everything."

"She's amazing, Kurtis," Kyle said, his eyelids drooping. "You oughta . . . you oughta marry her before I do."

Josie chose to ignore that statement as she prepared a needle to stitch Kyle's wound. But Jessica apparently wasn't about to let something like that lie.

"Marry her?" she repeated in a very interested tone. Then her gaze took in Josie's T-shirt, and her eyes widened a little.

Kurtis cleared his throat. "Josie, this is my sister, Jessica. Jessica, Dr. Josie Reed."

Josie smiled up at the young woman. "Pleased to meet you."

"And a doctor, no less," Jessica said, her fine black brows arched. "Where exactly did you find this *amazing* woman, Kurtis?"

"She, uh, sorta found me."

Josie took her first stitch, and Kyle remained in a quiet, drugged slumber. "He was about to have his leg cut off," she said.

"I don't think I want to hear this," Jessica responded.

"And then she barged in and poured whiskey on my leg," Kurtis replied. "She apparently likes to do that to her patients."

Josie gave him a dark look. "I saved his leg and his life, and he growled at me and made me unlock his manacles."

Kurtis shook his head. "I beg to differ with you, my dear. You unlocked those manacles purely on your own steam—because you were so damn fascinated by me."

"You were manacled?" Jessica asked.

"The marshal thought he might escape in the middle of the night," Josie replied, returning to her stitching. "Regardless of the fact that Kurtis had recently been shot."

"You were shot?" Jessica said, an octave higher.

"Only because they mistook me for Kyle, Jess."

"Oh, and that makes me feel better," she replied. "I'm assuming they eventually set you free?"

"Not exactly," Kurtis responded.

"He escaped," Josie supplied, keeping her eyes on her work.

"How?"

"By kidnapping me."

"All right, that's enough. Don't say anything more. It's bad enough being related to two men who can't find enough excitement around their own home, I don't have to sit and listen to stories of their insane exploits. I'm going to go back into the kitchen and finish lunch. Kurtis, thank you for bringing our brother back home. Josie, welcome to the family."

Welcome to the family? Josie stole a glance at Kurtis. He was watching her with another one of those expressions of his that always made her nervous. She quickly returned her attention to Kyle.

"I think he's going to recover. Give him a week or so, and he'll be causing trouble again. Just try to keep him away from marauding outlaw gangs."

Kurtis said nothing. She looked over at him and didn't like the hardness that had suddenly come up in his eyes. "What is it?" she asked.

"I'm going after Bonney."

He rose to his feet, and she leaped up in front of him. "Isn't one half-dead Mitchell enough?"

"You know," he said with a wry smile, "I really do appreciate your faith in me, Josie. I really do."

"Kurtis, I know you don't believe I'm from the future, but you have to listen to me. I know for a fact that Pat Garrett eventually kills Billy the Kid. Just let history run its course. If you go chasing after Billy now, you'll only end up getting yourself killed!"

He paused, his hand resting on the butt of his gun at his hip. "How can Garrett kill Bonney if Bonney gets Garrett first? Garrett doesn't even know the Kid is heading for Fort Sumner, Josie. This is our only chance to catch him. If I don't warn Garrett, me and Kyle will be running for the rest of our lives." He lifted his hand to cup her face. "Could *you* live like that?"

Nobody could live like that, Josie realized. And what if Kurtis was right? What if his warning to Garrett was an integral part of the history she was throwing in his face? But if Billy the Kid caught even a glimpse of Kurtis Mitchell near Fort Sumner he'd shoot first and ask questions later. The fairy had told her that Kurtis might be killed, and Josie couldn't take the chance that his ride to Fort Sumner would endanger him. This, then, could be her opportunity to save him.

"I understand," she said softly. "I'm going to go in and see if I can help your sister with lunch."

He pushed his hands into her hair and forced her to look up at him. "I love you, Josie."

She nodded, sudden tears filling her eyes.

"I'm doing this for us as much as for Kyle. Do you understand that?"

For us? she repeated to herself. She sniffled. "Do you prefer wheat or white bread—"

He bent down and kissed her, slow and sweet, then pulled back and brushed away her tears with his thumbs. "I'll be back so fast, you'll never know I left."

"First, lunch. Okay?"

He smiled again. "Let me see to a fresh horse. Then I'll join you and Jessica in the kitchen."

As Josie watched him stride out the front door, regretful tears burned her eyes. She wasn't sure he'd ever forgive her for what she was about to do.

Kurtis walked into the kitchen, and Josie and Jessica exchanged a glance. Josie had convinced her to go along with her plan, but only after assuring Jessica that she knew exactly what she was doing.

Kurtis smiled at both of them and took a seat at the table in front of a plate of steaming smoked ham. "Looks incredible, as always, Jess."

Jessica managed a smile and turned toward the dry-sink.

Josie took a steadying breath, gave Kurtis what she hoped came across as a warm smile, and handed him a glass of water. "I've already eaten," she said. Her first but not her last lie of the afternoon. Her stomach was too tied up in knots for her to eat a thing.

He wolfed down two thick slices of ham and then drained his glass of water. "Just in case Josie hasn't told you, Jess. I'm heading off for a day or so over to the fort. Be"—he shook his head as if a fly were buzzing around his nose—"be sure to let Kyle know that I'll be back in time to pound him for getting in the way of that . . ."

He shook his head again, then looked up at Josie.

A tight lump caught in her throat. "I'm sorry, Kurtis," she whispered.

His eyes widened. "What did you do?"

"I can't let you go!" she shouted, praying he wouldn't hate her. "Billy will kill you—I know he will. I can't let you go!"

He braced both hands on the table, trying to fight the effects of the morphine she'd put in his water.

"But don't worry. I plan to ride to Fort Sumner myself and warn—"

"No!" he bellowed, his head rolling back.

"Billy knows me as Joe, Kurtis. If I ride to the fort as Josie, I stand a much better chance of reaching Garrett than you do!"

He tried to push himself to his feet. "You can't . . . you can't—" Then he fell out of his chair to the floor, and Jessica let out a gasp and covered her mouth with her hands.

Josie rushed to his side and dropped down beside him. "I'm sorry," she whispered. "I'm so sorry. It was the only way."

He tried to touch her face, but his hand fell limply to the floor beside him. "Don't go. . . . "

His plea brought tears to Josie's eyes. In the final instant before he slipped into unconsciousness, she bent forward and kissed him sweetly. Somehow he had broken through the solid wall surrounding her heart.

His head fell to the side, and she brushed her fingers tenderly over his face. Then she stood to face his sister, who looked nothing short of stricken. "He'll be all right. He'll wake tomorrow morning with one hell of a headache, that's all. Now, I need a dress."

"Dear Lord, Josie, are you sure you know what you're doing? Kurtis is going to be madder than a wet cat when he comes around."

"After all this, I'm not backing out now."

"But what do I tell him tomorrow morning, when he wakes up and demands to know where you are?"

Josie looked down at the man she'd actually come to love. "Tell him to trust me."

Jessica shook her head and led the way from the kitchen.

Josie paused and looked down at Kurtis one final time, then hurried after her.

25

The road from the Mitchell ranch to Fort Sumner was easy to follow, even for Josie. It was the clothes she had on that were driving her insane.

She was dressed in a pink cotton dress—to bring out her eyes, Jessica had said—and shoes that put the Wicked Witch of the West's to shame. Her toes were all piled up on top of each other, and Josie doubted it had anything to do with an improper fit.

She'd refused to wear any underwear but her own beneath the dress. Big mistake. Those long white bloomers would have come in handy against the bugs nipping her bare calves as she raced onward.

The wind whipped at her face, and her pink satin hair ribbon flopped into her eyes again and again. She shook her head to move it back where it belonged. In her opinion the ribbon had been a little much, but Jessica had insisted that if Josie wanted to pass as a woman, she had to look like one—a remark that still pissed her off. She *was* a damn woman, for crying out loud!

She had also refused to wear the white, lace-edged gloves, and after struggling to keep her speeding horse in line for two straight hours, she was regretting that as well, as her fingers were practically raw from working the rough leather reins.

Josie rounded a bend in the road, and there, at last, in the distance, lay Fort Sumner—at least she hoped to hell it was Fort Sumner. She certainly wasn't in the mood to find out she'd taken a wrong turn somewhere.

The ramshackle wooden gates were open, and by the looks of them when Josie passed through, she doubted they were capable of closing. She paused just inside the entrance to the town and stared at the utter chaos in front of her. Chickens were darting everywhere, flapping and squawking. Running behind them were hordes of small Mexican children, with sticks in their hands and dogs nipping at their heels.

The street was crawling with people dressed in colorful serapes and wide-brimmed sombreros, some calling out wares, others just trying to get wherever it was they were headed. The noise was deafening.

She nudged her horse forward into the crowd, hoping people would have sense enough to move out of her way. They didn't, and she ended up having to shout what little Spanish she knew in order to get their attention.

"¡Vámonos! ¡Vámonos!"

Not a single person budged or even looked up at her.

She tried again. *"¡Ándale! ¡Ándale!"*

She was using her best Speedy Gonzales voice but began to think maybe she was dealing with an all deaf town.

People jostled up against her, and she felt her horse stumble. "Damn it." Either she was going to end up trampling a few of them or they were going to end up trampling her!

"¡Tu madre usa botas de militar!"

That was just a little something she'd picked up as a kid growing up in San Jose, but it definitely did the trick. Silence fell over the crowd surrounding her. She supposed even in 1881 folks didn't appreciate being told that their mother wore army boots.

"¿Vámonos?" she said in a kinder voice. *"¿Por favor?"*

The crowd let out a collective grumble and went on about their business. They still weren't moving out of her way, but at least they hadn't sicced those children with sticks on her.

It took her fifteen minutes to work her way through the crowd and turn down another, less populated street.

And the first thing she saw there was Dave Rudabaugh, leaning casually back against a post in front of a run-down building with a sign out front that said Beaver Smith's Saloon.

Josie's breath caught in her chest at the sight of him. She almost whirled her horse around and charged back into the crowd, but Dave was staring up at her and she was transfixed by the look in his eyes.

Their stare could have held for five minutes or five seconds for all Josie knew, but in that time she felt the burning sensation of a hundred imagined bullets as they riddled her body. She'd end up dead in the street, wearing a bloody pink dress, with that damn ribbon hanging in her face. And nobody would ever know or ever care who she'd been.

And then Dave did the strangest thing. He smiled, a smile that actually made his unremarkable features almost handsome, and tipped his hat. "Ma'am," he said to her in a drawl.

Josie blinked. She knew Dave well enough to know that if he suspected her at all, man or woman, she wouldn't still be sitting her horse. She smiled faintly and nodded her head. "Sir," she answered, and nudged her horse forward once again.

Josie smiled to herself, thinking this was going to be easier than she'd originally thought. She'd just find the local jail, ask for the whereabouts of Pat Garrett, and give him the good news: Billy was in town and could be Garrett's for supper.

And there it was. The sign was big and painted in bright red letters outlined in black. CITY MARSHALL. EMMETT TUNSTALL.

She cast a glance back at Dave Rudabaugh and saw that he'd gone back to sucking on the end of a bottle. The sun was low in the sky, casting long shadows on the ground, as Josie reined up in front of the marshal's office and dismounted. The boards beneath her feet thudded a hollow sound as she walked over them and reached for the door.

"This is for you, Kurtis," she whispered to herself. She pushed the door open.

The interior of the marshal's office was lit by two

open windows at the front of the building. As she stepped inside, she glanced at the stove in the corner, the gun case on the wall, and then the skinny man sitting behind the desk.

"Kin I help ya, ma'am?"

Josie smiled at him and moved farther into the room. "Yes. I'd like to speak with Sheriff Pat Garrett, please."

The man raised his gray brows. "Sheriff Garrett ain't here, ma'am. Last I heard he was resting up at his home in White Oaks."

"Then I need to get a message to him immediately. It's very—"

"Well, well. What have we here?"

Josie turned around. She couldn't believe her eyes—or her luck. Marshal Riggs and Deputy Green were just coming out from the back room. And, unlike Dave Rudabaugh, these two men knew her as a woman.

Riggs was grinning triumphantly. "Walked right into jail for us. And all gussied up, too."

"That's mighty nice of ya, Doctor," Deputy Green said, smiling.

Josie gave the marshal a look that summed up her feelings for him. "I'm here to speak with Sheriff Garrett."

"He ain't here," Deputy Green answered.

"We told you before, the sheriff isn't interested in anything you or Mitchell have to say. Speaking of that breed, you wouldn't happen to know where he is, now, would you?"

"Too bad he weren't with her, Marshal," Green said. "We could've shot him and had done with the thievin' injun."

Every ounce of guilt Josie had felt from having drugged Kurtis and come to Fort Sumner in his place vanished with that little piece of information. He might have been dead before ever finding Garrett.

The marshal moved toward her, and she slowly backed toward the door. "Come on, now," he crooned. "Don't make this harder than it has to be, honey."

She spun around and grabbed for the doorknob, but Riggs had her by the arms before she even saw sunlight. Josie wasn't about to give up, though. She put up quite a struggle before Marshal Riggs and Deputy Green could subdue her long enough to get her into a jail cell.

In the end, she stood behind the locked bars, glaring them both to hell.

"I have to talk to Sheriff Garrett!" she shouted. "It's about Billy the Kid!"

"Yeah?" Riggs said, grinning. He tossed the cell keys to the fort's marshal, who looked a little dumbfounded by what he'd just witnessed. "She's a wily one, Tunstall. Don't take your eyes off her for a second."

Then the two lawmen left, and Josie leaned her head against her cell door with a dull thud. She'd been the Mitchell brothers' last and only chance to escape being hunted criminals for the rest of their lives. And she'd failed, miserably.

Darkness fell over the bustling little town of Fort Sumner. Josie was lying on a narrow, lumpy cot in her cell, staring out her barred windows at the moon and stars, as she and Kurtis had done after making love only the night before. It was almost eleven o'clock.

Marshal Tunstall had long since left her with a bull-
dog of a deputy to guard her for the night, and the
chances of Garrett capturing Billy the Kid were growing slim.

The front door opened and closed, but Josie didn't
pay much attention. People had been coming in and
out all evening for one reason or another, and she'd
gotten sick of facing their stares.

"What in the tarnation is that woman doing in that
cell?"

Her head snapped up and she peered at the lean,
tall man looming over the deputy, who was sitting
behind the marshal's desk.

"She was brought in by Riggs and Green, just this
afternoon. They said she's a member of that Mitchell
gang."

"What Mitchell gang?" he asked in a harsh voice.

"That gang that runs with the Kid. She's their doctor or something."

"There is no Mitchell gang, Deputy. Now, I want
you to get your ring of keys and let that woman out
from behind those bars right now. Do you understand
me?"

Josie sat up on her cot, trying to make out the features of the man who was so upset by her incarcera-
tion. The two men walked toward her cell, and the
lamp by her door caught on the unforgettable face of
Pat Garrett.

"Sheriff Garrett!" she blurted out. "Thank God you
came!"

The deputy opened the door, and Josie dashed out
and took the sheriff by his arms. "How did you know I
was here?" she asked.

"Marshal Tunstall didn't appreciate the way those

two men treated you, so he thought it might be wise to send me a wire."

"God bless the man!" Josie cried. "Listen, Kurtis Mitchell has lived up to his half of the bargain, Sheriff. He's lured Billy the Kid here, to the fort, and he and his gang are in town as we speak—"

"Now, that ain't so," the deputy spoke up. "We'da known if the Kid had ridden in."

"I saw Dave Rudabaugh at Beaver Smith's Saloon just this afternoon," Josie said. "Billy doesn't go anywhere without Dave, Sheriff. Billy's here. And he's here to kill you."

The tall lawman man blinked. "I think you better start from the beginning, Doctor."

Josie pulled him aside and explained to him the plan that Kurtis and Kyle had put into action, how they'd played on Billy's own need for glory to lure him to Fort Sumner but had underestimated just how dastardly Billy was.

"Now the rest is up to you," Josie concluded.

The sheriff nodded thoughtfully. "Fine work. Where is Mitchell? I'd like to congratulate him on his daring and smart thinking."

"Oh. He's, uh, he's taking it easy, lying back and waiting for you to come to him with the news that Billy is in jail."

She hoped he hadn't detected the apprehension in her voice.

He put a hand on her shoulder. "You know, I think I'd have to say that you are the most amazing woman I have ever met, Dr. Reed."

Josie broke into a smile. "Thank you, Sheriff Garrett. Thank you very much."

"Deputy, escort the doctor to the hotel down the

street, and make arrangements for her to stay the night."

Josie thanked the sheriff again as he left the office. She would have wished him luck, but she knew in her heart he wouldn't need any. This would be the night. The night Pat Garrett went down in history as the man who killed Billy the Kid.

26

At nighttime in Fort Sumner, New Mexico, there were only three things on any hombre's mind: women, getting drunk, and finding trouble.

Pat Garrett strode down the street, away from the marshal's office and jail, with his two best deputies following close behind. He was unusually watchful of the press of people around him this night, having just been told, by what he felt was a fairly reliable source, that there was a very dangerous young man in town who planned to see him dead.

He walked until he came to Pete Maxwell's cabin. Pete was a friend and local rancher who always kept abreast of the various comings and goings in the fort. If Billy Bonney was hiding out anywhere nearby, Pete was bound to know about it.

Sheriff Garrett posted his two deputies outside on the front porch and went inside the house to wake Pete.

*   *   *

It was after midnight when Billy kicked open the bunkhouse door and barged into the small room, laughing. He'd spent the evening celebrating the forthcoming death of his nemesis, Pat Garrett.

"Where's the food?" he shouted at the startled men. "Come on, you Maxwell boys always have somethin' lazin' around waitin' to be drunk or eaten!"

"You're a little late tonight, Billy," one of the ranch hands replied. "Ox over there ate most of everything there was."

Billy narrowed his eyes at the heavy man across the room, and Clyde Olinger—Ox, as he'd come to be known—went pale. "You ate my share?" Billy asked menacingly.

"S-sorry, Kid. I didn't know you was comin'."

Billy eyed the butcher knife stuck nose down in the table in front of him, evidence that meat had been there earlier. He snatched the knife up and waved it at Ox. "I oughta hack you up and fill myself up on you."

The man pressed back against the wall, and then Billy burst into laughter as Ox wet himself in front of God and all his friends. "Just kiddin', Ox. Don't ya know when a man's pullin' your leg?"

"There's a quarter of beef hanging on the porch of the main house, Billy. Pete won't mind if you help yourself."

"I think I'll do that, Jim. Thank you very much."

Knife in hand, Billy left the bunkhouse and crossed the yard. He was about to round the corner to the porch of Pete Maxwell's cabin when he saw something stir in the darkness. He quickly pulled his gun and decided to sneak into the house by a side door.

That side door led directly into Pete Maxwell's bedroom.

In the inky darkness, Pat Garrett couldn't make out the face of the man who entered the bedroom. He held perfectly still, however, and Billy didn't detect him sitting there on the side of Pete Maxwell's bed.

Billy moved closer and leaned both hands on the bed, his right hand almost touching Pat Garrett's knee, and said softly, "Who are they, Pete?"

At that moment Pete Maxwell whispered to Pat Garrett, "That's him!"

Billy the Kid raised his pistol and pointed it directly at Pat Garrett's chest. He retreated back across the room, crying in Spanish, *"¿Quién es? ¿Quién es? Who's that? Who's that?"*

Pat Garrett drew his revolver and fired, dove to the side, and fired again. The first shot had been enough, though, and William Bonney hit the floor, dead without even a cry.

Billy the Kid had gone down the same way as many of his victims: violently, and taken unawares.

The door to Josie's hotel room flew open and she lurched up in her bed, holding the sheets to her chin. She almost let out a scream, until she saw Kurtis standing there. "Jesus, Mitchell! Don't you know how to knock!"

The morning sun was shining brightly through the window, marking the beginning of another day. She slowly backed up against the headboard of her bed; Kurtis looked mad enough to snap her neck.

"What the hell did you think you were doing?" he said in a voice so low and so tight that Josie could barely hear him.

He strode into the room and slammed the door shut. She flinched at the loud bang and sat up straighter in the bed.

"First you pretend to go along with me riding out after Garrett . . . and then you drug me and do it yourself!"

Josie remained silent in the bed, her teeth clenched to keep herself from crying. When the hell had she become so emotional?

"Of all the stupid things I've ever seen done in my life, that one, Josie, that one takes the whole goddamn cake!"

"Don't you dare stand there and call me stupid!" she shouted back.

"Oh, I didn't call you stupid. I called what you *did* stupid!"

Regardless of her state of undress, Josie threw aside the covers, climbed out of the bed, and began pulling on the dress she'd borrowed from Jessica the day before. Kurtis remained silent behind her as she tugged the garment up and over her arms and jammed the buttons on the front into the holes. Then she grabbed up the "torture shoes" and headed past him for the door.

His hand shot out and grabbed her by the arm. "Where do you think you're going?"

"If you think I'm going to stay here while you insult me"—she shook off his hold—"then you don't know me very well at all, *Mister* Mitchell." She reached for the doorknob.

"That's it, Josie, run, just like you always do," he threw back at her. "But first, tell me something . . . what the hell is it that you're so afraid of!"

She whirled around to face him. "Of men like you who feel they can bellow at me whenever I do something *they* think I shouldn't! Of men like you who'll spend their whole lives trying to run mine!"

"You charged off and almost got yourself killed," he said, his look now incredulous. "What the hell do you expect me to do, pat you on the back?"

"You were planning on doing the exact same thing, Kurtis," she replied. "Care to point out the difference?"

He advanced on her, his arms crossed. "Everything's always a war with you, isn't it? You always have to turn everything around so it fits your need to be terrified of me and everything I might represent."

"And you have made what you represent very clear to me this morning." She looked up at him, not bothering to hide the tears falling from her eyes. "You don't know how badly I wish things could be different for us, Kurtis. I—I have to get out of here," she stammered, and hurried from the room.

She ran down the hotel stairs, out the front door, and into the street. She raced, heedlessly, in front of a milk wagon that almost ran her down and pushed through a crush of people milling around Beaver Smith's saloon. She barely caught a glimpse of a body laid out in an upright coffin, but she felt sure the dead man was Billy Bonney.

She kept moving, barefoot, down the splintery boardwalk, until she came to a small white church at the northeastern side of town and stopped to catch her breath. She was running, just as Kurtis had said she always did, but she wasn't sure what from anymore.

She rested her hands on the sharp points of the white picket fence circling the church yard, and then suddenly the little fairy woman was there, frowning at her from beneath a maple tree, her pearls glinting in the sunlight.

"Congratulations. You've managed to change history."

Josie gave her a baffled look. "I don't see how. Billy the Kid is dead, isn't he?"

"Oh, yes. And now residing exactly where his black soul belongs. I was speaking of Mr. Mitchell. Originally he did manage to warn Garrett about William Bonney, but he was shot in the back by Marshal Riggs that very night."

Josie nodded. "Then I've done what you asked? I saved Kurtis one final time?"

"Yes. I take it you're ready to leave now."

Josie couldn't speak, emotion had such a tight grip on her throat. She was surprised she could even breathe. Was it the fourteenth of July already? How had she lost track of time like that?

She swallowed, thought of Kurtis, looked one last time at the blue sky and the people walking past her, and reluctantly nodded again.

"I'm afraid I can't hear the rocks shaking around in there, Doctor. If you want to return to 1994, you'll have to say so."

Josie licked her lips. She steeled herself against the tears threatening to fall and opened her mouth to speak.

"Josie!" Kurtis raced up behind her and wrapped his arms around her waist.

"Let me go, Kurtis," she managed to say. "It's better for both of us this way."

"Better for who?" He spun her around to face him.

"Better for the man who loves you, who'll never touch you or see your beautiful face again? Better for you, Josie? Is that it? Will it be better for you to never see me again?"

She looked deeply into his eyes and let out a small gasp. "Do you believe me?" she asked, stunned.

"I believe *in* you, Josie. And I believe that something is about to happen that could take you away from me forever." He took hold of her chin and forced her to look at him. "You love me. Can you honestly look me in the eye and deny that?"

She shook her head. "But sometimes love isn't enough."

"Why?" he demanded. "Why can't two people who love and respect each other work out anything that might come their way?"

Respect. There was the key word. "How can you say you respect me when not five minutes ago you were shouting at me for doing something you didn't want me to do!"

He actually broke into gentle laughter and then shouted, "Because I love you, Dr. Josie Reed! And any time you choose to put yourself in danger I'm bound to lose my mind with worry!"

She hesitated, staring into his eyes. "But how can I ever be certain that someday you won't try to stop me from doing what I choose? How can I be sure?"

He cupped her cheek and leaned his forehead against hers. "Faith in each other, Josie. That's all anybody ever has."

"Trust him," she heard the woman behind her whisper.

Josie turned to look behind her. "Can you tell me what will happen if I stay?" she asked the woman.

The woman shook her head. "Destiny is a fickle thing, Dr. Reed. Depending on your minute-by-minute decisions, the possibilities are continuously changing."

"But will I be happy?"

The woman gave her a warm, genuine smile. "I think the important question is: Are you happy now?"

Josie turned to look at Kurtis, who was watching her carefully. The idea of seeing that handsome face grow old and distinguished was very appealing. To always have these strong arms available to hold her was a very comforting thought.

"Make your decision, Doctor," the woman said. I haven't got all day. A lot of other, much more *appreciative* people depend on my services as well."

Kurtis leaned closer to her. "What's your answer, Josie? Do you leave this dream behind? Or do you stay here with me and make it come true?"

Epilogue

Josie tucked a stray piece of long, dark hair back behind her ear. The day was unseasonably warm for early May, and already her clothes were beginning to stick to her. She stood up from her desk to stand at the window and take in the spring breeze.

"You're next patient is ready, Doctor. He's waiting in room three."

Josie turned and nodded to her nurse. "Thank you, Judith. I'll be right there."

This heat was swelling her ankles to the size of tennis balls. She wiggled her bare toes against the polished wood floor and hoped her state of undress wouldn't bother her patient. Dreaming of a tall glass of Pepsi, she left and headed down the corridor to room three.

The patient sitting on the examination table gave her a warm smile as she entered the room. She sighed and leaned back against the door. "What is it today?"

He shook his head, as if not understanding his own pain. "I've got this ache"—he brought his hand up to his chest—"right about here."

She arched her brows. "Really?" She put her stethoscope in her ears and listened to his heart. "Everything sounds okay to me."

His hands slipped behind her and locked around her back. She replaced her stethoscope on her neck and smiled at him. "You know, you can't just come in here and bother me every time you get a little bored."

"Oh"—he kissed her once on the mouth—"I'm sorry. I didn't realize my ailments were a bother to you."

"I have other *real* patients who need my attention."

His hands slipped around to rest on her ever-expanding waistline. "What about this little patient right here?"

Josie rolled her eyes. "You've been talking to Jessica again, haven't you, Kurtis? I told you, I can work right up to the delivery. It's actually good for both me and the baby."

"And that delivery could be any second."

"Just because Jessica had such a time with her baby last month does not mean that I'll have problems with this one."

"My love, there is no doubt in my mind that you'd work until the baby dropped to the floor, and then just pick it up and keep on moving. Your dedication to your profession is known across the land. I'm only asking that you slow down a little. For both of you."

Josie smiled and shook her head. "You know, if we'd had this conversation ten months ago, I would have . . . "

"Panicked?"

She put her arms around him and moved closer until their unborn child pressed between them. "Tell me more about this ache"—she pointed to his chest— "right here."

"It's a love ache."

She arched a brow. "A love ache?"

"You left this morning without giving me a kiss. Snuck right out of my bed, leaving me feeling cheap and used."

She laughed. "The spring branding will start soon, Kurtis. Then you'll have so much to do, you'll forget all about your fat, pregnant wife, and these love aches."

"Yeah, but in the meantime I cook, I clean, I slave—"

"You pay the stable boy to clean our room every morning, Kurtis. Jessica ratted on you months ago."

He frowned. "I cook?"

She shook her head. "Jessica."

"Well, surely I must slave?"

She leaned up on her toes until their lips were practically touching. "You built me this clinic in less than a month. You managed to convince people from all over the territory to come and see me, despite the fact that I'm a woman in a man's profession. And you are the most wonderful, loving husband a wife could ever have."

He nodded. "I slave."

"I love you," she whispered against his lips.

Kurtis kissed her tenderly, plucking the willing strings of her heart. Their child stirred between them, and they both knew that destiny had truly been fulfilled.

Author's Note

Billy the Kid was killed by Sheriff Pat Garrett in Fort Sumner, New Mexico, on July 14, 1881. While it's true that Garrett made claims that he'd given up on the outlaw in order to lure Billy out of hiding, no one is exactly sure how it came to his attention that the Kid had ridden into the fort. Many rumors persist surrounding William Bonney's death, but evidence indicates that Billy the Kid does, to this day, rest in a grave just outside the ruins of old Fort Sumner.

For purposes of entertainment, Billy and his gang held up a bank in this story, but in real life the Kid never did rob banks—or even trains. He stuck, for the most part, with cattle rustling and horse stealing: two very unlucrative ventures.

A fascinating, detailed account of William Bonney's short but eventful life can be found in *The Complete and Factual Life of Billy the Kid,* by William Brent.

Let HarperMonogram
Sweep You Away

❧❀❧

AMERICAN DREAMER by Theresa Weir

Animal researcher Lark Leopold has never encountered a more frustrating mammal than handsome farmer Nathan Senatra. But Lark won't give up on her man until he learns to answer her call of the wild.

BILLY BOB WALKER GOT MARRIED
by Lisa G. Brown
A HarperMonogram Classic

Special Price only $2.99

Shiloh Pennington knows that Billy Bob Walker is no good. But how can she ignore the fire that courses in her veins at the thought of Billy's kisses?

SHADOW PRINCE
by Terri Lynn Wilhelm
A HarperMonogram Classic

Special Price only $2.99

Plastic surgeon Ariel Denham is working at an exclusive, isolated clinic high in the Smoky Mountains when she meets and falls in love with a mysterious man who stays in the shadows, a man she knows only as Jonah.

DESTINED TO LOVE
by Suzanne Elizabeth
A HarperMonogram Classic

Special Price only $2.99

In this sizzling time travel romance, a guardian angel sends Dr. Josie Reed back to the Wild West of 1881 to tend to a captured outlaw. The last thing the doctor expects is to go on the run—or to lose her heart.

And in case you missed last month's selections...

TALLCHIEF by Dinah McCall
Bestselling Author of *Dreamcatcher*
Ever since Morgan Tallchief lost the only woman he would ever love, he has struggled to seal away the past. But now she is back in his life, and Morgan is helpless against his own rekindled desire.

THE SEDUCTION by Laura Lee Guhrke
Desperate to restore the family's fortune, Trevor St. James seduces heiress Margaret Van Alden. But he realizes this American has awakened dreams of love he has long denied—until now.

ALWAYS IN MY HEART by Donna Valentino
Time Travel Romance
When a diary transports Matt Kincaid back to the Old West, he becomes the reluctant groom in a shotgun wedding. His bride can handle a gun, but is she prepared for Matt's soul-searing passion?

CHANCE McCALL by Sharon Sala
A HarperMonogram Classic
Jenny Tyler has been in love with Chance McCall for years, but the hired hand wants nothing to do with his boss's daughter. When Chance leaves the ranch to discover his forgotten past, Jenny is determined to find the man who has stolen her heart.

MAIL TO: **HarperCollins Publishers**
P.O. Box 588 Dunmore, PA 18512-0588

Yes, please send me the books I have checked:

❑ *American Dreamer* by Theresa Weir 108461-1 . . . .$5.99 U.S./$7.99 Can.
❑ *Billy Bob Walker Got Married* by Lisa G. Brown 108550-2 . . . .$2.99 U.S./$3.99 Can.
❑ *Shadow Prince* by Terri Lynn Wilhelm 108551-0 . . . .$2.99 U.S./$3.99 Can.
❑ *Destined to Love* by Suzanne Elizabeth 108549-9 . . . .$2.99 U.S./$3.99 Can.
❑ *Tallchief* by Dinah McCall 108444-1 . . . .$5.99 U.S./$7.99 Can.
❑ *The Seduction* by Laura Lee Guhrke 108403-4 . . . .$5.50 U.S./$7.50 Can.
❑ *Always in My Heart* by Donna Valentino 108480-8 . . . .$4.99 U.S./$5.99 Can.
❑ *Chance McCall* by Sharon Sala 108155-8 . . . .$4.99 U.S./$5.99 Can.

SUBTOTAL . . . .$_____
POSTAGE & HANDLING . . . .$_____
SALES TAX (Add applicable sales tax) . . . .$_____
TOTAL . . . .$_____

Name _____
Address _____
City _____ State _____ Zip _____

Order 4 or more titles and postage & handling is **FREE!** For orders of fewer than 4 books, please include $2.00 postage & handling. Allow up to 6 weeks for delivery. Remit in U.S. funds. Do not send cash. Valid in U.S. & Canada. Prices subject to change.   http://www.harpercollins.com   M05911

Visa & MasterCard holders—call 1-800-331-3761

Would you travel through time to find your soul mate?

TIME TRAVEL
ROMANCE

DESTINY AWAITS by Suzanne Elizabeth
Tess Harper found herself in Kansas in the year
1885, face-to-face with the most captivating,
stubborn man she'd ever met—and two precious
little girls who needed a mother. Could this man,
and this family, be her true destiny?

A WINDOW IN TIME
by Carolyn Lampman

A delightful romp through time in which Brianna
Daniels trades places with her great-grandmother,
Anna. She arrives in Wyoming Territory in 1860
to become the mail-order bride that Lucas Daniels
never ordered.

THE AUTUMN LORD by Susan Sizemore
Truth is stranger than fiction when '90s woman
Diane Teal is transported back to medieval France
and must rely on the protection of Baron Simon
de Argent. She finds herself unable to communi-
cate except when telling stories. Fortunately, she
and Simon both speak the language of love.

MAIL TO: **HarperCollins Publishers**
               P.O. Box 588 Dunmore, PA 18512-0588

Yes, please send me the books I have checked:

❑ *Destiny Awaits* by Suzanne Elizabeth 108342-9 . . . .$4.99 U.S./ $5.99 Can.
❑ *A Window in Time* by Carolyn Lampman 108171-X . . . .$4.50 U.S./ $5.50 Can.
❑ *The Autumn Lord* by Susan Sizemore 108208-2 . . . .$5.50 U.S./ $7.50 Can.

SUBTOTAL . . . .$_____
POSTAGE & HANDLING . . . .$_____
SALES TAX (Add applicable sales tax) . . . .$_____
TOTAL . . . .$_____

Name _____
Address _____
City _____ State _____ Zip _____

Order 4 or more titles and postage & handling is **FREE!** For orders of fewer than 4 books, please include $2.00
postage & handling. Allow up to 6 weeks for delivery. Remit in U.S. funds. Do not send cash. Valid in U.S. &
Canada. Prices subject to change.   http://www.harpercollins.com   M05711

Visa & MasterCard holders—call 1-800-331-3761

Let Your Imagination Run Wild

DREAMCATCHER by Dinah McCall

"A gripping, emotional story that satisfies on every level."
—Debbie Macomber

Amanda Potter escapes her obsessive husband through the warm embrace of a dream that draws her through time. Detective Jefferson Dupree knows his destiny is intertwined with Amanda's and he must convince her that her dream lover is only a heartbeat away.

CHRISTMAS ANGELS: Three Heavenly Romances by Debbie Macomber

Over Twelve Million Copies of Her Books in Print

The angelic antics of Shirley, Goodness, and Mercy are featured in this collection that promises plenty of romance and dreams that come true.

DESTINY'S EMBRACE by Suzanne Elizabeth

Award-winning Time Travel Series

Winsome criminal Lacey Garder faces imprisonment until her guardian angel sends her back in time to 1879. Rugged Marshal Matthew Brady is the law in Tranquility, Washington Territory, and he soon finds Lacey guilty of love in the first degree.

MAIL TO: **HarperCollins Publishers**
P.O. Box 588 Dunmore, PA 18512-0588

Harper Monogram

Yes, please send me the books I have checked:

❏ *Dreamcatcher* by Dinah McCall 108325-9 . . . .$5.50 U.S./ $6.50 Can.
❏ *Christmas Angels: Three Heavenly Romances*
   by Debbie Macomber 108690-8 . . . .$12.00 U.S./$16.75 Can.
❏ *Destiny's Embrace* by Suzanne Elizabeth 108341-0 . . . .$5.50 U.S./ $7.50 Can.

SUBTOTAL . . . .$_____
POSTAGE & HANDLING . . . .$_____
SALES TAX (Add applicable sales tax) . . . .$_____
TOTAL . . . .$_____

Name _____
Address _____
City _____ State _____ Zip _____

Order 4 or more titles and postage & handling is **FREE!** For orders of fewer than 4 books, please include $2.00
postage & handling. Allow up to 6 weeks for delivery. Remit in U.S. funds. Do not send cash. Valid in U.S. &
Canada. Prices subject to change.   http://www.harpercollins.com/paperbacks   M04811

Visa & MasterCard holders—call 1-800-331-3761

ATTENTION: ORGANIZATIONS AND CORPORATIONS

Most HarperPaperbacks are available at special quantity discounts for bulk purchases for sales promotions, premiums, or fund-raising. For information, please call or write:
Special Markets Department, HarperCollins Publishers,
10 East 53rd Street, New York, N.Y. 10022.
Telephone: (212) 207-7528. Fax: (212) 207-7222.